DEATH SHIP

Jim Kelly

CRÈME de la CRIME

This first world edition published 2016
in Great Britain and the USA by
Crème de la Crime, an imprint of
SEVERN HOUSE PUBLISHERS LTD of
19 Cedar Road, Sutton, Surrey, England, SM2 5DA.
Trade paperback edition first published
in Great Britain and the USA 2017 by
SEVERN HOUSE PUBLISHERS LTD

British Library Cataloguing in Publication Data
A CIP catalogue record for this title is available from the British Library.

ISBN-13: 978-1-78029-090-4 (cased)
ISBN-13: 978-1-78029-573-2 (trade paper)
ISBN-13: 978-1-78010-818-6 (e-book)

All Severn House titles are printed on acid-free paper.

Severn House Publishers support the Forest Stewardship Council™ [FSC™],
the leading international forest certification organisation.
All our titles that are printed on FSC certified paper carry the FSC logo.

Typeset by Palimpsest Book Production Ltd.,
Falkirk, Stirlingshire, Scotland.
Printed and bound in Great Britain by
TJ International, Padstow, Cornwall.

This book is dedicated to the Royal National Lifeboat
Institution at Hunstanton.
Guardians of the Hundred Mile Beach.

Donations please to: www.justgiving.com/ForHunny
Cheques to 'RNLI Hunstanton'
Hunstanton Lifeboat Treasurer
Hunstanton Lifeboat Station
Sea Lane
Old Hunstanton
PE36 6JN

ACKNOWLEDGMENTS

Death Ship is the seventh Shaw & Valentine mystery, and the 'team' is now well-established. I would like to thank all at Severn House for their work on the manuscript. My agent Faith Evans has again provided unflinching guidance and vigilance. My wife, Midge Gillies, found time in her own writing schedule to help out when the plot was foundering, and the characters sketchy. I would like to extend my thanks to Lynn Museum, and Lloyds of London, for their help, and – especially – Roger Bridge, tunneling manager with Balfour Beatty, for finding the time and patience to outline the basic principles of engineering which underpin the narrative – particularly the construction of the underwater 'caisson'. While he provided broad guidance, all the detail and the specific operations described are entirely the products of my own imagination. Anyone tempted to build the resulting structures will be living very dangerously. The support of the RNLI at Old Hunstanton is appreciated, and I hope readers will note the dedication to this book, and give generously if they feel they can.

ONE

I t was no surprise to Donald Ross that his three sons had decided to mark their first day on holiday by digging a hole on Hunstanton beach. Digging was in the Ross family DNA: a hardwired urge to disappear underground. A distant relative had earned a Victoria Cross in Crimea, leading two hundred men out at night to dig zigzag trenches across no-man's-land. Donald's father had worked on the Channel Tunnel, commanding a TBM – a tunnel boring machine – one of the mechanical worms that had eaten its way through the chalk to France. Donald had a job on the London Underground, as a maintenance supervisor, trawling the dark tunnels at night, tapping rails.

His boys worked with an almost manic intensity, digging down into the damp, cloying sand. The pit, as it deepened, collected the shadows of the day and seemed to pack them tightly away, consolidating their darkness into a single black void, within which anything might lay hidden – a treasure, a fiend, a tunnel entrance, a mystery. The boys had brought spades with them, each one suited to their respective ages of five, eight, and thirteen.

The sand flew while Donald and his wife, Eve, watched from their vantage point in the lee of the concrete esplanade, a sinuous miniature cliff which would offer shade until midday, and a comfortable surface on which they could later lean back and enjoy the eventual, inevitable sunset. Hunstanton, Donald had gravely informed the boys, was unique in this one (literal) aspect of its geographical position, being the only west-facing East Coast resort, tucked into the great estuarine bucket-shaped bay of the Wash. The consequence of this strange inversion – a seaside town facing its own coast – was that the place felt humid and enervating, haunted by dead air.

More sand flew from the deepening pit. Eve and Donald sipped stewed tea from a thermos flask. Above them, on the seafront, they could hear the unmistakable sound of coins being ejected by a one-armed bandit. A small amusement arcade and café operated in what was left of the old pier entrance hall, a stubby remnant of what had once been one of the finest Victorian structures ever built on the English coast: eight hundred yards of wrought-iron tracery, as graceful as an arrow, flying west towards the setting sun.

Storms and fire had reduced this fine landmark to a series of stunted wooden piles, visible only at low tide, two dotted lines leading out to sea: a fleeting reminder of a more graceful, splendid past. It was between these rotting stumps that the boys had dug their pit.

By mid-morning the children had disappeared from sight. The fact that she could not see her boys prevented Eve from sleeping, although her eyelids weighed heavy. Her problem, which kept her nervously vigilant, was that she found it very difficult not to equate holes with graves. The Ross family enthusiasm for dark pits left her cold. She'd been just fifteen at her mother's funeral. Encouraged to stand at the graveside, she'd been told to take a handful of dust and let it fall to the coffin lid. But the soil had been substantial, a claggy, clay clod, so that the sound, the dull echo of the percussion from within the casket, had marked her for life.

Donald intermittently heaved himself up on his over-large feet and went down the beach to survey the work, advising his eldest son, Marc, appointed gangmaster, to widen the hole so that it didn't tumble in on the 'navvies' as they dug down. The children's spades made an increasingly harsh, quartz-on-metal clatter.

'A fat man told us to stop, Dad,' said the youngest, Eric, grains of sand in his eyelashes. 'He said it was dangerous between the old pier posts. It's not, is it? He said he might call the police.'

'Course it's not dangerous,' said Donald, checking again that there were no signs. Besides, the boys were within sight of a lifeguard hut, from which a yellow 'all safe' flag flew.

'Mind you – you have hit rock bottom,' added Donald. 'So you could pack it in and wait for high tide.'

The boys said they could go deeper, and their father was stupidly proud of their stubborn endeavour. Marc, a keen photographer, asked his father to bring his camera down to the pit so that the excavation could be recorded and then posted on Instagram. The boy took a picture at about two o'clock, the last of the hole itself, as it turned out. (This would prove a vital piece of evidence in that it revealed a small metallic blemish, the colour of fish skin, in the west wall of the pit.)

Lunch was chips, and Donald had to pass the greasy parcels down, because the boys wouldn't come up to eat properly on the picnic blanket, complaining that they might lose their pitch to interlopers. Besides, the moment of drama was less than an hour away: the sea, which at Hunstanton did not so much go out as go missing, was – at last – about to make its dramatic return. A warning sign next to the lifeguard's hut, dutifully studied by Eve, explained that because of the shallow declination of the sands, the sea, when it arrived, would race landwards, flooding acres in seconds, swirling into pools, bubbling over sand banks. This was the moment for which the pit had been dug, the moment of biblical inundation.

Donald, mildly dazed by a pint of lager from the Golden Lion, the pub up on the clifftop green, snuggled down for a nap, leaving Eve to tackle the *Daily Mail* crossword, asking only that she wake him in time for high tide.

It was Eric who struck metal first: the sound of a beach spade striking iron ringing out as distinctively as a church bell.

Donald sat up, unsure what had snapped him out of his half-sleep. Anxious, unsettled, he rummaged in the picnic bag and found his binoculars. Between thumb and forefinger he turned the serrated dial until an image came sharply to his eye. Out at sea a structure resembling an oil rig bristled with cranes and girders, a miniature maritime Manhattan. Mechanical noises had reached him earlier in the day: had this been what had woken him now?

Hunstanton had been chosen for the Ross annual holiday because Donald's younger brother had secured a contract to work on the construction of the new pier. Robbie, a bachelor aged just thirty, was a member of that elite known as the 'tunnel tigers'. For nearly ten years he had worked for one of the big multinational construction companies, responsible for bridges, oil rigs, coastal defences and tidal barriers. Now the company had won the contract to build a new pier at Hunstanton. The pier head, more than a mile out to sea and standing in the deep water channel, would be of itself, Donald told the boys, a feat of twenty-first-century engineering.

The magic, Donald had explained, lay below the surface. A concrete caisson, manufactured in Holland, had been hauled across the North Sea and lowered, by crane, to the seabed, two hundred feet beneath the rig. At bath-time in their rented cottage he'd illustrated the principal qualities of a caisson to the boys by taking one of their beach buckets, turning it upside down, and forcing it down into the water so that Eric could put his hand on the top, countering the buoyancy of the trapped air.

'See?' said Donald. 'There's air in the bucket. Men can work in the bucket on the seabed, digging away, and then the bucket settles into the sand, and they put the metal pillars on the top of the bucket, and on top of those you build the pier!'

'There's men under the sea?' asked Eric, astonished. 'Uncle Robbie's underwater?'

'It depends on which shift he's working. But he will be. It's really safe. The paper says they've sunk the caisson, but now they're working on the pipe that goes down for the men – that's what they call a manlock – and the bigger pipe for the gear and the stuff they dig out, that's the mudlock. The men who go down are all tunnel tigers – just like Robbie.'

Eric, delighted, liked the sound of the mudlock and the tunnel tigers. He'd tilted the bucket until a glistening bubble of air had broken free to pop to the surface.

The new pier was not, however, a universal source of admiration.

Driving into town, they had passed under an old railway bridge adorned with graffiti: no urban childish scrawl, but a work of art, six feet high, in bulbous multicoloured letters: *STOP THE PIER*.

The town was plastered with posters calling supporters to an anti-pier meeting at the theatre. Graffiti seemed to mark every bus shelter, every wall. Protestors claimed that the original idea of rebuilding a classic Victorian pier had been hijacked by big money and vested interests. They wanted the work on the pier halted so that there was time to take the case to Westminster and Brussels. All sorts of allegations were made in technicolour: fraud, graft, corruption, incompetence, and reckless pollution of the historic Norfolk coast.

The anti-pier campaign had not stopped at graffiti. The construction company's trucks had been vandalized, and a floating demo in the spring had attempted to prevent the lowering of the great caisson. Only yesterday Donald had bought the local rag to check on cinema times for *Interstellar* and read the splash story: *ARSON FEAR OVER FRESH PIER ATTACK*. Police were, apparently, trying to track down a man who had swum out to the rig at night and dragged an oil drum into the fuel store and left a paraffin-soaked rag smouldering, stuffed into the open cap. An explosion, and the clear danger of injury or worse, had only been averted by an alert lookout on night watch.

Even here, on the beach, they couldn't shake off the protestors, who worked the crowds, collecting tins in hand, giving out STP stickers.

A wave of screams swept the beach, and, lowering the binoculars, Donald saw that the sea had breached the leading sand bar and was rushing inwards, the white-edged waves advancing at a running pace, leaving children in its wake, suddenly paddling in a foot of water. The boys had already scrambled out of their pit and were sitting on the edge throwing stones. It was Marc's turn next, and as he drew back his arm, his father saw that he'd chosen a half brick, smoothed by the sea.

The sound of it hitting its target took a second to reach Donald, but he knew instantly what had woken him up, and it hadn't been the cranes on the distant rig. He stood, fell, stood, tripped, then finally found his running feet, calling out Eric's name, because it was his youngest son's turn next and he had his hand up, ready to strike. Donald got to the pit just as the sea funnelled down, carving a miniature valley, creating a whirlpool which spun their plastic buckets wildly in a circle and threatened to suck them back out to sea.

For a fleeting moment, as the wave retreated, Donald saw the boys' target. Their stones had dislodged part of the pit wall, to reveal a shiny metal surface which, for a surreal moment, he thought looked as if it might be scaled. Then the sand wall gave way, spilling out the object within, as if giving birth. In less than a second it was gone, lost in the frothing spume, but Donald sensed its weight as it tumbled, its sheer mass: a giant silvery metal fish, almost instantly concealed within the hissing whirlpool of white surf.

TWO

D S George Valentine had always felt that there was a distinct criminal class – a *type* – each individual member of which was fated to follow certain predetermined and irresistible urges. This somewhat Victorian view had been tempered by nearly thirty years in CID, but its essential contours still formed the bedrock of his own attitudes and methods. One tenet of this view of the lawbreaker was that he, or she, always felt the need to return to the scene of the crime. Most criminals were stupid and getting no smarter – a fact that Valentine understood to lie behind the steady increase in the rate at which they were being caught. It was now standard practice, for example, for CID to discreetly film the crowds gathered behind the yellow-and-black SOCO tape at the crime scene, and especially those who stole to the spot to lay flowers and notes of condolence and support in cases of murder.

Valentine rummaged in the pocket of his raincoat and found his dark glasses, slipping them on his narrow skull, which from either side followed the outline of a hatchet; his face, in fact, seemed almost entirely constructed of profile, so that when he said 'no', it seemed to flip from left to right, without an intervening full-face image. Thinning hair, a widow's peak, a suit, an ironed white shirt, dark tie, and black slip-on shoes completed the unvarying ensemble. The raincoat, worn in winter, was simply carried in the summer, folded like a priest's maniple over one arm.

Valentine eased the collar on his shirt with a finger as a trickle of sweat ran down his neck.

Sitting opposite Hunstanton's modest bus station in the summer sunshine, he watched a queue beginning to form for the T45 service to King's Lynn railway station, fifteen miles south along the zigzag route that hugged the coast. The bus, a single-decker, was due at three thirty. Folding out a copy of the *East Anglian Daily News* with a crack, Valentine peered over the top of the newspaper and noted the faces of the eight would-be passengers waiting for the bus: two men, six women, none a match for the widely distributed police 'wanted' poster, a copy of which he had between the pages of the paper. He forced himself to scan the other queues, at the other stops, reminding himself that his surveillance shift would be over soon with the departure of the T45, and that he should remain alert. He sensed, however, with all the cynicism of his thirty years of service, that he was wasting his time.

It had not been a good day: he was bored, uncomfortable, hungry, thirsty, and hot. Valentine was newly married for the second time, to Probationary Police Constable Jan Clay, the widow of a former colleague, who had brought up a family out here on the windswept north Norfolk coast. Valentine was, by contrast, a man of the town. His two-up two-down lay in the tightly packed terrace streets inside Lynn's London Gate, a warren of corner shops, backstreet boozers, and the Gothic remnants of the port's whaling past.

Jan wanted to start a new life, in a new house, out here in sight of the sea. They'd spent the morning viewing identical Barratt boxes on faceless streets, each estate agent desperate to meet Jan's desire for that glimpse of the ocean. One property had boasted 'a much sought-after view' – which turned out to be an apology for the fact that to see the sea you had to stand on tiptoe at one of the dormer windows.

Valentine didn't want to move. He'd spent his life on Greenland Street. Late at night he'd sit by his first wife's grave in the nearby cemetery of All Saints'. It pleased him, oddly, to be a ghostly presence. Moving out to the coast felt like an act of betrayal, although even Valentine was able to discern behind that simplistic summary other, less accessible emotions: a fear of failure perhaps, and a stunted, atrophied expression of the concept of home.

He caught the soft whisper of the distant crowds on the beach, a gentle pulsing scream marking the onward rush of the tide. There were so many things he loathed about the seaside: the sun and fresh air, the irritating sand, the salty tang of burnt flesh on the breeze. Even the sound of it made him feel anxious.

Snapping the paper open again, he took his hundredth look at the wanted poster.

The crime in question had occurred at precisely this time a week earlier. An elderly woman standing in the queue for the T45 had, at first, done nothing to attract attention. Her fellow passengers had outlined a surprisingly consistent picture of her face. Several

said they might have seen her before, on the bus, but they couldn't
be sure. Valentine's boss, DI Peter Shaw, was a trained forensic
artist, and having interviewed the witnesses in the queue to form
an overall visual impression of their suspect, he had been able to
produce the wanted poster. The ghost of lost beauty lay in the fine
features, the wispy white hair, and the choice of earrings, noted by
three of the female witnesses: two small classic cameos, set in silver.
Pushing a wheeled shopping bag, she had worn a crisp white blouse
and pale cream pleated trousers, with brown leather court shoes.
She was neat, respectable, and, as it turned out, lethal.

A few minutes before the scheduled arrival of the bus, she had
started offering those in the queue a sweet, her hand held out with
a few wrapped toffees and chocolates cupped lightly in her fingers.
Working her way up and down the queue, she'd approached
everyone. The brand of confectionary was unknown, but was later
identified from a discarded wrapper as TopChoc, a discount product
sold through supermarket chains. Five of the nine passengers had
taken the sweets, but only four had eaten them. One of these
had been Jack Roach, a sixty-eight-year-old former train driver, on
a day out from his home in Norwich. Roach, a widower, had two
grandsons, and the trip was in part a recce ahead of a planned outing
the following week. Visiting the town's Sea Life Sanctuary, he had
purchased three advance tickets, later found in his wallet.

The T45 had arrived on time and the passengers had climbed
aboard, all of them alighting at Lynn railway station, or the next,
and final, stop, at the bus terminal. Roach chose the railway
station and waited for the 4.17 to Ely. Feeling unwell, he bought
a bottle of still water on the train from the trolley. At Ely he
bought a packet of paracetamol before getting on the 5.22 to
Norwich. At Wymondham, Roach had quit the train and run for the
station toilets, where he was sick. Complaining of nausea and
cramps, he asked station staff to call an ambulance, which arrived
promptly, and took him to the Norfolk and Norwich Hospital, where
he was admitted. Sitting in A&E, he was sick several times, this
time vomiting blood. His condition deteriorated rapidly and he was
unconscious by the time doctors were able to make a full examination. Suffering a violent attack of muscle cramps in the hospital
lift, he entered cardiac arrest and, despite the attentions of medical
staff, was certified as dead at six fifteen p.m.

Valentine's mouth was dry, and so he retrieved a bottle of water from his raincoat and wet his lips. Checking his watch, he noted that the T45 was two minutes late.

The Ark, West Norfolk's forensic lab, had examined the contents of Roach's stomach following a full autopsy. The toffee was located and found to contain nearly four grams of strychnine – an industrial mix, with other chemicals, probably purchased wholesale. The Ark's electron microscope revealed traces of water and flour in the choco-late, suggesting that the poison had been injected into the sweet in the form of a sticky solution.

West Norfolk's serious crime unit had been on the case for six straight days. The priority was to make sure there were no more victims, and so the poster had been mass-produced, and Shaw had made several TV appearances to appeal for witnesses to step forward with a name, or information leading to a name. Every possible facet of Roach's life had been investigated in the hope that he was the *intended* victim. Two of the passengers said they'd been allowed to pick their sweet, while another said the woman had handed him one she had nominated. None of the other passengers was ill. Shaw's unit was visiting care homes, sheltered housing, and churches, armed with the poster. Meanwhile, the media, including the national tabloids, had covered the case, labelling the suspect the 'sweetie killer'. Shaw, ever-cautious, had been the first to suggest the killing might be accidental: had the sweet been doctored *as* vermin bait? Had a tragic error led to death?

Valentine was happy to leave bizarre accidents to his superiors, while he volunteered to run a surveillance unit of six officers providing cover here at Hunstanton from six to ten – the last bus leaving at nine fifty-six for Lynn. So far he'd sat through a dozen three-hour slots. Not a naturally contemplative man, the vigils had given him time to consider the question: Why do criminals return to the scene of the crime? Did the nervous offender haunt the scene in order to gain some brief advantage of time if a clue was found? Some, he felt, must believe they were superior beings to common detectives, and the return merely offered an opportunity to gloat, to watch poor uneducated coppers like George Valentine missing vital clues. Perhaps he was being watched now. Swiftly, he stood, his hatchet skull panning the scene, but nobody hid, nobody looked away.

Valentine had shared the perplexing question with Shaw. It was a mark of their developing relationship that he could bring himself to ask his young superior officer a question at all. In another life, before Valentine had been busted back to DS, he'd worked with Shaw's father – DCI Jack Shaw. Valentine had once been a whizz kid too. So this current partnership had been a wary, edgy, and occasionally ill-tempered affair. But some of the jagged edges had come off, especially now that Valentine realized that for Shaw the difficult truth was that his detective sergeant had once known his late father better than he ever would.

'It's emotional, George. Criminals – especially violent ones – register a palpable thrill when they commit a crime. How can they get that buzz again? They can kill again, or rape again, or disfigure again. But there's another way. They can *relive* it, if they can get back to the scene. Take my beach,' said Shaw, aware that Valentine knew it well. Shaw's wife ran an up-market beach bar and café at Old Hunstanton, a mile distant along the coast from the bus station. 'I played there as a child with Dad. Now I watch Fran play on the same sands. I'm happy at that precise spot because it's associated in my mind with freedom, joy, beauty, and family. I can feel that – all of that – every time I set foot on the beach.

'If a criminal enjoys a crime, they'll come back in just the same way. It's a facet of the place, burnt into the mind, a trigger which releases the emotions into the bloodstream. If they're smart, they'll find somewhere with the same attributes as the original place – a path through woods, a sand dune, a back alley. But sometimes it has to be the *same* place. Exactly the same place.'

Valentine felt that Peter Shaw, a clean-cut father of a young daughter, with a fancy degree and a beautiful wife, had an unhealthy grip on the murkier facets of the criminal mind.

The T45 swept into the tight turning circle that formed the heart of the bus station, the hiss of expelled air marking the release of pneumatic pressure which allowed the bus to lower its doorway to the curb.

'Christ,' said Valentine, standing, the newspaper falling from his knees to the pavement.

The little queue was uncurling to climb aboard and as it did it revealed what he had missed, a woman, halfway down, holding out her hand to a child who was on tiptoes to see all the individually wrapped chocolates on offer. Given the circumstances, Valentine later felt, it was unsettling that at the time he thought the elderly woman, a close match for Shaw's portrait, had a remarkably sweet smile.

THREE

D I Peter Shaw gazed out to sea from the lifeguard's high chair set on the sand in front of *Surf!*, the wine bar run by his wife, Lena. Beside it, they'd converted the Old Boathouse into a shop, selling everything from ninety-nine-pence beach windmills to £5,000 wind yachts. Back in the marram grass lay the family cottage, linked to the café by a modern extension. The three buildings formed a miniature outpost of Old Hunstanton, set on the beach a mile north of the lifeboat house, reached only with a four-by-four or tractor along the rough track below the dunes.

In a minute, maybe two, he would swim in the water which was now flooding the beach, brimming over from the deep water channel offshore and sweeping towards the dunes in a series of hypnotic surges, covering half a mile in less than a minute. Southwards, where the beaches were crowded at Hunstanton, he could hear the gentle hum of the holiday crowds. Locals knew this was the time to swim, as the chilly waters of the North Sea soaked up the heat of the sunbaked sand, forming a lake of lukewarm water, just a few feet deep.

The water horizon in front of Shaw now comprised more than 180 degrees, so that peripheral vision would have been needed to capture the entire sweep of the waters of the Wash in one panoramic snapshot. The East Anglian coast, especially at this precise point, boasted this strange, rare quality. On a map, the north Norfolk shoreline seemed to suggest a great bay window, looking out to sea, north towards the pole. The sandy, littoral coast, unencumbered by rocky headlands, gave a sense that the sea was not only ahead of you but stretched behind you, over both shoulders.

The sea was calm. An extraordinary spring of gentle winds and clear skies had given way to an even softer summer. The unruffled waters had allowed the sand to settle so that the visibility below the surface was extraordinary, the water holding that degree of pure light more reminiscent of the Greek islands than the normally turgid, murky North Sea. The calm weather had seemed like a benediction after a cruel, stormy winter, which had seen the tides remake the sand bars and channels of the Wash, sculpting new creeks and rivers, and remoulding the beaches with ridges and banks. Sitting now, eager to run into the waves, Shaw felt that this was just one of the reasons he loved the place, that it was a work in progress, the result of a shifting balance between land and sea.

Shaw closed his eyes and enjoyed the sounds of an English seaside beach. Memory was most vividly stimulated by those senses that did not change with age. We don't see, we perceive, and images alter from year to year, depending on our experiences. The past is overlaid by newer, more relevant versions of the same picture. But sound was constant, unalterable, and by closing his eyes he could access the past directly, by-passing the intervening decades. He felt himself drawn to the edgeland of memory, playing as a ten-year-old to this identical soundtrack. There was no doubt he was haunted by the past in this spot, but he never saw ghosts, even in the long dusks of summer, because he'd written his own story on the landscape, partly obscuring what had gone before.

Opening his eyes, he looked out to sea, the world behind him and nothing in front of him. Swinging a small pocket telescope southwards, he noted two jet-skiers, a lone red-capped woman, and three men hurling a rugby ball water-polo-style. Shaw's personal marine horizon was actually just less than 120 degrees, due to a blind right eye. He'd lost his sight in an accident on the beach five years earlier, trying to haul a small child away from a toxic barrel of waste into which she'd been prodding a stick. The screaming girl had inadvertently pierced the sclera of his right eye with the point of the stick. The resulting white iris – a *mooneye* – was in stark contrast to the blue of the left.

Blinking, exercising the good eye, he looked down at an open police file on his knee, the cover marked *MISSING PERSON: Case no. 45998 M/EU/A.*

Shaw had never been good at losing things, not in the simple binary sense of winning and losing, but in the sense of objects *misplaced*, or its more final, brutal partner: *lost*. The concept of 'missing' left him deeply anxious. In childhood he had often been able to picture the lost object – a favourite toy, a treasured watch, a fossil from the cliff foot. The sheer power of his imagination was enough to conjure up the lost object in a palpable form. It was intolerable to consider the hard reality that he could not actually find it. This had led, throughout his life, to interminable and increasingly bitter searches. He had once spent an entire university vacation intermittently engaged in a forensic sweep of the family home in search of a black moleskin sketchbook, six inches by three. The problem was that every time he imagined where the lost object might be, *he could see it* – right there, where he pictured it to be. Lena had long abandoned him to these infatuations, which had persisted into adult life. It was as if his character was defined by the opposite of the maxim 'out of sight, out of mind'.

The missing object currently tantalizingly just beyond Shaw's reach was a sixty-three-year-old Dutchman called Dirk Hartog. An enlarged black-and-white picture of his passport headshot showed a heavy face, with bags under oyster-like eyes, furled like the sails on a galleon.

Hartog was an electrician from Harlingen on the Frisian coast. He had taken a room at the Lancaster Hotel, on one of Hunstanton's Edwardian squares, insisting, in the manner of the great English landscape painter Joseph Mallord William Turner, that he be allocated a bay window, with a sea view. In apparently flawless English, he had informed the hotelier by email that he wished to see the sun set in the west. Arriving in early June, he had spent a month in the town, initially restricting himself to his room except for meals, which he took in various pubs and cafés in the town. In the evenings, at sunset, he took a window seat in the Wash and Tope, a pub on the front, and drank three pints of Guinness, each with a single whisky chaser.

Breakfast was taken on a tray in his room. The landlady, cleaning when he went out, found the room's round table set by the window and covered in Admiralty charts of the seabed offshore, extending to the distant Lincolnshire coast. By the bay window a small telescope soon sat in a fixed position on an expensive metal tripod.

After a week Hartog started going out for most of the day, always with a rucksack (distinctively marked with two sewn-on Dutch tricolour flags) and a metal hiking stick, and wearing worn walking boots. The wardrobe in his room now accommodated a summer wetsuit, purchased locally. By the start of the second week it had been joined by a full scuba kit (marked *Hunstanton Marine*), including an air tank and face mask. The owners of the hotel had spotted him on three occasions: once on the beach to the south, just beyond the pleasure park, drying himself after a swim; once on a bench in front of the sailing club; and, finally, emerging from the sea in the scuba gear, right here, on Shaw's beach, a mile north of Old Hunstanton.

Then Dirk Hartog had disappeared, and nobody seemed to care, except the owners of the Lancaster Hotel, keen to clear his room. Inquiries revealed he was divorced, with two grown-up children, whom he never saw. His father had died when he was a child, and his mother, a long-term inmate in a mental institution in Arnhem, had finally passed away that very winter.

The missing-person file had landed on Shaw's desk at St James' a week ago. The Dutchman's room at the Lancaster was Shaw's first port of call. The diving gear was gone. The CID team had spent some time in the room and noted several details: the Admiralty charts were new and marked with the price – £143 each, comprising a set of five; and the telescope was focused on the floating crane and rig of the pier head. And while the cupboard no longer held the diving suit and gear, it wasn't empty. Two items were removed for forensic examination: an urn of ashes and a piece of driftwood bearing the hand-painted letters *Cala*: a ship's nameplate, with the first letter C, and letters possibly following the second A, as the wood had sheared at that point. The wood was wrapped in oilskin. Shaw speculated that Hartog had been searching for more wreckage of this partially named ship. However, the online Lloyd's register listed eight ships lost in UK territorial waters since 1900 with a name beginning *Cala*; none lay off the East Coast.

Despite an all-points alert, there was no trace of Hartog at ports or airports: according to online Stena Line records, he had an open return ticket on the Harwich ferry to the Hook of Holland. Dutch police reported that his flat in Harlingen was deserted. Hartog's life, superficially reconstructed, appeared bleak, except for a lifelong passion for swimming. He'd won a silver medal for the hundred metres backstroke at the Dutch national championships when he was nineteen, and was an instructor at a swimming club in his home town. A season ticket holder at Anderlecht, he also coached an under-eights junior football side.

Shaw had the case file open at a page containing a translation of a letter from Hartog's doctor to the Dutch police in response to inquiries about his patient's health. Had his mental state been fragile in the period leading up to his disappearance? The answer was unequivocal: his mental health was *stevig* – 'robust'.

Suicide seemed unlikely. An accident while diving was the obvious, lethal scenario. But where was the body? This question seemed to bother nobody except Shaw.

The Wash consisted – at low tide – of nearly 150 square miles of maze-like sand banks and tidal creeks; high tide transformed it into a treacherously shallow sea, bounded on three sides, but wide open to the north wind. Within this vast space a man's body was a micron. Shaw's superiors at St James' had resigned themselves to the idea that Hartog's body lay out in this liquid wilderness, lost for ever.

Shaw's perspective was very different. For five years he had been a volunteer on the lifeboat at Old Hunstanton, more recently the pilot of its small inshore hovercraft, which was designed to thread those self-same maze-like channels and sandy cuts. His relationship with the Wash was more intimate than most. History showed that this eerie lagoon *always* gave up its dead. Of the eighteen deaths recorded since 1950 on the coasts of the great inlet, only one body had *not* been washed up within forty-eight hours, and that had been found at Brancaster, just round Holme Point on the open north coast, on the third day.

In the days after Hartog's disappearance Shaw had piloted the hovercraft over the sands and mudflats in search of the Dutchman or his kit. The sluices and drains feeding the coastal marshes had all been checked. The beaches had been walked. There was no sign of the missing body. To Peter Shaw, this meant one of two things: either Hartog was alive or someone had weighted down his dead body.

Lifting the telescope now to his good eye, he scanned the sea.

Footsteps on sand are silent, so he didn't hear Lena approaching and he jumped when she touched his foot, reaching through the opening between two slats of the ladder.

Walking slowly – Lena never rushed – she rounded the lifeguard's high chair to face her husband. She had a sinuous, cat-like step, Jamaican black skin, and a face made up of a collection of curves, which Shaw always felt reminded him of an African tribal mask, with its wide cheekbones and arched eyebrows.

She was smiling, but a tear escaped from her left eye. 'It's Mum,' she said. 'She's gone at last.'

Lena had been brought up in Brixton, with younger siblings, while an estranged stepfather lived in north London. Her own father had died young, shortly after her own birth. Her mother, Muriel, still only in her mid-fifties, had been suffering from kidney failure for three years, living in a care home in Tooting.

'She won't see it now,' added Lena, turning on her heel to encompass the beach. They'd planned to drive her up to see *Surf!*, although her mother seemed increasingly fearful of the world outside Lily House. Lena had showed her pictures, of the café and the shop, and the wide beach, hemmed in by the dunes, and her mother had seemed genuinely captivated. She'd asked for one of the images – of Fran and Lena standing in the shallows as the sun went down – to be framed and set beside her bed. Despite her relative youth, she had treated her illness as terminal from the moment of its diagnosis. This sense of inevitability had infused the entire family, and her death had been anticipated as a release from pain.

For the last two months she had suffered from severe vascular dementia, brought on by a series of strokes, and failed to recognize Lena on her final visit, but for a lucid final few seconds as her daughter stood at the open door.

Lena sat on the ladder, two steps below Shaw. 'They called me because I'm the oldest, so I'll have to tell the others. I'll do it now. They'll be angry – with the doctors, the nurses, me. They're always angry. I wonder sometimes – when I hear them speaking to each other in whispers – why the anger seems to be reserved for me. I've always felt like an outsider.'

The rest of the Braithwaite family was dysfunctional, harbouring a familial sense of injustice that had entirely bypassed Lena. Shaw had met the brother and sister at a family christening. They seemed to resent Lena's path in life: the law degree, a high-profile job with the Campaign for Racial Equality, and finally her marriage to a detective, working out of New Scotland Yard.

'Jessie will want the flat. I don't have the energy to fight her over it. Marcus wants a cremation at Streatham, and the ashes scattered locally, so he can visit. But I've told him, she hated the idea that she'd be ashes on the wind. I just hope she left a will. I told her enough times that if she didn't get it down in black and white, Marcus would do what he wanted, for himself.'

What, at that moment, prompted both of them to turn south, towards the distant pleasure beach?

Shaw recalled later that his left eardrum creaked, signalling a sudden change in air pressure. Was there a flash of fire? The sound – a dull, buffeting thud – reached them a second later, shaking the lifeguard's high chair. Lena recalled the bottles behind the bar in *Surf!* tinkling softly.

A plume of water rose up a mile distant, sand at its heart, as if the guts of the earth had been ripped out.

Shaw, already running, heard a ripple of screams, and then – the worst moment of all – a shocked stillness, which seemed to encompass the sea itself, so that even the waves were silent.

FOUR

Shaw was thirty yards along the beach before he stopped, checked his mobile, and, finding no signal, called back to Lena to use the landline to ring emergency services and DS Valentine. 'Tell George there's been an explosion,' he shouted. 'Could be anything. You stay put. I'll see him by the old pier.'

About to turn away, he had one last question. 'Fran?' he asked, both palms open and held out to the side.

Their daughter was on a day trip with a friend's family to Norwich, but somehow he needed to hear an external confirmation that she was safe.

'I'll double-check,' called Lena. 'She'll be miles away.'

'Tell her to stay put until we call again.'

It was enough, so he ran. Running was Peter Shaw's obsession, punctuating every day of his life with two sub-five-minute miles. To the lifeboat house at Old Hunstanton, and the parking space for his Porsche, he averaged 4.32 seconds. That was the *workwards* leg, while *homewards* he averaged 4.28 to the first step of the *Surf!* verandah. Today, he knew he'd broken his best time as he passed the lifeboat house and began the climb up the coastal path that skirted the edge of the cliffs.

Ahead, the cloud of sand launched skywards by the blast was still drifting in the air, the particles fine enough to produce an interior rainbow. By the stone ruins of St Edmund's chapel Shaw stopped, doubled over, then checked again for a mobile signal. A single bar came and went like a heartbeat, but there was a 3D digital signal from the aerial on the old lighthouse, so he picked up BBC Radio Norfolk. Securing an earphone, he ran on, past the old radar station, towards the outskirts of the resort.

The pips on the radio announced four o'clock, the news leading with an item about holiday traffic chaos on the Norfolk Broads. The afternoon programme of music and chat was interrupted thirty seconds later, just as Shaw reached the distinctive pyramid-roofed clifftop café above the town.

The BBC had a radio reporter at Hunstanton compiling a feature on the pier construction project. 'We have reports of an incident at Hunstanton. We can go live to our business correspondent, Rupert Bloom.' They cut to the scene by mobile.

'Everyone's running,' said Bloom, without preamble, as if in mid-sentence, struggling to make himself heard against the white noise of scattered voices and a persistent backing track of what sounded like car alarms. Shaw was unsure if he was hearing the soundtrack on the radio or via his free ear.

'Just running,' said Bloom, as if this fragment made sense in itself. 'There was a bang and the sand went up, and seawater too, and it's still coming down, like rain. A lot of people have got their hands to their ears. The sound really hurt. It still hurts. I can't see any blood.'

Shaw heard the reporter's laboured breathing and a young child crying.

'Everyone's trying to get off the beach. I'm at the edge of the esplanade now and I can see, looking back, a . . . a shell hole. It's the only way I can describe it. About – what? – thirty feet long, but narrow at the centre, and then splaying out. There's a lot of smoke maybe, or sand – I can't tell. Everyone's running and they've left loads on the beach – pushchairs, and tents, and picnics, and towels. I can't see any casualties, but it's chaos, so I don't know; I can't confirm that. There's a lot of glass too, so people are carrying children without shoes. I'm going to try to talk to someone . . .'

Shaw stopped, now looking down on the beach below, which was indeed scattered with abandoned belongings, a set of cricket stumps standing in the middle of an acre of empty sand as the tide swept the outfield. Ahead, on the low clifftop by the old pier head, a crowd stood crammed into the triangular green at the centre of which stood the town's war memorial.

The reporter's incoming feed was distorted as if they were listening to his mobile from a handbag or pocket. Shaw readjusted his earphone to try to improve the signal.

The broadcast cleared, the sound suddenly sharp and immediate. 'Yes. Sorry. It's the BBC. Did you see what happened? An explosion?'

'Yes. My God. Oh my God.' A woman's voice, stressed, but already laced with a sense of relief. She must have turned away to a child because the next thing she said was distorted. 'Yes. It's all right. Hold your brother's hand.'

'Where were you?' said Bloom, trying to regain his witness's attention.

'Just close. Some kids had dug a hole and everyone crowded round to see the sea come in and fill it up. Then everybody ran. Then there was this thud, and the sun just blacked out, like a shadow was thrown up, and it went completely quiet. And dark, like the sun was behind the clouds. And then people just tried to get off the sand. Like, it's not panic, is it? But I'm scared and everyone's upset. You can see that. It's such a shock. And my ears hurt . . .'

'Were the kids OK? Did you see anyone with injuries?'

'I don't know. I don't know. Well, I can't say. I feel so sorry for the parents . . .'

A piercing police warning alarm made the radio broadcast screech with feedback. Shaw stopped at the top of one of the zigzag metal staircases that led down to the beach, his good eye scanning the debris and detritus, locking on to anything red: a discarded swimsuit, a ball. He phoned the control room at St James' but found the switchboard jammed. The nerves in his legs kept sparking, as if they wanted him to run, but he made himself compose a text to Valentine: *Where you? Bomb blast at beach. Services alerted. Heading for crater. Get bomb disposal. No copters on beach till all-clear. Alert IPCO.*

IPCO was the coordinating unit for terrorist information for the provincial police forces. Shaw didn't believe this was such an attack, but after a year of atrocities across Europe they needed to make sure the Home Office was alerted.

A police squad car swung off the coast road and parked by the cliff edge, disgorging two uniformed constables, one with a radio mike already to his lips. The crowds, jammed along the esplanade, pressed up to the iron railings.

Shaw ran to the squad car and showed his warrant card. 'What do we know?'

One of the constables was short, with steel-rimmed glasses, and said his name was Harrison. 'St John's Ambulance were here. Control room says they've got five casualties on their way to Lynn. Condition unknown.'

'Loud hailer?' asked Shaw, noting a fire engine, lights flashing, forcing its way between two lines of stationary traffic on the street leading to the green.

Harrison went to the boot and retrieved a hailer, and a warning beacon and a drum of scene-of-crime tape.

Before he shut the boot, Shaw had another thought. 'Evidence bags?'

Harrison held up two bundles of sealable plastic bags, with red zips.

'Right . . . We don't have much time,' said Shaw, forcing his voice to stay flat, matter-of-fact. 'High tide's pretty close, so we have a brief window to collect any surviving evidence. Our first priority is the safety of the public. For now you two are what passes for authority. You need to impose it. Harrison, take the hailer down on to the beach. Ping it to get through the crowd. Don't run. Tell the crowds the emergency services are on the way and that anyone with injuries should make themselves known. In the meantime, everyone – *everyone* – needs to move away from the railings, and, when the paths are clear, make their way up to the green, or back to their cars. The beach is closed for the day. Got it?'

Harrison nodded.

'Don't say the word "bomb". Don't say there might be others. Try to sound like an airline pilot. Got it?'

Harrison nodded again.

'Right. Lead the way. You come with me,' added Shaw to the other officer. 'Name?'

'Wright.'

Using the hailer, they parted the crowd and made for a set of stone steps which cut down through the esplanade to the sands, at the foot of which a pushchair on its side had disgorged a child's toys and a bag of soiled nappies. Towels and a line of wetsuits hung drying on a breakwater.

Shaw surveyed the beach, alert to any movement that might indicate an injured victim. The problem was the wooden break-waters, which effectively hid the view north and south. Were there casualties out of sight? An unnatural silence still shrouded the coast, and Shaw noted that the Ferris wheel at the fun park a half mile south was stationary. Out to sea, a blue warning light flashed silently on the construction rig, while the crane stood frozen in the sky, the great arm poised at forty-five degrees, dangling a steel girder over the water.

The crater caused by the blast was awash.

Harrison began to broadcast to the crowd behind them, his voice – Shaw noted – even and calm. The fire engine had reached the esplanade, and with it an ambulance.

Shaw and Wright headed for the crater. It did not form a neat Western Front shell hole, but rather a sinuous bow-tie-shaped trench, the blast point at the knot, indicating how the force had been directed north-west and south-east, leaving two rims of the original children's pit partly intact. The pit was half full of seawater.

As they approached, Shaw turned to Wright. 'You got kids?'

Wright nodded. 'Two. Boy and a girl. They're—'

'This might not be pretty,' said Shaw, cutting him off, making eye contact. Wright was six foot two, about level with Shaw, and although he appeared calm, his eyes seemed to skitter over the scene, unable to rest. 'There were children playing near the hole. Maybe *in* the hole. We need to check the sand. Sift through all this stuff. You understand that? The tide's nearly full but it might fill the rest of the hole. You need to be ready. We need to collect evidence. If you find anything, shout. Got it?'

Wright nodded, distracted by stuffing his pockets with the evidence bags.

Shaw used his iPhone to take pictures of the shell hole. 'Look out for anything suspicious,' he called. 'Fragments, metal shards, a priority. Human remains – you shout, I'll come and help.'

Wright turned, nodded, his face as pale as candle wax.

Blood was red for a good reason. Shaw, like all human beings, was hardwired to see it, to react, his nervous system poised to flood with adrenaline. His good eye scanned the sand around the crater. Shreds of plastic were dotted within the blast zone – a few red, but mostly yellow and blue.

Spotting flesh, or bone, on the pale yellow sands would be less straightforward. Shaw realized that his good eye, under stress, was blurring at the tail and hypersensitive at the focal point. What had he expected? A scene from the Somme – shattered bodies slumped in the hole? Now that they were at the edge, they could see that some of the sand on the sides of the pit was black, discoloured by the blast.

Shaw jogged quickly along the waterline, surveying the area, his mind actively shielding his consciousness from hellish images of torn bodies. His pulse rate had hit a thudding, steady high, but as each minute passed, he began to sense that they just might have been lucky, unless the blast had vaporized the victims in the force of the explosion – terrorist bomb victims often went to the grave in empty coffins. Or had they been buried perhaps, in the falling veil of damp sand? Were the dead beneath his feet?

Picking a spot, Shaw knelt and swept the surface layer of sand aside. The tide surged and salt water sizzled around his knees and boots. The next wave was much stronger, sweeping clean over the shell hole, so that he had to retreat. With the water came the spume, like old candy floss, carrying ice-cream wrappers and an empty beer can, and something else, asymmetrical, weighty.

Shaw's still hyperactive eye fashioned it into the shape of a head, and his heart stopped a beat, then two. Straps and a zip redefined the object: a rucksack perhaps. At the next wave it came within reach, so he plucked it out of the water and saw that it was a diver's net bag, decorated with two sewn-in Dutch flags.

FIVE

Shaw set up a missing-person checkpoint on the green by directing four West Norfolk squad cars to park in a square. Inside, anyone lost could wait to be found. A female constable from the town's police station arrived with a clipboard and took names. Within ten minutes a huddle of eight lost children had been reunited with tearful parents. A seventy-two-year-old pensioner was claimed by his grandson, and a thirty-two-year-old female patient from the psychiatric ward at the Queen Elizabeth Hospital in Lynn was reunited with her nurse, and six other patients, on a day out to the resort.

Shaw's mobile rang, and he brought up a text from St James' control room: *Family of five at QE2. No threat to life. They dug hole. No other casualties reported. HH*

HH was Sergeant Harry Hunter, a copper who'd been a byword for streetwise policing when Shaw's father was a DCI, which helped to explain the precision of his message. There might be other, unknown, casualties, but it looked increasingly likely that the explosion had claimed no lives. It left two questions unanswered: What kind of bomb had it been, and were there any others?

Shaw called the crews of the four squad cars together for a one-minute briefing, establishing that the priority was to keep the crowds off the beach until the sands could be surveyed by the army. One of the squad cars was nominated as a control centre, the doors thrown open, a flashing light set on the roof. What they needed was manpower, and the control room at St James' was directed to pull in all off-duty uniformed officers and get them to the resort as quickly as possible. An on-duty DS from CID was given the job of organizing food, admin back-up, and transport. Road traffic was warned to brace itself for an exodus from Hunstanton, with holidaymakers heading for other beaches, or just taking the direct route home. Conversely, there were already reports of cars crammed with sightseers heading *towards* the danger zone.

Shaw dismissed the team, setting five o'clock for a regroup, and turned away to see Valentine's Mazda mount the curb and trundle down the grassy slope. The car, with a 1980s registration plate, was Bakelite brown and dinted in the bonnet. Even though he knew his DS had given up smoking, Shaw could never quite dislodge the image of the Mazda as a four-wheeled ashtray.

Hauling himself out of the driver's seat, Valentine pressed a hand to the small of his back. Then they stood, polar opposites, almost toe to toe: Valentine defined by the suit that seemed to hang off his bones; Shaw, four-square, in shorts and T-shirt, hair spiky and straw-blond.

'Welcome to the frontline,' said Shaw, looking out to sea, his face broad and open, with high cheekbones, as if an outrider of the Mongol hordes had fetched up on the north Norfolk coast.

'Injured? Dead?' asked Valentine, licking his lower lip, as if trying to recollect the tang of nicotine.

'Not so far. It's looking good. But no doubt it was a bomb – well, an explosion. Kids were digging a hole.'

'Wartime. Got to be,' said Valentine.

'Maybe,' said Shaw, nodding. 'Question is: one of ours, or one of theirs? And if it's ours, is that British or US? Americans didn't pack up until the early sixties. Up to then this place was pretty much a military town. When they did go, they were in a hurry, so who knows what got left behind.'

Shaw had grown up in the seaside resort. His childhood had been full of stories about the war, and the fifties, when one in six residents had been American – mostly air force personnel at the nearby base at Sculthorpe. Infamously, the town had provided services of all kinds, including a string of brothels, set up in the resort's fading hotels, an attraction that had won Hunstanton unwanted publicity in the racier newspapers.

'So who do we need to give the all-clear?' asked Valentine.

'Bomb disposal, I guess. They're on their way.'

A uniformed PC arrived with a tray of a dozen Costa coffees.

'For the sake of argument,' said Shaw, 'if it's not a UXB, what are our options, George?'

'Our anti-pier campaigners have decided to crank up the odds?' Valentine, with obvious distaste, examined the white froth on the top of his coffee, dappled with chocolate. 'What have we had? Graffiti, road blocks, vandalism, arson . . . Maybe someone's prepared to push things a bit further?'

Shaw looked doubtful. 'I can't see it. It's early days, and an open mind is a wonderful thing, but *really*? A bunch of Barbour-wearing environmentalists plant a bomb on a holiday beach? They kill some three-year-old and that's the end of their campaign. I know they've got fanatics on board, fellow travellers, but a bomb?'

'The arson attack out on the rig wasn't exactly a nursery crime.'

'But it *was* amateur. Trademark eco-extremists. Half-cocked. It isn't that easy to make a bomb, George. And why target the beach?'

'It's where the power cables run out to the rig,' said Valentine.

Shaw turned back to survey the scene. Valentine's bluff, old-fashioned copper routine hid a first-class grip on his manor. Occasionally, Shaw had to remind himself that while he'd been at school, DI George Valentine had once been the bright young thing in CID. 'OK. I didn't know that.'

'Yeah. They dug a trench six weeks ago, then filled it in. Perhaps this was half-cocked too.'

Shaw played with that idea but then caught a movement in the back of the Mazda. Squatting down, he saw an elderly woman in the back seat, looking straight back at him with a profoundly disorientated sadness, like a lost child.

'She's why I'm late,' said Valentine. From the front seat the DS produced an evidence bag containing the carton of wrapped toffees he'd found in her shopping bag on wheels. Another bag held three wrapped sweets, plus an unwrapped toffee.

'You're kidding,' said Shaw.

'Nope. Same queue, same bus. She'd given out four, one opened.'

Shaw took another look, trying to recall the details of his artistic reconstruction of their suspect. 'Doesn't look *that* much like her, does it? Or maybe she does. What does she say?'

'No idea what's going on. Didn't notice the posters. She gabbled a bit; now she's shut up. Insists she's not herself – her words. Hip replacement op, apparently, and she reckons the painkillers make her dizzy.' He unzipped the evidence bag and held the carton of sweets up for Shaw to sniff. 'Thing is, I reckon you can smell it.'

'Almonds,' said Shaw.

'Yup. I've checked. There's one – an almond cluster. But it's the *only* smell. What about the orange swirl or the rum truffle. You can't even smell the chocolate. Just almond.'

Shaw was close enough to pat Valentine on the back, but he

resisted the urge; George Valentine had backed a hunch and followed through. There was a good chance he'd struck lucky. He didn't need, or crave, Shaw's validation. And he had a rare smile on his lips. 'What did she say before she stopped gabbling?'

'Name's Keeble – Esther. Aged seventy-two. Lives with her husband in one of the old prefabs down on the South Beach. They don't have a TV – the Keebles – never listen to the radio, and she doesn't get the local paper, so, like I said, she says she's no idea we were looking for someone giving out sweets in a bus queue.' Valentine bent stiffly to look at his suspect. 'I'd say she was in shock.' Straightening up, he took a few paces down the slope. 'But there's something else going on, behind here . . .' He pointed at his eyes, left then right. 'It's not fear. It's not disappointment. It's like she's working something out, Peter. Calculating.'

'I know the Keebles,' said Shaw. 'Know *of* them. Husband's George Keeble. They ran the newsagents down Empire Way for years. Maybe that's why they avoid the papers now. George was a volunteer in the lifeboat – in the fifties, sixties. He used to turn up for open days, fundraisers. Good bloke. Dad used to say he was salt of the earth.'

'I'll run her back to St James', get her a duty solicitor,' said Valentine. 'And I'll have the doc give the once-over. Don't want her keeling over on us.'

'Right,' said Shaw, opening up the boot of one of the squad cars and retrieving a large evidence bag, inside of which was the diver's bag he'd picked out of the sea, emblazoned with Dutch flags. He gave it to Valentine, wanting him to make the link.

'Hartog? Where?'

'On the surf line twenty minutes after the explosion.'

'So what are we saying – that it's linked to the explosion, or it's a coincidence?'

Shaw was unhappy with that most illogical of explanations: *coincidence.* 'More to the point, why does the kit turn up, but not his body?'

SIX

The shadow of the dogfish, shark-like, skimmed over the ribbed sea sand, heading shorewards, called from its feeding grounds in the deep sea trench by the single shock wave of the exploding bomb. The fish's slate-grey back, pitted with scars, twisted with the torque required to power the tail fin, driving it forward on a three-dimensional path it had swum all its life, out of the cold water of the channel, into the warm shallows. Sunlight, filtering down in shimmering columns, created micro-currents, which gently churned the grains of quartz and chalk, sandstone and shell on the ocean floor, creating a thin underwater sea mist, through which the fish sliced a path.

In the deep channel along which the ships plied, the dogfish could slide untroubled within the sandy walls of the canyon, while above it the iron propellers churned towards the Bentinck and the Alexandra, the Boal and the Fisher Fleet. But here, in the waters above the sand bar, it was troubled by the white scratches of skidoos, hauling water skiers, or a paraglider, cutting silently across the surface above, or the paddling feet of swimmers in pursuit of drifting inflatables, blown west and out to sea. But there was enough water, even here, to muffle the shock waves these intruders left above.

It slid past a bony fish, past a smack of jellyfish, hanging like a chandelier, and a suspended wreath of sea wrack, until its target came within sight, the shape within the sand even clearer this spring, after the winter storms had stripped away the sandy blanket that had lain over it like a shroud.

The prow, forced up by the sinking of the engines, stood proud still, clogged with clam shells and weed, so that it looked like a lone rock, encrusted. The deck, steel-plated, pitted with sea snails and limpets, lay twisted, its graceful oval lines skewed, running to the stern, just visible now, revealed to the light by the winter currents.

That first night, the dogfish had circled the boat as it sank, hurtling in slow motion to the seabed, the water above white with the storm. Seething, the power of the waves had been felt below, creating a maelstrom of silt, through which the falling hull was no more than a shadow passing, crumpling on impact without a sound. The lights had flickered within, circular beams striking out from the portholes, the bridge bright with polished metal, until a small explosion shook it like a cough, deep in the bowels of the superstructure, and darkness had fallen.

Despite the collision with the seabed, the rivets had held, preserving the outline of the hull, the hold, the deckhouse, and the forward winch. All that first winter the wreck lay unvisited, until the dogfish returned, nosing its way along the bulwark rail towards the hatches of the hold, sensing perhaps what lay within. Plankton, crabs, and small fishes had already inveigled their way into the dark space through air vents and the narrow slits between the buckled plates.

But the dogfish had to wait. The dogfish was patient. It had a memory of sorts, so that it had returned along the path over the years, nosing at the shattered portholes, the twisted plates, but always denied.

Until today. The shock wave had sprung the rivets and a plate had fallen from the starboard hull. The dogfish hung, motionless in the lazy current, analyzing the chemical messages hidden in the brine. A lobster hauled itself out through the gap. Finally, the dogfish slipped within. Once, there would have been sweet meat, but no more. Only this: the shadowy hold and an audience of skulls.

SEVEN

'**M**iracle Escape!' is an overused newspaper cliché, and as a result the media struggled, in the hours after the explosion and after the truth was known, to make their readers appreciate the startling fact that no one had been seriously injured in the explosion on the beach. Witnesses interviewed on the radio and TV suggested that it had been the in-rushing tide that had saved so many lives, driving the crowd back from the lip of the hole, so that when the blast came it had driven upwards through the sea itself.

The major incident paramedic team, assembled at the Queen Elizabeth Hospital in King's Lynn, braced for casualties and severe trauma wounds, was astounded when the rear doors of the ambulance opened outside A&E, to find the Ross children in a communal hug with their parents. Only Eric had been injured, pulling on his father's hand and turning back towards the pit at the vital moment, suffering second-degree burns to his left leg below the knee, and severe abrasions to his left shoulder, where he'd been thrown against a cooler box and a child's pushchair. Marc complained of a 'flutter' in his left ear, but this disappeared within an hour of his arrival at the hospital.

An army bomb disposal unit, scrambled from Sheringham, was on site within three hours, and a spokesman informed *BBC Look East* that it was not uncommon for survivors of bomb explosions to be very close to the point of impact, due to the fact that the force of the blast tended to be concentrated within narrow angles of dispersal – leaving odd pockets, or 'lacunae' – very close to the epicentre of the explosion itself. The spokesman, Captain H. Wharram, was less helpful when asked to identify the bomb itself. Further east on the Norfolk coast, UXBs were common, left over from military training during the Second World War. Although Hunstanton's beach had been fortified against possible invasion in 1940, there was no record of the live firing of ammunition or enemy air raids.

The question for DI Shaw, and one reiterated by the chief constable in a series of persistent text messages, was whether there might be other devices in the area that could represent a threat to public safety. Should the beach remain cordoned off from the public? It was late summer, the weather was hot, local businesses were making financial hay. The town council wanted the beach reopened without delay, although they were, of course, unwilling to take responsibility for such a decision themselves.

The army set up floodlights at dusk and used a pump to drain the shell hole as the sea retreated. Two bomb disposal experts, working in wet suits, retrieved several plate-like sections of molten sand, cooled by the seawater, which had been created in the fierce heat that for a nano-second had been generated at the base of the pit.

The receding tide also allowed a thorough search of the western extension of the bow-tie trench, and the recovery of one other shard of metallic material, to add to the three collected by Shaw and PC Wright in the last few minutes before high tide. An ordnance expert from Catterick had been ordered south to assist the inquiry. The West Norfolk's own diving unit was being assembled and would survey the seabed off the shoreline for further bomb fragments at first light.

By the time Shaw reached his office at St James' in Lynn, it was after nine, a glorious late-summer sky turning from blue to star-studded black. He told Valentine to assemble the squad 'off-site' – CID code for meeting at the Red House, a pub just inside the London Gate, lost in the narrow terraced streets of the old town.

It had been Shaw's father, DCI Jack Shaw, who had chosen the Red House as CID's official 'other office' back in the 1980s, in cahoots with his then DI, George Valentine. Once a bustling back-street boozer, it was now largely dependent on trade from St James' to keep it solvent. Local slums had been cleared, the Red House's customers shipped out to the new estates. It was so out of the way, and so rarely used by anyone but CID and a handful of regulars, that the landlord had put a visitor's book on the bar. An ex-boxer from the East End known universally as Jez, he was happy to give CID a room at the back, and – on request – exclusive access to a back yard, which had seen intermittent attempts at gentrification.

Tonight, Shaw noted some palms in pots, a string of fairy lights, and a chalk 'specials' board which bore two words: *Food off.* Shaw rubbed it clean and used a stick of white chalk from the dartboard to write *1939–1945?*

'Let's get this straight right now. At the moment we have no evidence whatsoever that this was a Second World War unexploded bomb, but common sense tells us it almost certainly is – and we're having the beach checked tomorrow by the army to see if there are others.' Shaw surveyed the team. 'Common sense almost always points the way ahead. But we mustn't be blind to other options. There's a good chance, for example, that while it might have been made for the war, it was actually left behind when the Yanks pulled out in the early sixties. They had to pack up their gear all along the coast: ammunitions, stores, barbed wire, anti-tank devices, the lot. Who knows what got buried. Don't get me wrong – the Americans didn't think they were leaving live shells. But bomb disposal says even if they were made safe at the time, corrosion could make them unstable now, and we know from witnesses that these kids were pelting whatever they'd uncovered with pebbles – and a half brick . . .

'The Ark will have results tomorrow. With luck, we'll know what we're dealing with by first thing. I'll see the Ross family at the hospital and try to get some idea what this device looked like. We need the beach to stay off-limits to the public until the all-clear – half a mile in either direction.

'Uniformed branch are there now. And . . . sorry about this, but the CC wants us to man a call line, twenty-four/seven, in case members of the public have information. Switchboard will vet the calls, but we need someone tonight for the first shift . . .'

The yard's floodlight came on, casting them all into deep relief. Moths began to make the shadows dance. Two or three hands were raised.

'Great. So: that's theory number one: wartime bomb,' said Shaw. 'Either dropped between 1939 and 1945, or left behind by the Americans up to 1963. Theory number two. Anti-pier activists.'

A groan greeted the suggestion. A chaotic conversation broke out while drinks were brought out from the bar. The Stop the Pier campaign – and its various 'paramilitary' wings – had soaked up valuable police time for more than two years. Sympathy for the protestors – an uneasy alliance of green activists and local shopkeepers and business interests – had been stretched to breaking point as the campaign had escalated, from non-violent protest to criminal vandalism and finally arson.

When the project won planning permission and secured EU funding, CID had thrown a party, in the mistaken belief it marked the end of hostilities. Far from it. The STP had promptly launched a two-pronged attack in an attempt to stop the construction work and force both Brussels and the local council to go back to the original 'Victorian' blueprint first mooted by the consortium behind the project. They claimed the plan for a 'super-pier' had been sneaked past MPs, MEPs, and local councillors, and insinuated that financial backhanders had smoothed the way. Lawyers fought a continuous campaign to get Brussels civil servants to put the case before the EU's auditors, while STP activists were preparing to stand as candidates at the next local elections unless councillors agreed to an inquiry. The STP argued it wasn't too late to stop work and go back to the original design, pointing out that an elegant theatre pavilion could stand on the caisson just as easily as the planned fairground super-rides.

Shaw called for order. 'I don't think any of us believe a bunch of local shopkeepers or butterfly hunters is going to start a bombing campaign. But what about our green warriors? We know outsiders have been flocking to the demos – activists, veterans from other campaigns. What if this device is home-made – cobbled together to make a point? Maybe it wasn't a rusty old thousand-pounder; maybe it was an old fridge full of fertilizer.'

DC Jackie Lau raised her voice above the general hubbub. 'Maybe it didn't just go off. Maybe it was triggered.'

The yard fell silent. Lau was ethnic Chinese, a career copper who wanted to be the force's first female DI in operational CID – not traffic, or, unbearably, child liaison. She had a reputation for working hard, and playing harder, largely in fast cars. Nobody doubted she was smart enough for the job.

'Go on, Jackie,' said Shaw.

'Maybe they didn't want to kill anyone. So the device is in the sand; they watch it being dug up, and then, when everyone runs, they trigger it off. That way they get the publicity, but don't cross the line. No one empathizes with murder.'

'Right. So triggered by someone in line of sight. How are we fixed for CCTV, Mark?'

Mark Birley, ex-uniformed branch, had a genius for sifting through evidence, and a straightforward approach to the job which matched his rugby forward's physique. Shaw's theory was that Birley's incessant physical activity – he worked out in the gym every day and was a manic weightlifter – gave him that rare human skill: an ability to remain still. Birley could review CCTV footage for hours, maintaining a high level of focus.

'I'm on it,' said Birley. 'Six cameras on the front – plus one outside the amusement park, and one by the sailing club. I've got data requests in for the lot.'

'Good. But let's take Jackie's idea one step further. If it is a home-made bomb, and it is the anti-pier campaign, then it may well be the same people who got out to the rig and lit that oil drum. Where are we on the arson, Paul?'

Paul Twine was graduate entry, a smart copper good at keeping the unit from information overload. He worked as 'point' – the officer designated to review all data, and circulate anything of significance to his colleagues: effectively a human data filter.

'Forensics gave the rig a once-over, but even they admitted it was perfunctory,' he said. 'The rig's got three decks, two accommodation blocks; then there's the tug, the crane, and the sea platforms down in the water. So they had to focus on trying to isolate the accelerant used.'

'Right,' said Shaw. 'If the Ark can nail the device as military – and historic – then that's all fine. If not, have a word with forensics; let's get a second SOCO sweep of the rig. Maybe they missed something first time.'

Valentine, leaning against the yard wall, stepped forward. 'Home Office has been back on. What with the Brighton attack, they're jumpy. Can't blame 'em.'

Six weeks earlier, an off-duty soldier suffered a fatal knife attack while sitting on a picnic blanket by Brighton Pier. The assailant had recently returned from Syria where he had fought with ISIS.

'I told them it looked like a wartime bomb, maybe,' Valentine continued, 'but they're spooked by the coincidence, right? A pier. A beach. Maybe it's a summer campaign – hit the Brits on the sands. Crazy – but they want twenty-four-hour updates. I'll do it.'

Shaw sipped some more Guinness. 'Good. But let's not be too dismissive. What little we've got so far is second-hand testimony, or third-hand. So let's be careful. We want theories, but we need facts. Until we get some, nothing's ruled out.'

'What about the construction work?' asked Twine. 'They're working on the seabed now. They use explosive bolts. Or did I make that up? Plus, if they're shifting rock, maybe they need charges . . . Springtime, they were hauling all their stuff down to the shoreline. Laying cables. Maybe they got careless.'

'Check it out, Paul. In fact, forget what I said just now. Let's organize a trip out to the rig and get forensic to do a fresh sweep whatever.'

Valentine looked at his black slip-ons. No doubt he'd be included in the boat trip. He hated the beach because of the sand and the salt, and the moving, nausea-inducing water. Actually floating was his idea of hell.

Shaw stilled a buzz of chatter with a raised hand. 'Which leaves us with one other case. Congratulations to George. We have an arrest in the Roach murder inquiry. A woman's in custody. A chemical analysis of the chocolates she was handing out at the bus stop has identified rat poison.'

Applause drew a short, curt bow from Valentine.

'No doubt George will get a medal. He deserves one.' Shaw left that hanging in the air. He wasn't quick to praise, and his relationship with his DS could be tetchy, so the commendation was duly noted by all. 'He'll get another medal if we can work out why the hell she did it.'

EIGHT

The website post was timed at precisely one thirty-four a.m. British time, two thirty-four Dutch time.

Marine Projects Inc., the construction company undertaking the building of the Hunstanton Pier, was a wholly owned subsidiary of the multinational giant Blue Square, which operated a website hosted by a server in Rotterdam. It encouraged visitors to post comments. Given that Blue Square operated in 131 different jurisdictions on four continents, many of the posts were in Spanish, Arabic, and Chinese. One block of interrelated posts marked the opening of the new Ghoung Dam, 125 miles upstream from Beijing. The last English entries celebrated the award of certificates of merit awarded to six of the company's designs for flood defences in Guyana.

The tone of the post timed at one thirty-four was very different. *Stop the pier. Next time people will die.*

The word 'die' triggered the site security and the post was removed three minutes later. Dutch CID rang a standard nightline number at the company's corporate headquarters in Bremen, and the guard on duty contacted the senior board member with responsibility for digital communications. He rang Interpol, who in turn emailed Scotland Yard's terrorist response unit. Over the previous year the Met had compiled a 'digital crime' register which listed officers in regional forces who had undertaken a two-week course at Hendon Police College.

The West Norfolk's officer was listed as DC Jackie Lau.

Lau was in bed, her bed, with a man called Milo whom she'd met at a stock-car racing event the previous weekend in Lynn. Lau liked cars, motorbikes, anything that could impart to the word 'speed' a streak of glamour. She liked danger, chaos, and movement. Milo had driven his car – a Fiat shell with a Merlin 3.1 litre engine – off the track and through a wall of straw bales six metres thick. Lau had been standing twenty feet away, cradling a half bottle of vodka, as he extricated himself from the wreck.

Over a few shots Lau had told Milo she was a fan, and, when asked, volunteered that she worked shifts at the Campbell's soup factory on the edge of town.

The first time the phone rang she thought she'd dreamt it, but the second woke Milo.

'What the fuck . . .'

She stretched a hand across his bare chest and captured the buzzing mobile, recognizing the incoming number as New Scotland Yard.

'Detective Sergeant Jackie Lau,' she said, and, in the moonlight, saw Milo's eyes widen.

NINE

Esther Jayne Keeble was not the oldest suspect ever held over-night in the cells at St James'. Her date of birth had, however, been entered by the desk sergeant with some difficulty, as the drop-down computer option list had not immediately offered 1944. Given her birthday – 3rd April – she was booked in as aged seventy-two. The record was ninety-one, but that was in the case of a man suspected of dangerous driving, who had driven round three of the town's roundabouts anti-clockwise, and couldn't recall his own name, let alone trivial aspects of the Highway Code.

The Lynn force seemed to specialize in apprehending the ancient. Popular prejudice held that the ageing burglars and petty thieves who seemed to crowd the magistrates' courts had come to Norfolk in the 1960s, part of the great exodus encouraged by the govern-ment, keen to rehouse the East End in the then thriving port. The locals maintained that the town's OAP crime rate was entirely imported from West Ham and Poplar, Bethnal Green and the Isle of Dogs.

Shaw, however, noted that the pensioner criminal was just as likely to be Norfolk born and bred. In fact, the port had a long medieval history of seedy, waterside crime which seemed to take no heed of age. Perhaps the phenomenon was a nationwide one, as the average lifespan lengthened, accommodating the professional thief unwilling to contemplate retirement on a dwindling state pension.

Keeble had been regularly plied with cups of tea and biscuits. Generally, grey-haired villains got short shrift, clogging up the justice system and wasting police time. But Keeble's stoic silence had engendered a rare atmosphere of guarded sympathy.

A woman PC brought Keeble into the interview room, one hand supporting a fragile elbow. Shaw wondered if it was vanity or just plain bloody-mindedness that made her eschew a stick after her hip operation. Sinewy, with white knuckles, the suspect did have remark-able eyes, the spider's web lines seeming to suggest the imminent arrival of a smile. Making a perfunctory effort to sit up straight, the very slight vibration of her skull on her slim neck betrayed the stress that seemed to hold her bones together, like piano wires.

One of the canteen staff brought her yet another cup of tea, and a small plate upon which had been arranged three wrapped sweets, which Shaw thought betrayed a macabre sense of humour. They remained untouched.

Valentine activated the tape and made the usual announcements, Shaw jumping in with the first question without preliminaries. 'Have you ever seen a poisoned rat die?'

Keeble shook her head, then seemed to try to disguise the movement after the fact, rearranging the collar of her spotless linen blouse. She had turned down her legal right to a solicitor, and Shaw wondered if she'd begun to regret the decision because she kept looking at the door as if assessing her chances of a dash for freedom.

Shaw offered her a brief summary of the last six hours of her victim's life, reportage in style, but replete with the medical detail that made it clear he died in pain, surrounded by strangers, both confused and terrified.

Then he put a newly purchased carton of TopChoc on the table. 'Our forensic laboratory staff are working on the ones you were offering the child. And the carton from your trolley. Fifty in that box, thirty tested so far, one containing rat poison. So a two-in-a-hundred chance – at the very least – of this child dying in a similar fashion.'   •

Shaw's capacity to see in the abstract was highly developed. Fran, his daughter, appeared to his mind's eye, buckled over at the waist, trying to cough up the corrosive poison.

His voice, which was usually light, suggesting the ability to hit a note at will, was a revelation now. 'I want you to tell me why you did this, Mrs Keeble. I want you to tell me before you leave this room. Do you understand me?'

The hairs on the back of Valentine's neck rose. He'd heard this voice before, many years ago, at his first suspect interview with his then DCI, Jack Shaw. It wasn't loud, and it wasn't aggressive or threatening, but it was loaded with a sense of moral justice and conveyed vividly an entitlement to the truth.

She almost told them then – they could see in her eyes the utter relief it would have brought – but she seemed to choke back a word, as tears began to fall.

The woman PC offered a Kleenex. The cup of tea stood untouched, a fatty, milky, undisturbed film on the top.

'I do want to say I'm sorry,' she said. 'I'm sorry it ended like this.'

'Why?' asked Shaw. 'Why did you want to kill these people? Were the sweets handed out on a random basis? Did this child have a chance, or was she a victim already? Did you know Roach? Was he your target, or could any of them have died?'

'I can't say any more,' she said, looking towards the door, as if this simple statement would release her instantly. She tugged at the fold of skin beneath her chin.

Shaw leant back, and Valentine took up the thread. 'I spoke to your husband, Mrs Keeble.'

Shaw saw it then, behind the eyes, as conflicting emotions struggled for some kind of closure. *This is about the husband*, he thought, about George Keeble, retired newsagent and one-time lifeboatman.

'We obtained a warrant to search your house but were unable to find any evidence of rat poison at the house or in the garage. Mr Keeble says he's always used humane traps. He said he had no idea where you obtained the poison. He is shocked by what's happened, and adamant that he didn't know, or assist you in any way. Is that true, Mrs Keeble?'

They sat in silence.

'You were a nurse, of course, for many years,' said Shaw eventually. 'The cottage hospital in Hunstanton – that's right, isn't it?'

She nodded quickly, as if scared that one admission might lead to another. 'A volunteer; I'm not qualified.'

'So you spent your life looking after others, and now this . . .' Shaw stared at the sweets on the plate. 'Mr Keeble says he can't think why you should want to kill anyone, let alone an apparently random victim. You're a "good wife" – his words. An articulate man, your husband: an *aberration*, he says – a mental storm, brought on by the strain of caring for him, on a limited budget, in a cramped prefab on a windswept piece of estuary beach. And the disability allowance has just been cut back, so that's made life harder. Is that what did it, Mrs Keeble?' Shaw left a gap in which they could hear the wall clock tick. 'But none of that really fits, does it? The slow accretion of strain and stress is unlikely to lead to a fairly meticulous and pre-planned attempt to poison a group of total strangers. That smacks, surely, of much darker motives.'

Again, the effort *not* to speak seemed to overwhelm her, until she visibly set her jawline, teeth clamped. 'I want to speak to my husband. I want to see him. Is he here? I thought I heard his voice . . .' The eyes again, flitting to the door and then back to the cup of tea.

Valentine rearranged his black slip-on shoes beneath the table, leaving the answer to Shaw.

'Mr Keeble has attended for interview, voluntarily. His solicitor has advised him not to see you. If he did, we would have to insist at this point on a police officer being present. That option was declined; in fact, I have to tell you that Mr Keeble said he did not *wish* to talk to you, or see you – not today, and perhaps not ever.'

TEN

The naming of hospital wards had always been a source of irritation to Shaw. The transparent attempt to instil a message always ensured a deadening effect: Nelson Ward was oncology, and therefore a desperate plea for courage and a reminder of mortality; Rosemary Ward – geriatric – a tired Victorian effort to conjure up the English country garden in which old age consisted of the scent of herbs; and now Sunshine Ward, for children, invoking the spirit of summer adventure and the distant, thrilling susurrus of play.

The reality was starkly at variance with the bright poster colours of the shiny walls. Eight beds, six taken, two surrounded by the screens which in themselves were tangible euphemisms, in that the imagined, unseen suffering was often far worse than the obscured reality. Somewhere, off stage, a child cried. In the bed by the doors a small boy blinked through a swollen face marred by a gravel-rash, one eye bloodshot.

Eric Ross, five, was transfixed by a game on his brother's smartphone, his small thumbs working the controller with preternatural dexterity. His bare right leg, marked by a red blotch, exhibited a livid burn. The rest of the boy's family sat round on plastic chairs, except for Jonah, the middle son, who had inveigled his way on to the bed beside his brother to see the screen. Marc, the eldest, took snapshots with his Canon, ostentatiously swapping lenses to take a shot out of the window.

That morning's daily national newspapers were spread over the rest of the bed: the *Daily Mail*'s headline read: *TERROR LINK TO BEACH BOMB OUTRAGE* – a story cobbled together from anonymous sources and one – unnamed – member of the Cabinet. *The Guardian*'s front-page coverage avoided the hysterical: *POLICE PROBE WARTIME RECORDS IN WAKE OF BEACH BOMB BLAST*. Only the *Daily Express* seemed unable to rise above cliché with *MIRACLE ESCAPE FOR THOUSANDS ON BOMB BLAST BEACH*. None of the papers had gone with the trickier storyline involving the anti-pier campaign, although both local radio and TV had quoted the force media spokesman, who had refused to rule out any line of inquiry, and speculated that detectives would undoubtedly investigate possible links with environmental extremists.

Shaw's eye encompassed the newspapers, as he considered again the email he'd just received from DC Lau outlining the overnight posting of threats on the Blue Square website. He'd authorized time and personnel to track down the person responsible, or at least the computer responsible, and set finance aside to bring in an IT specialist to help. If the claim made was valid, then the bomb was indeed home-made. *If.* But it was far more likely that anti-pier campaigners had simply decided to make the most of a totally unexpected turn of events. Shaw's money was still on a wartime UXB. He hoped that his junior eye witnesses could provide the key evidence.

'You're all famous,' said Shaw, pulling up a chair and showing their father his warrant card.

For ten minutes they chatted about what the family would do with the rest of their holiday. Doctors had advised that Eric should be kept in for forty-eight hours, so they were going to stay in Lynn and go to the pictures (*Interstellar* in 3D), and Nando's or the drive-through McDonald's.

Shaw's interview style was disingenuously laconic. The techniques used he'd studied at Quantico, the FBI training college in Virginia. Shaw had taken a degree in Fine Art at Southampton University, which included a term out to study forensic ID reconstruction. The three-month sojourn in the US had been a vital component in developing his skills, so that by the time he joined the Met he was one of only fifty officers in the UK qualified to create sketches of suspects, or age the faces of missing children or adults, or 'vitalize' the features of the nameless dead after accidents or crimes, allowing the police to print posters and appeal to family and friends, neighbours or workmates, to step forward with the identity of the victim.

The principal skill in gathering information from witnesses was to understand that memory – *any* memory – is, in fact, a series of images, not a bundle. Flashbacks are rarely total, but more often jigsaw-like fragments. The Quantico technique involved identifying these frail half-memories and using them to try to retrieve others, slowly rebuilding a face, an image, a sentence. Each remembered image was used to lead to the next, in a daisy chain of related snapshots. The mistake was to think that memory was binary: present or absent. Often, witnesses who professed to recall nothing could – if skilfully handled – eventually remember vital evidence.

Quickly, he established the basic facts: Jonah spotted the object first, Marc cleared away a little sand, and then they decided to try to knock it out of the sandy wall using pebbles and stones from the shoreline.

'You touched it, Marc?'

'Yeah. It was like really cold – icy, metal.'

'Sure?'

Marc just nodded.

'So how much of it could you see? Show me on my hand,' said Shaw holding out his palm. The boy sketched an area about the size of a jam-jar lid with his finger.

'That small? Rusted?'

All three brothers shook their heads.

'Shiny,' said Marc.

'And how far down from the surface? It was a big hole, right? So five feet down, four feet?'

The boys exchanged glances but deferred to Marc. 'I reckon two feet.' He punched a button on the back of his camera and showed Shaw the image his father had taken on the lip of the pit.

'See. It was near the surface,' he said.

Shaw was no ballistics expert but he was pretty sure a falling bomb should make a bigger impact in sand than two feet. And even an abandoned wartime shell case should be rusted, even friable, not a lustrous, shiny silver metal.

'What did you think it was?'

'A round biscuit tin,' said Marc.

'The metal was thin, then. Flexible?'

'No. We thought it was full of sand. It was kind of lodged in. Good for the game.'

'You played before on the beach . . . What did you find then?'

'A boot. A bit of scaffolding – like the joint?'

Shaw nodded.

'An old thermos flask,' said Eric, glancing up from the phone.

'Rivets,' said Marc.

'Find anything else in this hole?'

'No – but I heard it tick,' said Jonah.

'No, you didn't, idiot. You just think you did,' said Marc.

'I did hear it,' said Jonah, his eyes flooding with tears. 'I put my ear to it – right, Eric?'

'Yeah, he did,' said Eric reluctantly. 'I heard it too – but like, not tick-tock – just a tick, a few times, not like a clock.'

Shaw thought about the hole. 'Where was the object? Which side of the hole: north, south, east, west, or points between?'

The boys conferred and then agreed on west. Shaw thought it unlikely there was a clock mechanism in the bomb. Ticking bombs were a myth from the early days of cinema. Marc had said the object was icy cold. Exposed in the west wall of the pit, it would have been heated by the sun till past noon. Is that what they'd heard: the metal expanding, *creaking*?

They talked about all the people who'd come up to look in the hole. The boys remembered one man, in lifeguard's red shorts, who'd taken a look and asked where their parents were; and another with a camera, who'd taken a picture and said they should keep their eyes on the sea at high tide because there'd been reports of seals offshore. And one teenager, barefoot in jeans, who'd asked to join in, but they'd said they were OK.

And, finally, an overweight man in swimming shorts.

'He spat in the hole,' said Eric. 'He said it was dangerous digging between the old pier posts, that the police would be angry. We said our dad said it was OK.'

'He was wet, like he'd just come out of the water, and he came back too – twice,' said Marc.

'The last time you could see he was trying to be nice. He said it was a prize-winning hole but we should stop now. Did we want ice creams? We said no. We've been told to say no.'

'Good boys,' said Donald.

'So he was overweight – anything else?' pressed Shaw.

'Strong,' said Marc. 'Like, not just fat; he had muscles, so he was wide too. Bald. Kind of *fleshy* . . .'

'All right. So – back to the metal box,' said Shaw. He'd bought a packet of wine gums on the hospital food court and handed them round. 'So the surface was curved?' Shaw used the palm of his hand, rotating his wrist, to indicate the classic ogive shape of a bombshell – the aerodynamic, tapering cone.

'I reckon it was curved, but like big enough that the bit we could see didn't look it at first sight,' said Marc, and Jonah nodded. Shaw thought that sounded like a classic case of twenty/twenty hindsight.

'But Dad saw it,' said Jonah. 'We were all scuttling back, like, when the sea came in, but he said he saw it for a second – right, Dad?'

'That right, Mr Ross?'

'Half a second – less. The sand wall collapsed and it kind of spilt it out into the surf. Yeah. I saw it, I guess.'

Shaw imagined what a good defence lawyer would make of that half-hearted eye-witness account. 'And . . .'

'A big silver fish!' shouted Eric, bouncing slightly on the bed springs.

'That's it,' said Donald, embarrassed now. 'I just saw the surface, the curve of it, and the sheen off the skin. A bomb, I reckon. Maybe . . . but like new.'

Which, if true, was another awkward detail. *If it wasn't a wartime bomb, it shouldn't be curved*, thought Shaw. A modern device had no need to be aerodynamic.

The boys' eyes suddenly swung away from Shaw to look over the detective's shoulder. A man walked down the middle of the ward carrying a selection of large, wrapped parcels. Shaw judged he was six foot three, heavily built, but with no visible fat. His fists hung from his arms like knuckles of bone.

There was a cry of 'Uncle Robbie!' and the presents were handed out.

Robert 'Robbie' Ross was introduced to Shaw as the boys' uncle, Donald's brother. He worked out on the pier head and, according to the boys, was a real-life tunnel tiger.

All the boys crowded round Robbie on the edge of the bed as he opened up an iPad.

'So, like, that's *under* the sea?' asked Eric, letting the phone slip from his hand.

Robbie nodded and flipped the screen further back, so that Shaw could see a video running.

'What are we looking at?' asked Shaw, intrigued by the scene of a large, almost cavernous concrete room, with a rough, sandy floor, lit by a series of overhead neon beams.

'I took this inside the caisson, the concrete box on the sea floor. We were down there yesterday for the first time. It's dropped with the valves open so she fills up with seawater. Then it's pumped out. So it's still pretty damp.'

The picture was oddly distorted by what looked like condensation on the lens. The fleeting pictures of the men working reminded Shaw of the first live pictures from the moon landings in the sixties. There was something almost alien about the shuffling figures, linking cables, operating a Caterpillar digger, a series of pneumatic pumps. The noise level was high, grating, with a heavy-metal bass beat from the machinery. Somewhere, on an additional high-screeching note, muzak played.

'You use explosives down there?' asked Shaw.

'Yeah. Can do. But that's a whole other job, right there. Company flies in the experts, and the gear is signed out, signed back in. It's a big deal. We've just started and the seabed's sand. But if we hit rock, then maybe . . .'

Shaw thought this answer to his question was strangely formal, if not defensive.

Robbie's camera must have tipped forward because suddenly the image was of the sea floor. They could see a crab there, high and dry, and the carcass of what looked like a rock salmon. Then the image shifted again to show a workman, in protective glasses, walking forward, offering a thermos and a cup. The idea that these men were working under the sea, enclosed in their concrete shell, made small globes of sweat form on Shaw's forehead.

'All this is pressurized,' said Robbie. 'So, boys, what's the big danger?'

'The bends,' whispered Jonah.

'Right. When we come up, we have to rest in the manlock. Otherwise, your blood can boil.' Robbie wrapped his legs and arms in an agonized knot. 'OK – this is it, boys; this is when it hits,' he said, resting a fingertip on the screen.

For a moment nothing happened. The slightly out-of-focus figures trundled about at their tasks, but then the image shook, the neon lights swung, and the picture went black.

'We lost power for thirty seconds,' said Robbie. 'I tell ya, that isn't pleasant. No power, no pumps, no air compressors. Pretty quickly, you're going to fill up with seawater. Then you got a choice: run for it and take a chance on decompression sickness, or stick around and drown in the dark.'

Shaw noted the slight mid-Atlantic twang to Robbie Ross's accent, and guessed being a tunnel tiger was a skill that could get you an air ticket to construction sites on five continents.

'That was the bomb blast striking the caisson?' asked Shaw.

Robbie tapped the screen in the lower right-hand corner: a digital clock read 15:31.

'Yup. Well, the shock wave. That's the thing about water, right; it's a medium through which energy passes without losing a lot of its power. You get a decent wave in Cornwall, chances are the storm that built it was off the Grand Banks of Newfoundland – that's a three-and-a-half-thousand-mile fetch, but the wave's still twenty foot high. So your beach explosion was like a punch.' Robbie sank a bony knuckle into a massive palm. 'We felt it, all right. Believe me, that thirty seconds, it's the longest year of my life.'

Although the screen was black, the audio was clear: voices, not panicky, but insistent, one man's in particular: 'Use mobiles, guys.' A single pool of light appeared, the beam quickly lighting a man's face in the gloom, then others bloomed in an eerie undersea garden of coral flowers, until the darkness was studded with faces, each one a small study in chiaroscuro.

The emergency lighting flickered, and a steady warning buzzer sounded. The machinery coughed back into life, the pumps thudding. A single red light on the wall of the chamber flashed in time with the buzzer.

'That's the signal to go aloft,' said Robbie.

'What did you do for those thirty seconds in the dark?' asked Shaw.

'I prayed.'

ELEVEN

As a schoolboy, Valentine had learnt to swim, reluctantly, at the Gladstone Street baths in Hunstanton. The class, bussed weekly from Lynn, had filled the tiled, windowless pool with murderous screams. Those boys and girls identified as reluctantly buoyant were thrown in and kept away from the edge by a schoolmaster armed with a bamboo pole. It had been the first, vivid episode in Valentine's long distrustful relationship with water. He remembered it now and tried to push away the thought that in all likelihood he'd end up living out here, on the edge of the land, with nothing to see but water.

Although Hunstanton's seafront was now dominated by Waterworld, an Olympic-sized pool with wave-making technology, the town's old baths were still in business, rebranded as Flume! – not so much a refurbishment as a transformation: plate-glass windows now filled one side, giving a distant view of the Norfolk hills behind the town. The white tiles had given way to technicolour designs. The *pièce de résistance*, the flume itself, projected above the pool roof, a spiral in see-through plastic scaled by a circular steel staircase, allowing howling children to plummet into the pool's deep end from outside the building.

Valentine had braced himself for the usual liquid cacophony, but the pool was totally silent, if not empty. In the water, embedded but breaking the surface, were six divers, in full wet suits. Each lay face down, limbs splayed, as if in free-fall flight. Valentine's creaking heart froze for a beat: in any other situation, in any other place, he would presume the divers were dead. None wore breathing gear, none moved; while a few breached the surface, all floated with their airways submerged, mouth and nose beneath the mirror-like surface, the lethal boundary between water and air.

A man stood on the poolside in a lifeguard's bib, holding a stopwatch, his eyes on the floating bodies in the water, but beckoning Valentine closer with his hand. Up close, Valentine realized he was a teenager, with the cherubic face of a fresco angel: slightly plump cheeks, tight fair curls held close to the rounded skull, and pale skin.

'Moment, please,' he said, the voice light and airy, with a definite East European accent. 'Tad? He the manager. In office . . .' He extended his arm along the poolside, his eyes – remarkably – still on the divers. Valentine tried to place the foreign inflection: Bulgarian perhaps, or even Russian.

Valentine turned away towards a windowed cubicle, where an older man sat with a landline phone pressed to his ear, but as he padded the stippled poolside tiles, a hiss came from the water, a strangely alien sound which made Valentine's skin suddenly rise in goosebumps.

One of the suspended swimmers had turned turtle, swivelling along her body axis, so that her face stared up at the vaulted roof. The sound had been an almost inhuman exhalation, far from the gasp Valentine would have expected. She lay still, her chest rising and falling slowly, the spine arching to press the body upwards; her face was colourless, the lips invisible. Valentine recalled an image from science fiction, the long-distance astronaut waking from suspended animation, unfurling creaking joints, flexing bloodless fingers.

The pool manager stood now at his office window, watching the scene outside: he was elderly, florid, calling to mind the white-haired, high-stepping fisherman of an 'It's so bracing' seaside poster.

His name was Tad Atkins. 'Swum all my life,' he said, in an attempt to answer a question unposed. 'Live in the water, if I could, but this . . .' He indicated the pool and the wet-suited swimmers, shaking his head.

'Sorry,' said Valentine, holding out his warrant card. 'I'm here on business – but what exactly is *this*?'

Atkins retrieved a rock from the room's second desk, about the size of a bowling ball, made of a strange mineral infused with thousands of small holes.

Valentine took it, weighing it in both hands.

'About twenty-two pounds – dead weight,' said Atkins. 'Theo will tell you the full story, but the gist is simple enough. The Med, places like that, when divers go down to look at wrecks, they find these – dotted about. First off, I guess, they thought they're rocks.' Atkins laughed, the inflated barrel-chest heaving. 'Then they figured it out, cos most of the time the seabed's just sand and silt.' He held the rock in his capacious hand. 'You get yourself a net, pop the rock in, and it takes you down to the wreck. Gravity does the work, even in water. We're talking way back – I don't know – the Greeks, whatever. Like I said, Theo's got it rote. Down there, on the bottom, you hold your breath, see if you can salvage the gold, or the silver, or the coins, from the wreck, then you swim up. Maybe they put a rope on the net and hauled the lot up, rock and treasure together. This one's volcanic, from Etna. They found it sitting in the sand next to a Roman trireme.' He made an effort to pronounce the word correctly, emphasizing the second syllable. 'Theo says that was in the Adriatic, five hundred miles from the volcano.'

'So this lot are just holding their collective breath?' said Valentine. Several of the divers had turned over now, and lay exhausted, spent, shaped like stars.

The belly laugh again. 'Yeah. But not collective. It's an individual sport, highly competitive. *Static apnea*, they call it: holding your breath but not moving. Dynamic's when you swim and hold your breath. It's all free diving really. Pearl divers and that. This lot are doing it natural, but you can take oxygen too, for half an hour before you start. Theo's competed, got a silver medal at some competition in Monaco. Yanks are into it too. It's catching on. This class –' he made a scything motion with a chubby hand – 'sold out.'

Atkins subsided into a wide captain's chair, his weight making the frame creak. 'Business, you said?'

Valentine retrieved an evidence bag from his raincoat pocket and let it flop on to the desktop in front of Atkins. It contained a swimmer's watch in matt black, with a white face, and the usual digital signals: time, depth, temperature, and a stopwatch to record the length of a dive, against a target based on the oxygen available. Set across the face was the blue insignia of Flume! – a fluid corkscrew – but this time entwined with the words *Leander Club*.

Atkins' rheumy eyes looked a little harder. 'Right, that's one of ours, Sergeant.'

'Sold to?'

'Members of the club. There's loads of clubs, right? Water Polo, hundred metres, high board, lifesavers – we do watches for the lot. Even this mob – static apnea. Leander is wild swimming. Again, all the rage. Every day on the beach, unless they've found somewhere odd – a moat, a canal, a lake. Ask me, they're a bunch of nerds, but it takes all sorts.'

'You?'

'Fair weather only.'

'You got a watch?'

He shook his head, shooting out his thick, muscled arms. The skin was tanned and weathered, with no sign of wrist strap. 'Can't wear a watch. They always stop on me.'

'Can't be cheap, either,' said Valentine, picking up the forensic bag.

'This version's a hundred and twenty-nine ninety-nine, I think. WaveCrest's the brand. We have 'em customized. The corkscrew's on everything – leisurewear mostly. But this is a good bit of kit. The key is the reliability of the stopwatch. Compass can save your life too. And . . .' He gave the watch a firm shake and the face lit up in fluorescent green. 'You swim?' he asked.

Valentine managed to keep a straight face. 'Not recently.'

'I reckon we sold fifty watches like this. Leander Club members only; there's an online form.'

'So there's a record of every purchase?'

'Yeah. I guess. We always say it's a one-off, every time we launch something – keeps the till tinkling. So Leander watches we did in 2012 – limited edition – that kind of crap. Always works. They love 'em; kids to pensioners – they all wear them. It's like a badge of honour.'

'I'll need a list, Mr Atkins. With dates.'

Atkins began to type laboriously on his PC keyboard.

Valentine, irritated by the pool manager's heroic lack of curiosity, filled in the background to his inquiry about the watches.

At first light, the Ark's forensic team had gone out to the rig off the beach and conducted a second sweep of the structure to try to locate evidence related to the arson attack. This subsequent search had extended to the rig's lower platforms, set just above the sea, which provided access to boats and divers. One of the pontoon's four tubular legs contained a staircase leading to an exterior port. The watch had been discovered there, the strap engaged and slotted through the metal gridwork of the exterior steps leading down into the water.

'Arson is a serious offence, Mr Atkins,' said Valentine. 'We need to find the person who did this. A wet suit, if they wore one, doesn't help. This stuff . . .' Valentine reached for a suit hanging on the wall and worked the material between thumb and forefinger.

'Neoprene,' said Atkins.

'Yeah. Doesn't flake or shed threads . . . nothing. But we can take a guess at what's happened. Diver gets on board, probably carrying an accelerant. Once he's up deckside, the whole thing's lit up like the Golden Mile, so there's no problem finding the fuel store. Or maybe he knows the layout. The oil drum's just gash gear in the store, so he stuffs it with cardboard, pours in the accelerant, and scarpers. A boat's unlikely, given there's a twenty-four-hour watch. So we're talking a swimmer. We think he'd set himself a time limit – ten minutes, whatever. So he sits in the dark and hangs the watch through the gridwork steel, counting the minutes. If the fire didn't take, he'd go back, try again. But the night watch spotted the smoke and hit the fire alarm. Given the dangers of fire at sea, you'll know what that sounds like – flashing lights too, and an immediate roll call on deck. We think chummy panicked, got off the platform, left the watch behind . . .'

Atkins' eyes seemed to bore into the PC screen. 'Nearly there,' he said.

'Nasty, really. Arson's always reckless, of course. Fuel explodes, we're talking severe burns for anyone close, maybe worse.'

Atkins hit a printout button, and the list began to chug out.

Valentine didn't have to count the list: each name came beside a number. 'Fifty-one,' he said.

Behind Atkins' desk was a poster: red capital letters proclaimed *Stop the Pier* and advertised the planned public meeting.

'Popular cause?' asked Valentine.

Atkins considered the poster as if he'd never seen it before. 'Locals don't like it – shopkeepers, people who run the fun fair, that lot. It's gonna take business away. And then there's the pollution, the ferry off the end – they're talking three hundred DWT – right, dead weight tonnes. That's big – really big. Bit of an eyesore too – you have to admit that.'

'Not me. I like ugly. Whose poster?'

Atkins shrugged. 'Mine, I guess. This isn't a pier to stroll down, is it? I remember the old pier, before it got swept away in 1978. Delicate, like a gangway. We used to dive off it,' he added, handing Valentine the list.

'Anyone I should be aware of, Mr Atkins? We'll run everyone through the computer, of course . . . but a head's-up always saves time.'

'One of the girls – Abigail Clore – she got done last year for a topless sprint into the sea. Indecent exposure. She's the club's criminal mastermind, Sergeant.'

'And there's no spare watches?'

'None. They were made to order – payment up front, like I said.'

'And you haven't got one?'

'Like I said. No.'

'The kid? What about him?'

'Theo? Hardly. Minimum wage, Sergeant. He has to work sixty hours a week in here plus overtime just to stay alive. That's why he hasn't got a suntan.'

Valentine considered Atkins' oyster-like eyes for a second, then turned to leave. Everyone was out of the water except a lone diver.

Theo, down on his knees, was using a stopwatch, calling the time out for the rest. 'Six forty, six forty-five, six fifty . . .'

At last the diver turned, the white face slipping from the water like a fish surfacing, and then it came again: the long slow hiss of the saved breath, spluttering and viscous.

There was a ripple of applause, strangely inappropriate to Valentine, who couldn't help thinking the audible breath sounded like a death rattle.

Theo's voice had taken on an official timbre. 'Six minutes fifty-five seconds. Club record.'

Atkins walked Valentine to the doors.

'I need you to do two things, Mr Atkins,' said Valentine. 'I'd like you to keep our conversation to yourself. Whoever left the watch doesn't know we found it; they may even not be sure where they left it. Second, I'd like you to let me know what the Leander Club is planning for tomorrow's wild swim. Time and place, please.'

TWELVE

Marine Court, a chalk-white art deco block of flats on the seafront, looked like an Atlantic liner of the Blue Riband era, shipwrecked on Hunstanton's clifftop by a freak wave. The ground floor, behind a wall of plate glass, housed a used-car dealership, the vehicles polished to a mirror sheen, like mechanical beetles, twinkling under artfully arranged halogen lights. The façade of the building was bisected by a thirty-foot-high 'thermometer' – designed to show how much cash had so far been donated to the Stop the Pier campaign. The rising red line had reached £210,000, within reach of the £250,000 target.

Marine Court, once regal, had seen better days. The original Crittall metal window frames were rusted, one of the flats on the second floor was boarded up, and a makeshift wooden sign by the lifts now matched flat numbers to offices: a solicitors' practice, an estate agent, a firm of financial advisers. Floor six – the penthouse – was marked *Stop the Pier*.

As Shaw and Valentine waited for the lift, they examined a large, framed vintage poster in the distinctive British Rail style reading *The Rock-Pool Coast*, showing a pair of Edwardian children – girl and boy – fishing with a shrimp net in a tidal pond amongst the seaweedy rocks below Hunstanton's famous red-and-white cliffs. Cleverly, the artist had created the surface of the pool, but also hinted at what lay beneath, with white lines sketching out a stationary fish, a curled lobster, a lurking crab, and the waving, pallid fronds of a sea anemone.

The lift decanted them into a lobby, beyond which the whole floor was open plan, the seaward wall glass, a balcony beyond with a steel rail and a sea view. Stop the Pier posters covered the walls, together with a large blow-up archive picture of the original Victorian structure – all ornate ironwork and graceful spindle pillars – next to an artist's impression of its replacement: a box-like structure, shuffling out to sea like an airport luggage conveyor belt. A dozen staff worked at trestle tables, filling envelopes, while others manned a bank of landlines.

Tom Coram, the chairman of Stop the Pier, sat behind a shoulder-height sinuous glass screen, in a private office pod. The wall here held a framed black-and-white picture of a tug, the powerful engines churning the sea in its wake. A note in copperplate read *Lagan*. The word stirred connections in Shaw's mind, and images set alongside flotsam and jetsam, but he couldn't place the precise definition.

Coram had a landline to one ear, a mobile on his knee, while he tip-tapped at a desktop PC, projecting a young man's energy with vital, rapid, decisive movements. But his hair was white, set off by a skiing tan, the eyes betraying the first hint of the glaze that can be a symptom of cataracts. There was a dynamic tension here, Shaw felt, between the bustling energy and the ageing body. He held out his warrant card and Coram's jaw set straight; tossing the mobile into an in-tray, he ended the landline conversation with an absent, half-mumbled 'Bye' and stood up, scanning the horizon outside the window, not his guests.

'Not sure I want to talk to you lot,' he said, the voice furred by a lifetime of cigarettes, alcohol, or both. 'Heard the radio this morning – local, not national, but still. Police are taking seriously – exact words – *taking seriously* the theory that the bomb was planted by campaigners keen to disrupt the building of the new pier. So what does that make me?' he asked, turning to face them. 'That's the deal, is it? I don't care about human life to the point at which I'd plant a bomb on a crowded summer beach. *My* beach. Fucking kids . . .'

The office had fallen silent during Coram's tirade. On his feet, he projected a very real sense of physical threat.

'Well? Spit it out. I rang into the radio station, and this oik had the gall to ask me to my face, live on air, did I think any of my supporters – *my* supporters – had planted the bomb? Fucking cheek.' Coram's voice had risen to a shout. A flush of cardiac red marked his throat. 'It's not going to be a sodding home-made bomb, is it? It's from the war. Any idiot will tell you that.'

'My sergeant scares easily, Mr Coram,' said Shaw. 'If you don't calm down, he may faint.'

'This isn't a bloody joke.'

'No. It isn't. People could have died, which is why we are undertaking a thorough investigation and pursuing several lines of inquiry.

Last night a further threat to the construction project, and those working out at sea, was lodged on the website of Blue Square, the developers. *Next time people will die* – that's not verbatim, but you get the thrust. So, maybe not a wartime bomb after all. And certainly not a joke. If you don't want to answer our legitimate questions, we can reconvene at St James'. Your call.'

Coram sat, arms folded.

'We've got a squad car outside,' lied Valentine.

Coram looked at Shaw, then back to Valentine. '*Your* warrant card?'

Valentine searched in his raincoat for his wallet, and hung it open a foot from his face.

Coram's eyes slid out to sea in a mildly childish show of indifference. 'I've got work to do. So make it quick. I'm on a flight this afternoon to lobby Tory MEPs. Ever been to Brussels? Chips are good. Rest of it is smoke-filled rooms, except you can't smoke.' Coram filled his lungs, as if weighed down by the prospect of tackling the bureaucratic inertia of the European Union. 'These MEPs have the power to put a stop on the grant made by the EU's cohesion fund. Like that.' He thumped his fist on his desk top. 'The original business plan envisaged a *reconstruction* – their word – of J.W. Wilson's fine Victorian pier. That was eight hundred and thirty feet long by the way – not a mile-plus. There was supposed to be a graceful pavilion theatre on the end, and a miniature railway running the full length. That was it: the pier was merely a means of getting out to the end. No shops, no rides, no nothing. No bloody Moonraker or Corkscrew. Not a white-knuckle ride in sight. That's the vision that secured funding. I—'

Shaw raised a hand. 'Forgive me. I live on the beach here – the café beyond the lifeboat house. I'm up to speed on the pier. So's my sergeant. The question is this: Are any of your supporters sufficiently exercised by this issue to put the lives of innocent people in danger?'

'Never,' said Coram.

'I've seen a few at the demos. Punches get thrown—'

'They're angry,' Coram said, getting to his feet. 'It'll kill the town. Cafés, pubs, shops – everyone can see the future now. The whole point of Hunstanton was that it was where the kiss-me-quick coast ended. Beyond this point there's a hundred-mile beach, yes?

A hundred miles of sand and dunes – all the way to Cromer. A natural wonder. The other way, down to Lynn, it's fun parks, caravans, and chalets.

'This,' he said, pointing out to the rig, 'this is the start of something else. This isn't a few dodgems and an amusement arcade. This gets built, you can kiss goodbye to Holme, and Brancaster, Holkham – the lot. And Hunstanton'll be as tatty as most pier resorts. People think we're the new Brighton. It's not Brighton – it's Southsea, Morecambe, worse, Blackpool. You been to the Golden Mile recently? It's a ghost town off the front. Wintertime, the street lights are on half power. It's like the Soviet bloc, for God's sake. They've pulled a fast one – the developers, and we're on their case.' He sat down, breathless. 'What we need is time,' he said, checking his watch. 'Even if we can get into the court in Brussels, we won't get a ruling before Christmas. In the meantime, we have to stop the work because every minute the rig's in operation . . . Every minute costs money. The more that gets built, the less likely Brussels is to call a halt. If we could raise the cash, we could go for a judicial review through the High Court; that would freeze the project until the legal issues are dealt with in full. But we need more time for fundraising. Lawyers – especially those expert in the minutiae of the EU's legal systems – cost a pretty euro.' Coram pressed the back of his hand against his lips, as if to steady himself.

'But you don't think any of your supporters are capable of taking violent action to buy that time in the short term?' asked Shaw.

Coram swallowed hard, perhaps realizing that he had just sketched a scenario in which it made quite a lot of sense for committed campaigners to try to stall the construction project. 'Of course it's bloody possible,' he conceded, his shoulders sagging. 'I just take exception to the idea that I'd condone it. This is a broad coalition of interests, Inspector. Loose cannons are inevitable. Frankly, loose doesn't get near it. But bombs – I don't think so.' He stood, a hand on the glass divide, calling across the office, 'Anna, a minute?'

Anna Roos, Coram explained, was STP's liaison officer with the environmental groups fighting the development, while Coram himself dealt with the coalition of business interests fighting the pier.

Roos wore beach shorts and a loose T-shirt with the Greenpeace logo. Her arms and legs were impossibly thin, so much so that the coffee mug she was holding seemed to threaten to break her wrist.

Shaw knew Roos – at least he knew what she stood for. Twenty years ago her father had founded a 'Free School' in the resort, an institution dedicated to letting children discover the world through play and adventure, not timetables and exams. Its motto – Freedom, not Licence – was taken from the famous – or infamous – school at Summerhill, down the coast in Suffolk. Hunstanton's version had been christened Winterhill in honour of its forerunner. The school, a set of 1960s prefabs, had a mildly risqué reputation in the town for spontaneous nudity and petty theft. Roos taught at Winterhill and had established herself as an advocate of green politics in the town.

'Sure. We've got our quota of crazies,' she told Shaw, after he'd outlined their concerns.

'Could one of the campaign's supporters have been responsible for the arson attack on the rig, and – possibly – for the explosion on the beach?' asked Shaw.

'I deal with organizers, right? Scientists, professional campaigners, English Heritage, the National Trust. They're not exactly environmental warriors, unless you count a cream tea as a lethal weapon.' She kicked off a flip-flop and effortlessly raised a foot to massage the instep, brushing away sand. 'Most of our time is spent putting together an application to have this whole coast designated an SSI – an area of special scientific interest. We get that, we can stop the work, and we're very, very close. If that happens, we don't need an expensive High Court action. But first we need to compile an ecological audit of the beach, the dunes, the seabed offshore – it's painstaking, skilled work. As a group, I'd say studious was the key word, not extreme. But we need support at the grass roots, and we don't turn away anyone. There's a spectrum – at one end there's what I'd call the romantics. They want to preserve the "rock-pool coast". They're all members of the Anchorstone Society – from the name of the town in Hartley's book?'

'*The Shrimp and the Anemone*,' said Shaw, who'd gone to school in the town and had the Edwardian classic drummed into him by devoted teachers, who'd breathlessly revealed that Anchorstone was based on Hunstanton.

'So, literary ladies who lunch – that kind of thing. Bird-spotters, walkers, watercolourists. Other end of our spectrum are the zealots, and for them this is personal. What do the Americans say? They've got skin in the game. The graffiti campaign was clearly in support of the STP – but totally unofficial, and we denounced it publicly. I hear stuff. Who knows what's true? There's links to animal rights activists, the anti-road demonstrators at Twyford: these people move around, looking for a cause. They may have found us, I admit that, but they're as shadowy to me as they are to you.'

Shaw thought that for all the flip-flop routine Roos was a shrewd operator who had just expertly distanced herself and the STP from any number of environmental extremists.

Valentine left with Roos to take a note of some names from an online register of supporters and fundraisers.

Shaw examined the framed picture of the tug on the wall. 'The name – something to do with salvage? Like flotsam?'

Coram's eyes softened as he examined the boat. 'Yeah. Flotsam's floating wreckage from a ship. Jetsam is stuff thrown overboard to keep a boat afloat – cargo, equipment, even bits of the superstructure if it's wooden. Lagan is stuff that's lying on the bottom of the sea, but you might get it back – maybe it's marked by a buoy on the surface. Derelict – that's stuff on the bottom you can kiss goodbye to. She was my first boat – well, my dad's – a salvage tug. We worked out of Wells – still do. Fleet of six now, worth millions. You could fit the *Lagan* in the hold of one of the new boats. The wind farms – off the Lincolnshire coast, off north Norfolk? We service them, stand by on construction, shift the heavy stuff. A good business. Son runs it now. Thinks he knows best.'

'There'll be some business on the pier project, then?' asked Shaw.

Coram rolled with the punch. 'Actually, that all went to a Belgian outfit, out of Antwerp. They undercut us. Anyway, neither here nor there. I don't let the company's commercial interests impinge on the campaign.'

'So why do this? Why run STP and take on the aggravation?' asked Shaw.

Coram's eyes narrowed. 'What's in it for me, Inspector? I'll show you.'

Out on the balcony they could see down to the beach, deserted for half a mile on either side of the blast site. The distant fun park was in full flow, the weaving, sickly, circus-ring music coming in waves with the breeze. On the water's edge the West Norfolk's diving unit was preparing to enter the water, ready to scour the seabed for any more fragments of the explosive device. A light aircraft, in military camouflage, flew the shoreline, a torpedo-like sonar device hung beneath in a wire cradle.

Coram watched the fly-past. 'Aerial survey, right? They'll find others, believe me. Wartime. You see.'

Shaw smiled, thinking of Donald Ross's silver fish spilling into the sandpit. For now, they'd let the STP hang on to the convenient theory that the bomb was military.

Coram turned abruptly and stalked off down the balcony towards the prow of the 'ship' that was Marine Court. Looking landwards over the roofs of the Victorian town, a maze of red brick and Norfolk stone and flint, he picked out a distant building on the horizon.

'See the tower?' He extended his arm, the whole limb seeming to vibrate with tension.

A line of large villas stood on the chalk ridge inland, one adorned with a high tower, octagonal, topped with a single room under a witch's-hat roof.

'The Old Lookout. My home, Inspector. From there I can see clean across to Lincolnshire, or north out to sea. I've been north, not in the *Lagan*, but in one of the new tugs. Far enough to see ice. We did a few jobs in Spitsbergen, beyond the Arctic Circle. Sometimes, when I look north from home – and I know this is an illusion – I think I can see ice blink – that's the reflection of the ice, bouncing light up on the clouds. It's as if I can see for ever. It's a view to die for. I don't want it polluted by an ugly eyesore of a pier.'

Shaw turned his good eye back to the sea, but Valentine, who had followed them both out on to the balcony, focused on the house and that lookout window in the tower. He thought he saw a figure there, and a pair of binoculars perhaps, catching the light.

THIRTEEN

The army established a command post with military precision on the green above the beach, commandeering the square of police cars set up by Shaw in the hours after the bomb explosion. A miniature encampment, it comprised three canvas tents, a jeep with trailer, and a five-tonne truck with a hard cover over the flatback. Another tent, set aside, was clearly for catering, as two cooks in aprons ferried food in and out. One soldier stood guard with a sub-machine gun held horizontally across his chest, a slender microphone extending from his combat helmet. Until the all-clear from the Home Office anti-terrorist branch, the military was, Shaw noted, determined to play with all its toys.

To one side, a group of five squaddies shared cigarettes, standing in a loose Arthurian circle, looking at their boots.

Shaw broke the ring. 'Captain Wharram?'

Led down the brick steps to the beach, Shaw was taken to the edge of the original shell hole, now smoothed into a dish by several high tides, but still clearly visible, its bow-tie-shaped scar aligned broadly north-west–south-east. At the pit's bottom, St James' head of forensics, Tom Hadden, was on his knees, trying to prize a piece of glass-like rock from the sand with a metal spatula, while beside him crouched an officer in fatigues.

Shaw slid down the pit face as Hadden held up a splinter of rock.

'DI Shaw,' said Hadden, by way of introduction. Captain Wharram introduced himself with a surprisingly limp handshake, which involved just the tips of his fingers.

The bomb site was six feet deep, and Shaw felt the familiar anxieties of the claustrophobic. The sound of the surf breaking seemed to retreat to the far distance. It was probably Shaw's imagination that added the astringent edge of cordite to the pungent earthy smell of the damp sand.

Wharram bit the piece of rock lightly, like a cat delivering a warning nip.

Hadden took it back. 'The blast melted the sand, forming glass,

but some bits contain tiny shards of the metal. We need all we can
get, Peter. The spectrometer eats the stuff up.'

Hadden, a former Home Office scientist who'd fled a messy
London divorce for the backwaters of the West Norfolk Constabulary,
ran one of the best-equipped forensic laboratories outside the capital.
Whitehall links and a string of academic papers on police methods
had helped to secure additional funding from several universities,
including Cambridge. The mass spectrometer, an item budgeted at
£470,000, analyzed material by incinerating it in a controlled crucible
and recording the signature colours emitted, each associated with
individual chemical elements. The instrument's major drawback was
that it destroyed evidence. Each experiment was an expensive
one-off.

'I've just given the captain here the bad news. You might as well
get to enjoy it too. The metal fragments we have so far put through
the flames indicate that the device – let's just call it that for now,
because we don't know it's a bomb – the *device* is not military
Second World War.'

'Right,' said Shaw. 'Eye-witness accounts concur. They say it
was silver, shiny, and curved. And you're right, it's not good news.'

'Military records sing from the same song sheet,' said Wharram,
checking a smartphone. He made eye contact with Shaw for the
first time: large grey eyes, a steady gaze, but with a certain liquid
depth. Shaw had worked with bomb disposal officers before and
had found that they fell neatly into two categories: those without
the imagination needed to realize what they did was lethal, and
those able to function by burying that truth, screening their conscious
minds from the potentially explosive truth. Wharram, he felt, was
in this second group. Nerveless, but thanks to a conscious force of
character.

'The Yanks dumped loads of military material along this coast,
but nothing explosive. Clapped-out vehicles, Jerry cans, Nissan huts,
sure. I know local rumour would have it otherwise, but there's no
way they dumped live ammo, or even decommissioned explosives.
Anything you could sell, they sold, and that was anything that wasn't
nailed down. The black market boomed. But anything *viable* went
back stateside. No German air raids, not within miles: rail yards at
Peterborough, docks at Ipswich – that's as close as we get.
Sometimes jittery pilots dumped their bombs and fled – but there's

no record. Our guys? Bombers turning back in damaged aircraft sometimes shed their load, but it was rare, and they had the North Sea as a target . . . You ain't gonna miss that. So – I agree. It's not a UXB, or at least it's not one from the Second World War.'

They hauled themselves up the pit face and surveyed the deserted beach.

'I'm bomb disposal,' said Wharram. 'As far as this one's concerned, I'm a bit late on the scene. My concern is a simple one. I need to know if there are any more. If this is not from the war, then that's actually pretty good news; it's much more likely to be a one-off because it suggests it wasn't dropped at all, but planted. What did the eye witnesses see, exactly?'

Shaw gave them a summary.

'A bomb would fail to detonate in soft sand, but it would plug deep – ten feet, fifteen. Not eighteen inches,' said Wharram. 'Our unit's priority is a magnetic survey of the beach. We're doing one from the air, and we'll get the results later this morning, although they may take time to analyze. If that throws up anything, we'll use hand-held detectors to locate anything suspicious in the sand. But – given the forensics – we can at least hope there won't be anything to worry about.'

Shaw held up a hand, turning to Hadden. 'Just for the record. Precisely – *chemically* – why *not* the war?'

'Impurities in the metal. Irregularities too – within very small areas of less than fifty microns. Suggests a process much less rigorous than the mass production of shells. We have a very small fragment of the surface material of the device and there's no sign of rifling, so if it is a bomb, it wasn't fired.'

'Help me out here,' said Shaw. 'If you had to guess—'

'Guess? I've just run a series of sophisticated tests through half a million quids' worth of kit and you want me to guess?'

'An educated guess.'

Hadden shrugged, his eyes switching skywards to track a flock of Canada geese. 'All right. A guess. Nothing more. It may have been made – constructed – of metal not cast for military use. Now, that might be a modern metal structure – I don't know, like a bathtub or a wheelbarrow.'

'We're saying this could be an amateur device? A metal box full of fertilizer. A terrorist device?'

Hadden held his hands up, and Wharram shook his head. 'Peter, Peter – slow down,' said the forensic scientist. 'We know virtually nothing. For analysis, we need more material. I've got the force divers in now trying to find fragments thrown out to sea. So we may get lucky. But if it's not the war . . . Also, we have been able to pick up a trace of the explosive itself. Indications are that it is related to TNT. Terrorist cells rarely have access to TNT, but it is widely used in the construction industry. We're shaking down the rig in an hour . . . again. That'll be the third time. This rate, we might as well move the forensics team offshore.'

Out at sea a Blue Square flag flew from the rig's radio mast.

'The CC's under pressure to keep the beach open,' said Shaw. 'It's summer and the sun's out. There should be two thousand people on the sands. At the moment there's us three.'

Wharram pointed seawards. Four divers in full wet suits with oxygen gear were emerging from the waves, knee-deep in modest breakers. The lead diver, his suit marked by a yellow stripe, held an evidence bag at head height and signalled to Hadden, the hand gesture rapid and urgent. Behind him, two of his fellow divers knelt in the shallows, pulled off their face masks, and threw up into the sea.

FOURTEEN

Valentine sat at his desk in the CID room at St James'.
'At his desk' was a flexible description, in that he rarely sat and liked to use the landline phone standing up – an old trick, which subconsciously gives the voice a tense, impatient timbre, effectively shortening any conversation. Today, his desk was covered in the latest batch of estate agent details Jan had left for him before going out on duty: a new-build in Heacham, a lonely cottage near Docking, a semi on the outskirts of Hunstanton. All boasted sea views, however distant, and the virtues of the wide-open landscape. Valentine gulped coffee, tidied them all up in a pile, and dropped them in his wastepaper basket.

He'd driven the Mazda back to HQ to review progress with the team. The West Norfolk's appeal for information concerning the explosive device on Hunstanton beach had resulted in 256 calls to the 24/7 emergency line at St James'. The majority had favoured the theory – now discredited by the forensic analysis of the metal fragments found on the beach – that the bomb was a discarded remnant of the US occupation of the town between 1942 and 1963. A lingering anti-American sentiment seemed to underlie these views, which had little basis in fact.

Several more flamboyant theories had been put forward to explain the explosion. The 'bomb' had been planted by a group of three Irishmen at the height of the IRA's mainland campaign in 1976; two 'Muslim-looking' men had been seen digging on the beach two weeks earlier at dusk; a cache of gunpowder had been hidden on the beach in the seventeenth century during the Civil War, and – finally – a single German bomber *had* attacked the town in late 1944, at midnight, but none of the six bombs dropped had exploded and the flight had been mistaken for a British aircraft returning to the Lincolnshire aerodromes after a raid on Berlin.

There was one other caller that morning, identifying himself as speaking on behalf of Squadron Leader Max Aycliffe. He refused to expound on the airman's theory, simply announcing that it needed to be laid out in person, if an officer could find the time to call at The Lodge, Gayton Road, King's Lynn, on any day before three.

DC Twine walked over with a copy of that morning's edition of the *Eastern Daily Press*: *POLICE BAFFLED BY BEACH BOMB*.

'Baffled,' said Valentine out loud. It seemed to sum up the day. 'I'm on my way back to the coast,' he added. 'A boat trip out to the rig. Hurrah. Two things, Paul. Check how we're doing on the list of Leander Club members – drop me a text. It's a priority, OK? I'm turning up at their swim tomorrow morning, so I'll need two other officers to assist with a roll call, and to check off the watches. Meanwhile, I'll drop in on Squadron Leader Aycliffe for you; he's on my way. No doubt he'll have some crackpot theory like the rest.'

Edging the Mazda through town traffic, Valentine cut west into the leafy suburbs. The Lodge came into sight, at the end of a cul-de-sac of Edwardian villas, the name etched in a stone lintel over the door.

Valentine pressed a bell and checked the time: twelve twenty-eight p.m.

A woman in a business suit answered the door, a smartphone in hand: mid-fifties, brisk to supercilious as she held Valentine's warrant card with the other hand while squinting at the photo ID.

'I wanted to speak to Squadron Leader Aycliffe.'

'Tricky. He's been dead ten years. I'm his daughter.' There was a moment's silence. 'Your move,' she said, tapping her left foot on the tiled floor.

Valentine explained why he'd called, noting that the hallway was hung with a series of prints of RAF aircraft – Spitfires, Hurricanes, Lancaster bombers.

She asked Valentine in, closed the door, and, standing at the foot of the stairs, one hand on the newel post, shouted, 'Guy? Guy? It's the police. *For you.*'

'Sorry,' she added, as they heard a door open on an upper floor, possibly the attic. 'I'll leave you to this. Guy can see you out.' There was something pitying in her eyes as she shook Valentine's hand.

Guy tripped down the stairs, taking the last three in a single vault. A smart public school blazer, with blue piping, hung loosely off the child's shoulders. Guy looked sixteen, with a trendy stand-up haircut and a Perspex brace on his teeth.

Valentine and his first wife, Julie, had never had children, so he didn't feel confident in such situations. He resorted to formality. 'Wasting police time is an offence.'

'I didn't think you'd come if I said it was me. Grandad would have known about the bomb, and that's why I know. I can show you, like, now . . .'

The hallway led to a kitchen with quarry tiles and an Aga, beyond which was an original conservatory, half brick, with a sloping roof, slightly green with moss.

Guy seemed uncomfortable in his blazer. 'School's out – but I get tuition after three. I have to go in.'

Valentine noted a lemon tree with one wizened fruit and an open laptop on a wicker table.

'This is one of Grandad's charts,' said the teenager, leading the way to a deal table covered in documents. The map showed the Wash and the coastal towns of Hunstanton, Heacham, and Snettisham. A dotted line weaved its way along the north Norfolk coast from the east, out into the Wash, and then back – making landfall at Hunstanton, before charting a course towards Lynn.

The boy's fingers edged nervously across the map. Valentine noted that the skin was marked by biro, an equation on the wrist, some numbers on one palm.

'Aircraft? German aircraft?' he asked.

'A Zeppelin L3. The first ever raid on Britain. They were aiming for Hull but hit the coast at Cromer. After that, they were basically lost for the whole flight. They bombed Lynn – people were killed there. I reckon they spotted the pier later, took it as a target, and went for it. But none of them blew up – the bombs – not one. Witnesses said they dropped three. I thought that was important, that you should know. Grandad would have called it *operational data*.'

Valentine had a curious feeling that the floor was falling away from his feet, so he sat down.

'Of course, he wasn't alive then,' said Guy, setting the map at an angle so that Valentine could see it clearly. 'But he heard first-hand accounts. I think that in a weird way he felt he'd missed out – that if he'd had his time again, he'd have chosen that war, and then he could have flown aircraft against the Zeppelins. That's January 1915. A lot of people saw it, and the bombs falling. Back then, they had a maid, and she told Grandad what she saw. Like, actually *saw*, right here.' He stood up and took Valentine out through a set of doors into a walled garden. Guy pointed up, above the roofline of the villas on the next street. 'Right there.' The boy's eyes were shining. 'An airship, a Zeppelin – that's five hundred feet long, bigger than the *Queen Mary* – that's what Grandad said – right there, hanging in the sky. It's like in *A Hitchhikers' Guide to the Galaxy,* right – when he says the alien spaceship hung in the air the way bricks don't. The maid, she was called Sadie, she said you could feel the engines, like a thud, thud, thud. And it had this observation cabin – a gondola, they call it – and she said you could see them – the Hun. It's like Nazi, isn't it – a word that makes them not us. That's what Mum says. Then it moved on – they're a lot faster than you'd guess, right? So – forty miles an hour or more. It would have been gone in seconds.'

'This is a century ago—'

'Sure. But, like, people die every year in Flanders – digging up old bombs. Chemistry's tricky – that's why I need the tuition – but basically the insides – the explosives – they turn to soup. Sometimes it's soup that won't go bang. But sometimes it does. The Belgians, they have squads of experts, full-time and everything. I went with the school, to the trenches, so I know.'

'And this is history. This is fact?'

'That raid, the first, it killed four people, injured sixteen, in Lynn – right here. I did a project for school. They said there were spies here and they used car headlights to guide them in – but, like, that doesn't work, because this was daylight. They were two hundred feet up, and freezing to death, so it wasn't pin-point or anything. Grandad said it was dead important because it was about terror, about causing panic. A terrorist attack. And it worked. There were loads of crazy stories, like the airships were operated from a secret base in the Lake District – yeah, right . . .'

Valentine studied the map. 'Three bombs? All on the beach?'

'That's where it's tricky. Accounts differ – that's what it always says when nobody knows the truth, right? A lot of people said they saw three fall in the sea. But I've checked and it was high tide – see? So they could have fallen in the shallows, gone in the water, and then the sand. The commander turned south – tracking the coast – so I guess they all fell in a line. I've got books, stuff – take what you need. These are eleven-hundred-pound bombs,' he added, collecting a pile of books under one arm. 'I've got to go to school now.'

On the step Guy looked up and down the street as if it was all new to him. 'Grandad, before he died, he ordered this car and it was just left here, outside. Hired it, I guess. Mum and Dad were out. I helped him get down the path. We went to this village, in Suffolk, where they shot down a Zeppelin – not the L3; this is later. Three of the crew survived, but one died in hospital. They booed the others, as they took them away in an ambulance. Grandad said that was shameful. They used bits of the wreckage to make stuff – ashtrays, cigarette boxes, stuff like that.' Guy held up the front door key and Valentine saw that the fob was metal and marked *L48*. 'We drove to the church,' said Guy, turning the lock. 'They'd buried them all in the same plot, the Germans, and there was a kind of memorial: *To A Very Brave Enemy*. The grave was dug by the local women, but the sexton said the bodies were gone. That upset Grandad. He said that dying in a foreign land was bad enough, without being dug up. But the sexton said that all the Zeppelin crewmen killed in the raids were reburied somewhere in the north, together. The German government wanted it done that way, and they'd found this bit of land which was rocky, with pine trees, and it looked like Germany, like home. I know why we went on that trip,' said Guy, looking at Valentine. 'Well, I know now. In the car coming back – it must have cost a fortune, right? – Grandad said when he died, he wanted to be buried at St Andrew's, with Grandma, and would I visit. I do.'

Valentine thought of Julie, and her grave at All Saints', a dank mossy square of graveyard surrounded by an old sixties housing development.

'Good lad,' he said.

FIFTEEN

Shaw slipped from the world of air into the world of water, and noted the dramatic shift from the sharp, treble soundscape of the beach to the muffled bass track of the sea. Despite the blood pumping in his ears, he felt the piston strokes of the marine engine on the divers' boat, an unhurried mechanical heartbeat.

Oxygen bubbles fizzed in a cloud, each miniature globe of gas catching the sunlight that cut directly down into the murky soup of the North Sea. Most of all, he felt the cloying density of water, as if he'd been embedded in a salty treacle, slippery but resistant. Countering this sense of confinement was the sudden loss of weight, gravity diminished to a mild sense of magnetic resistance, no more than the mere thought that up and down existed still.

He kicked his flippers once, twice, and cut downwards, aware that almost immediately there was an implosion above his head as one of the other divers tipped backwards off the bulwark of the inflatable, followed by another. The percussion reached his own ears like thunder, immediately followed by the sizzle of oxygen.

Shaw swam down in a vertical spiral, circling the anchor chain that had been pitched over the side from above.

The seabed, quickly visible, lay beneath him as a blanket of ribbed sand. The pre-dive briefing had stipulated a depth of seventy-five feet. Visibility, after the calm, stormless spring, was nearly fifty feet. Descending, Shaw could see now that the sandy bed was overlaid with a chaotic crisscross design, the legacy of generations of inshore fishing with trawl nets and pots, so that it resembled a classroom blackboard, the scrawled hieroglyphs of former years just visible. Here, well below the depths where surface waves moved the water, the sands were disturbed only by skittering crabs, a hundred of which were within sight, studding the seabed like rivets, set in oddly mathematical lines, as if organized for an invasion of the beach. Across this submerged desert, the stub-like rotten stumps of the old pier marched in parallel lines, thirty feet apart, westwards out to sea.

The visibility was striking: Shaw felt the briefing estimate was in fact an underestimate. Oddly, this Aegean-like clarity seemed to increase with depth. The soupy brown murk of the upper layer was like a lid on a crystal, almost glass-like transparency below. Shaw was aware of the science behind this phenomenon of layering, the tendency of water to separate into horizontal planes due to differences in salinity and temperature. Between the two zones – the soupy upper murk and the glassy depths – a mirror-like membrane glistened.

The sunlight from above drilled down in shafts of gold, catching shoals of small fish, hanging in bowls like marine mistletoe. A single eel, as thick as an arm, crossed the seabed in a series of alien, sideways inscriptions of the letter S. Above, descending, the two following divers left behind a pillar each of expelled breath, holding between them the dark, dolphin-like form of the underwater camera.

Below, on the seabed, a red light flashed where a marker had been left by the previous dive team. They'd moved out from the beach in hundred-yard zones, discovering quickly three fragments from the device, each one of which had created its own miniature crater. On the final sweep, just over 260 feet out from the low-water mark, they'd discovered a diver's torch, discarded on the seabed.

Shaw touched down by the flashing marker, noting the torch, still *in situ*, and looked seawards. Although he'd been briefed about their *second* discovery, the sight still held a visceral shock: the silhouette of a distant diver hung in the water, frozen still, embedded in the sea, like some exotic insect caught for ever in amber or jet, the falling, refracted light from the surface playing across the figure so that it seemed to shimmer, as if treading water.

Shaw executed three rapid dolphin kicks, bringing himself within ten feet of the diver, whose right foot was connected by a nylon blue rope to one of the old pier's footings, a knot tied through a hole which had once held a wooden peg. Arms stretched towards the surface, the chin up, the diver's clear face mask reflected the light of the distant surface. The free-floating left foot had lost its flipper, the foot obscured by a gorgon's head of crabs, interlocked in a nightmare of articulated limbs and claws. Around the body, a hazy miasma of rotting flesh hung like a shroud.

Shaw felt a slight pressure at his back and realized the current, immobile during the period of dead water between the tides, was about to turn, flooding out. The victim swayed on its lanyard. Shaw saw the image before him as an inverted execution: the hangman's victim dangling in the water, drawn up towards the sky.

He forced himself to paddle to within a few feet. The shoulder of the wetsuit sported a single emblematic Dutch flag. One of the diver's gloves, on the right hand, was missing, leaving swollen pale fingers, stiff and strangely inhuman. A single crab clung to the thumb. Shreds of skin floated free from the puckered flesh. Had it been from these dead fingers that the diver's bag had slipped, freed perhaps by the shock wave of the beach explosion?

Forcing himself to study the flesh of the hand, he noted a gold signet ring and a red diver's watch with Roman numerals. Of the hidden human face, the only visible features were a bearded, heavy jaw. The face mask and mouthpiece were in place, but the eyes were lost behind a trapped bubble of oxygen.

Circling, Shaw had little doubt they'd found the missing Dutchman, Dirk Hartog. On the dead man's back was a single oxygen tank, marked with the logo of Hunstanton Marine.

Shaw tried to energize the scene: seeing a struggle perhaps, the air pipe ripped away, an oxygen cloud enveloping the thrashing figure. The hair, which swayed to and fro, was infested with small scavenger fish. A jellyfish, the size of a cricket ball, had attached itself to the left ear.

The two other divers arrived with the underwater camera and a floodlight blazed, the scene lit in lurid binary contrast, shadow and glare. Circling, Shaw allowed the sluggish current to edge him closer to the dead man's face, so that he could peer through the bubble trapped behind the mask. The flesh was bloated, the eyes almost closed, the natural symmetry of the features in life cruelly lopsided in death, so that only one dead iris caught the light. The mouth gaped, the jaw bone extending to breaking point – and possibly beyond, so that the line of the skull seemed distorted by dislocation.

Shaw tried to imagine what would have happened to the body if undiscovered: the flesh eaten away, the bones encased in the suit, the skeleton moored to its wooden pillar, the skin dissipated in the muddy, sluggish seawater, the human molecules dissolved in the vast chamber of the Wash. One day, perhaps, a shred of wetsuit might have washed ashore, but nothing more.

A dolphin kick took Shaw out of the circle as the other two divers rotated around the victim with the camera, the shifting shadows giving a fresh illusion of movement, as if the dead man danced on a leash.

The image felt like an intrusion, and so Shaw turned away, to look further out to sea, along the line of the shorn pillars of the old pier. The gloom seemed to stretch into the heart of the sea, but there was no sign of the construction rig, or the great concrete caisson on the seabed, all of which must lay half a mile west. But could he hear a mechanical pulse? The great pumps, perhaps, squeezing air into the caisson. In contrast to the suspended, bloodless victim, the sea itself seemed to have gained a heartbeat.

SIXTEEN

Probationary PC Jan Clay parked her blue-and-white squad car inside the port gates on an acre of concrete that ran down to the side of the Alexandra Dock. A container ship, unloaded and high in the water, threw a narrow inky shadow over the quayside, but the rest of the scene lay baking in blinding light.

Clay slipped on dark glasses and adjusted her chequered neck scarf in the side mirror of the car. One of the many things she hated about the port in the summer was this quality of heat appearing to radiate from the very ground. There wasn't a blade of grass in sight, just concrete and red brick, and a giant metallic grain silo that seemed to buckle in its own private mirage.

Even a rat, following the old train lines sunk in the cobbles, seemed overcome by the deadening effect of the vertical sun, its progress an aimless ramble, nosing at lumps of old sugar beet that had fallen from trucks by the loading bay.

Clay's cork-heeled shoes clipped smartly on the tarmac as she made her way down the main dock road. She'd been in uniform for just fourteen months, but she had already begun to put in place various aspects of her own style, an approach to the job based on careful, studious preparation. She'd noted that turning up to interview people in the squad car was never as effective as arriving on foot. The car seemed to create a barrier between police and public, while also providing a clear early warning to anyone with something to hide that awkward questions were coming soon. Clay was also aware that the emerging elements of her approach to coppering were, invariably, the opposite to those of her husband. The car, for George, was a haven, a cradle, which he rarely left unless he had to. George was quite capable of conducting vital interviews with key witnesses *from* his battered Mazda: window down, elbow on the door ledge.

The dock road was deserted, leading down to the Fisher Fleet, a narrow, deep muddy cut in which the trawlers lay waiting for high tide to lift them up, and out, into the arrow-like channel that led to the sea. The smell was distinctive: a subtle blend of rotting fish, baking mud, and marine fuel. A dog, lashed to a rail, barked at Clay from the hot steel deck of a dredger. Settling back down as she passed, it put both its front paws in a dry water bowl.

Salt's, the wholesale fishmonger, comprised a front shop and a warehouse, which appeared to have been built from broken-down old ships' boards. The interior was a surprise: gleaming white sinks held silver fish, a row of spotless fridges humming along one wall.

The fishmonger was hacking at a cod with a chopper, cutting through the plastic spine with short sharp blows.

Clay went to speak, but her throat caught on the hint of blood in the air. The resulting cough didn't startle the fishmonger who spoke with his back to her. 'One moment. I'll be with you.'

When he did turn round, his hands were covered in fish blood and tiny glinting scales.

Joe Salt was Esther Keeble's brother. As soon as he saw Clay's uniform, the jaw set, and he promptly explained that he didn't have much time, as one of his big wholesale customers would be on site soon.

'Won't take a moment, Mr Salt. I'm sure you're as keen to find out why your sister should act as she did; it's hardly in character, is it? A very caring woman.'

CID had drafted in uniformed branch to check on all of Keeble's relatives. The clear danger facing the inquiry was that the accused would get to trial and at the last moment change her plea. Without her own brief admission to police, the DPP had a potentially precarious case. Would the defence team offer manslaughter, banking on the unpredictability of juries, in order to sway the Crown to accept a deal? If they sought psychiatric reports, Keeble might escape justice entirely.

The key problem was the total absence of a known motive.

So far the life revealed by these inquiries appeared blameless. Esther Keeble had spent her life being a dutiful wife to George – the holder of an RNLI bronze medal for bravery – and working as a volunteer at the cottage hospital in Hunstanton, and at the children's ward at the Queen Elizabeth Hospital in Lynn. Why would such a woman turn to random murder?

After a few preliminary questions Clay ventured an observation. 'She must have liked kids.'

Salt had the face of a man who spent his life under artificial lights. He rubbed his cheeks now, as if to conjure up some colour in the skin. 'She was the big sister,' he said, his voice softening. 'Four brothers, all of us with kids, grandkids. It's a tribe really – you should see us at Christmas. I've got four, and they've got seven. She loved it. And she helped bring us up. So you're right. She lived for kids.'

In the silence they heard something plop into the water outside, setting the dog off in a mad spasm of barking.

'But none of her own,' offered Clay.

'Nope.' Salt folded his arms.

'Why was that?'

'I don't know. We were close, we all were, but there's some things you can't ask.'

Clay tried several other tacks, probing the Keebles' perilous financial position, which explained their damp, drafty prefab on Empire Bank. 'They worked hard all their lives. Good people. Was she bitter, do you think?'

'Bitter enough to try and poison a six-year-old she'd never met, you mean. I think we're done here, don't you, Constable?'

Clay put her official West Norfolk Constabulary card on the counter.

'Anything occurs to you, please ring. We're just trying to understand. Have you visited?'

'Sure.'

'What did you think?'

'I don't think *she* understands.'

Outside, Clay stood on the quayside looking down at the boats that lay at angles in the mud. A rope opposite supported two rats, trying to get past the metal vermin shield.

An idea, as murky as the water in the muddy channels of the Fisher Fleet, made her skirt Salt's shop and put her head through the open door of the warehouse behind. Despite the old tiled roof and the dilapidated wooden structure, the interior was, again, spotless: tiles freshly hosed down, fish boxes stacked high.

Along each alleyway, traps were set at regular intervals.

She took a picture with her phone and then peered inside the plastic cage, noting the innocent white powder within.

SEVENTEEN

'Like this, I think, at the moment of the attack,' said Dr Justina Kazimierz, the West Norfolk's resident pathologist, the centrepiece of her own forensic tableau, as she took on the shape of the stricken diver. A sturdy fifty-five-year-old, she nevertheless retained the ghost of a more childlike grace, stretching out both her arms ahead of herself, her hands carefully cupped to reduce drag, while lifting one leg to extend it backwards, pointing the toe of her flat shoe, like a ballerina. 'The head back, the air pipe in place. Then I think the assailant strikes . . .'

She leant forward and lifted the right foot of the corpse as it lay on its metal mortuary table. Outside the Ark's lancet windows, night had fallen, but here within the old chapel the halogen lights blazed, depriving the corpse of the comfort of shadows. On the wall above, the single stone angel covered its face with its hands, as if it couldn't bear the sight below.

'The assailant rips the oxygen pipe away, and then as the victim tries to escape to the surface, he – or she – grips the foot . . .'

The sound of broken bones creaking in flesh seemed to bring a new depth of bleak grief to the autopsy suite. Valentine concentrated hard on the ticking hands of the clock on the wall. Shaw stepped forward, bending his knees to get closer to the foot, which was pale, but distinguished by the marbling effect of death, with blue veins splayed like a river system across the skin.

'The bones broken here are many,' she said. 'The leg, just here, the ankle, the talus fractured, the cuboid also, four cuneiform bones, all of the phalanges.' As she spoke, she ran her hand confidently over the surface of the limb. An incision had been made in the side of the foot, and without warning she flipped the limb quickly, so that a wound opened to reveal the flesh within. 'Here – the extensor tendons are ruptured, the Achilles broken . . .'

The members of the murder team were all present. DS Mark Birley, the CCTV expert, perched casually on an unused dissection table. 'So we're looking for someone strong, active, even an athlete, or a labourer, a bodybuilder?'

Dr Kazimierz dismissed the idea with a flick of the wrist. 'No, no. You misunderstand. Listen, please . . .'

The pathologist had been in the UK for more than ten years, but the linguistic patterns of her native Poland were still powerful. Shaw suspected she employed this trait to keep her emotional distance from those around her, and to maintain a crisp, detached persona. Perhaps, in a subconscious way, it helped her draw a boundary between her own life and the dead with whom she worked.

'I am not saying that the assailant uses this force. No – this force comes from our victim: he struggles, he twists, but always he is trapped here.' She held the ankle up one more time, before setting it down gently, like a china cup.

Shaw walked to Hartog's wetsuit which had been hung on the stone wall. The image of the victim, suspended in the strange prism of seawater, attached to the seabed by a nylon rope, seemed to lurk on his retina like an indelible stain.

'The loop, you see,' said Kazimierz, quickly reaching out to take the heel-strap of the suit in her hand as Shaw held it up. 'This, I think, is the key. The killer holds on to this, the victim struggles, but buoyancy – and the desire for oxygen – impels him to ascend . . .' She looked up into the beautiful curved beam roof of the old chapel. 'But to free his foot he must *descend*. This proves an impossible contradiction, certainly once panic has struck.' She stretched the heel loop out, then let it go with a crack.

'He drowned?' asked Shaw. 'No other wounds – abrasions?'

'None. Just the foot. Yes, drowned certainly, in seawater.'

'Time?' asked DC Twine, the only member of the squad taking notes, using his trademark Montblanc fountain pen.

'A wide window,' said the pathologist. 'The sea temperature varies. Perhaps between a week and two weeks. The deterioration is marked, and the action of crabs, fish – it is obvious. The bound foot was tethered to the wooden pile, but tight enough to hold the bone in place even after the flesh is gone. So for ever he is here, unless, or until, he is found.'

Kazimierz walked to the head of the table and considered the victim's face. 'We lose much here,' she said, moving the head from side to side to exhibit the skull. Most of the CID squad studiously stared at the tiled floor. Shaw focused on the exposed bone, the teeth revealed by the missing lips, and decided he'd been right to insist the whole squad attend. It was often too easy to think of murder in a surreal or metaphorical sense. Here, the reality of death was overwhelming, the irrefutable evidence of decay present in every inch of exposed flesh and bone.

'Is it our missing Dutchman?' asked Shaw.

'An appendectomy here is a match,' she said, indicating a livid abdominal scar. 'The flesh of the fingers is gone. Otherwise, yes, a good fit with the medical file. But Tom has better . . .'

She tapped briskly on the glass wall that divided the old nave of the chapel into two halves, the autopsy suite here at the east end, the forensic laboratory to the west.

Hadden brushed his way through the plastic strip curtain in the glass wall and placed a silver ring beside the victim's head. 'This was on the right hand, still on the bone of the index finger. The hallmark is Dutch – luckily for us, they have a different assay system, so we know the date of manufacture: 1974. And the place – the city of Harlingen, an old port on the North Sea. I rang Rotterdam and they made inquiries with the family – such as it is. His ex-wife says she bought it for him on his twenty-first birthday.

'Other than that, I can't help. Locard's principle is not a great deal of use to us here. At most crime scenes the killer leaves a trace of themselves behind, and takes with them something from the victim. There is an exchange of evidence. But that's in the world we live in, which is full of air. This victim's been hosed down by millions of gallons of salty water. Several tides have been and gone. It would have been less effective, from the killer's point of view, if he had run him through a car wash.'

Hadden retreated into his own kingdom, but Shaw followed.

Two members of the SOCO team were working at desktop PCs and didn't look up. Stills taken from the dive unit's underwater camera were illuminated on a whiteboard.

'He wants a word,' said Hadden, indicating a desk where Captain Wharram, head of the bomb disposal unit, sat examining a series of marine charts. 'I'm not sure it's good news.'

Wharram stood to shake hands and then produced an iPad from inside his flak jacket. Two touches brought up an image in grainy black and white: 'This is the L3, the Zeppelin that undertook the first successful raid on the British mainland in 1915. I had little choice but to pass on this theory to our archive unit at Catterick. They didn't waste any time. It is true that the airship passed over the beach on that raid, and it is certainly reported that it might have dropped three bombs, which did not explode. We should have gone back in the records. But it's a century ago.'

Wharram's fingernail, which had been bitten back to the quick, tapped at the tablet screen. 'Anyway, to cut to the chase, our junior historian appears to have solved the mystery, while simultaneously creating another.'

'It's a one-hundred-year-old bomb?' said Shaw. 'Really?'

'I didn't say that. Look . . .' Weighting a corner of the chart down with a coffee cup, he tapped the iPad again and called up a picture resembling the final slurred few inches of an old-fashioned fax: black-and-white images, made up of dots and dashes in spectrum rows.

Shaw got close, then stood back, trying to see the image held within the chaotic binary snapshot.

'What we'd like to see here are images that indicate two bombs still on the beach. That would give us a neat, crisp solution to our problem. Three Zeppelin bombs, one already reduced to smith-ereens. However, if you orientate yourself using these two lines here – see the double dots? that's the old pier – you'll see that we have *three* images: here, here, and here. These are fairly large metallic objects about eight to twelve feet down in the sand. They are still in the sand.'

'Three?' said Shaw.

'Indeed. Three *plus* our mystery device. Sorry.'

Shaw had been on his feet for fifteen hours, and he felt his head swim, so he pulled out a seat.

'So that creates various problems, I suspect, for both of us,' said Wharram. 'My priority is to get a team on the beach tomorrow to see if we can locate these objects. Then we have a set of choices. They've been in the sand for a century and done nobody any harm. But can we really leave them there, given that the eyes of the world are upon us? I doubt it. So, we either try to disarm them *in situ* or blow them up. Frankly, the second option is already the outright favourite.'

'Christ,' said Shaw. 'So we still don't know anything about the original explosion?'

Wharram shrugged. 'Well, given what we *do* know, about its depth and shiny metallic casing, I think it makes a lot of sense to set it aside from these three electromagnetic traces. They're a century old. But that leaves our initial explosion unexplained. My gut reaction is we're dealing with something non-military, and modern, but I don't have the science to back that up. Sorry.'

Shaw stood. 'How long will you need the beach closed?' he asked.

'A week? Ten days. I'd say sorry, but I suspect you're fed-up with the word.'

'Great. Don't suppose you'd like to tell the chief constable?'

EIGHTEEN

St James' at night was a second home for Valentine. In the years after Julie died, he'd thrown himself into the job, and he'd often work into the night, slipping out before closing time for a drink at the Artichoke, and then returning to plough on, reading statements, into the small hours, before curling up on one of the spare beds in the basement cells, until the canteen started cooking breakfasts at six. Tonight he was heading for the Red House with the rest of the squad for a late pint, as Jan was on a late shift. But he never left the building without touching base – checking his in-tray, emails, and voicemail.

The note was from Paul Twine and stuck to his PC screen: *This came up on trawl through members of Leander Club.* On his desk lay a manila file, one of the old ones from the records kept in the basement, too old to be transferred across to the new digital system.

A single newspaper cutting fell out. From the typography, Valentine placed it as the *Lynn Express*, one of the local papers.

FISHERMAN KILLED TEENAGER
WHILE DRUNK AT WHEEL

A forty-three-year-old Wells' fisherman had five times the legal limit of alcohol in his blood when he knocked a teenager off his bike, killing the nineteen-year-old.

James 'Tad' Atkins, of Windmill Way, Docking, pleaded guilty to causing death by dangerous driving at Peterborough Crown Court yesterday.

Atkins, a ship's engineer with Wells Marine Services, had been drinking in the Mariners' Arms on Christmas Eve.

Witnesses told the court he had consumed eight pints of beer, and several spirits at an impromptu party with workmates.

Driving a company van, he left the pub at closing time to drive the six miles home.

At the junction of the Docking Road and the B1220 at

Brancaster he knocked Josh Ridding, of Creake Close, Titchwell, off his bike.

George Pilling, an eye witness, of Roman Way, Brancaster Staithe, was walking his dog and saw the accident. He told the court that the van had not stopped at the give-way signs, but had crossed the coast road at around 60 mph, colliding with the bike and flinging the boy into the roadside ditch.

Defence counsel for Mr Atkins said his client had stopped immediately and tried to help the boy, but he had died at the scene from multiple injuries.

The court heard that Mr Atkins had lost his job as a result of the accident and that his marriage had broken up. He recognized that his behaviour had been unacceptable. He had written the boy's parents a letter of apology and condolence.

Atkins was jailed for three years.

Mr Martin Ridding, the victim's uncle, read a statement on behalf of the family after the verdict outside court: 'Mr Atkins has robbed us of our wonderful son. Nothing can bring him back, but we are gratified to see that the court has seen fit to send his killer to gaol, although we feel the sentence is pitifully short. Even in this brief time, however, we hope that he will endure the solitude in which to reflect on what he has done.'

Valentine couldn't help thinking there was something vindictive about the last line of the family statement. His own personal contact with Tad Atkins had lasted less than twenty minutes in his poolside office at Flume!, but he felt he knew enough to judge the man's regrets as genuine. The law had sent him down for three years. The degree to which he suffered in solitude was down to his own conscience. As the statement said, nothing was going to bring young Josh Ridding back to life.

And what did that feel like: walking, breathing, waking up, knowing you'd wiped out an entire life in a fleeting second of irresponsible speed?

NINETEEN

The Graveyard Club, brightly lit but always deserted, had become Shaw and Valentine's private joke, and a secret place. The small cemetery that surrounded All Saints' Church lay less than a hundred yards from Valentine's front door, and half a mile from St James', at the epicentre of the DS's compact, urban world. His first wife, Julie, lay buried by the church's west front.

Entering through the unlatched gate, Valentine searched his rain-coat pocket for his latest offering – a battered 1970 half-crown he'd kept for luck in his desk – and placed it on the narrow sill of the gravestone. The grave itself was crowded with urban flotsam, collected from the pavements of the town: a series of chestnut-brown conkers, a discarded dog's collar, and an iron rivet he'd found on the riverbank amongst the wreck of a houseboat.

'Mind if I join in?' asked Shaw, placing a smooth ironstone pebble beside the coin. As a child, he'd known Julie Valentine, a kind, still figure on the edge of the exciting world inhabited by his father. She'd once taken a ten-year-old Shaw down to the beach while the men drank whisky, celebrating the end of a tough case.

'Help yourself,' said Valentine.

They retreated to a bench, and Shaw opened two bottles of Estrella using a bottle opener on the Porsche keyring.

Since his second marriage, Valentine's visits to All Saints' had been less regular, but the spot still exerted an oddly magnetic attrac-tion, especially after dark. During their last case Shaw had tagged along one night, in the small hours, and they'd both found the spot ideal for discussing the case, or, more pertinently, their inability to make any sense of it. The Graveyard Club had been born.

'We've reached the point where things are supposed to start making sense,' said Shaw, watching a bat swoop out of the shadows and circle a stunted cypress tree.

The graveyard lay bathed in white light from a security lamp. The church looked cowed, its stained-glass windows obscured by security grilles. By the locked doors someone had lined up six bottles of Special Brew on a war memorial as if preparing a shooting range.

'Has to make sense, does it?' asked Valentine.

'Let's give it a try, George, shall we? The CC will want a briefing in the morning. It would be nice to have some kind of narrative arc, a story to tell, even if we have to make it up.'

Valentine drank from his bottle, a sharp Adam's Apple bobbing, then he spat in the grass.

Shaw took the lead. 'Two cases. First, the pier – an escalating litany of crime from graffiti, to arson, and now, possibly, a bomb – or at least a shiny, metallic explosive device placed a few feet below the surface of the sand. So – for now – we have to take seriously the idea that it was indeed part of the pier campaign. It's the only way forward. So, progress?'

Valentine stretched out a thin thigh until it cracked. 'Jackie Lau's confident we're going to be able to trace the post on the Blue Square website. Not that that's a red-hot lead – I reckon it's just some lentil freak jumping on the bandwagon. The watches – the Leander Club – that's much more likely to get us somewhere. We'll do the roll call tomorrow morning, first thing. Atkins, the pool manager, is the only one who knows what's coming. All we need is one to be missing. Anyone says theirs is at home, we'll get a warrant.'

'I'd say I'd lost it.'

'Yup. But it's a start, right – and they're expensive watches. So you'd expect an insurance claim.'

'OK. And Atkins says he never had a watch?'

On the walk from St James', Valentine had filled Shaw in on the pool manager's criminal record. 'That's what he says. And he's not on the list, which I double-checked with the watch company.'

'Right. But he's got a criminal record,' said Shaw. 'Does that help us? He got drunk, he drove a car, he killed a kid.'

'And he's a supporter of the anti-pier campaign,' said Valentine. 'First question, how'd he get that bloody job? One minute he works on trawlers, as a mechanic; next minute he's an ex-lag who lands a nice little office, pension, and the rest, care of the local council. I'll kick the tyres – see if anything smells bad.'

Somewhere close a car alarm began to throb in the silence.

'The team's all over the STP campaign,' said Valentine. 'That's our best chance, Peter. Got to be. Nutters, fellow travellers. Might be a link to animal rights, according to Mark. They've used explosives – there's several cases on the file. Mostly fire bombs, but, you know, it's not beyond them.'

A car's headlights raked the churchyard, flickering as the beams shone through the old iron railings.

'Then there's the Hartog case,' said Shaw. 'Missing man becomes murder victim. We need to up our game. What do we know? A loner, on holiday, with ashes to scatter. Any progress on that?'

'Amsterdam contacted the ex-wife. She says his mother died over the winter.'

'Why come here to scatter her ashes?'

Valentine shrugged.

'Anyway, we know he's looking for something, probably the *Cala,* or something related to the *Cala.* Is that where he wants to scatter the ashes – over the wreck of the *Cala*? Now that this is murder, we need to try harder on finding a record of that ship. Sorry, *I* need to try harder. I've contacts at Lloyd's; I'll ring in the morning. Maybe there's a Dutch link? I'll call Interpol, see if they've got a missing ship that fits the bill.' Shaw took a cool pull at the Spanish beer. 'He's murdered two hundred yards off the beach, presumably by another diver, and his body's tethered to the old pier footings. His dive bag washes up after the explosion. Your starter for ten, George. Are our two cases related?'

Valentine leant forward, elbows on knees. 'Got to be. Ask me, he's either a saboteur working with the campaigners or he got in the way. My money's on the second.'

'We need to keep an open mind,' said Shaw.

'Bollocks. Sorry – bollocks, *sir.*'

A moon rose over the roof of All Saints' and Shaw began to look forward to a swim before sleep. For the first time he realized that what he saw in his mind when he thought of the beach was the result of many images overlaid – like sheets of tracing paper on top of an old photograph, each layer depicting a scene from his life. The result was strangely three-dimensional, an object built from memories.

The thought of the physical exercise made him stand quickly, pacing the gravel path.

Valentine pulled out a dog-eared notebook. 'Paul's found three people who saw Hartog the day before he disappeared. I'll organize interviews. Maybe he said something – although he's hardly Mr Chatty, is he?'

'Let's dig deeper on Hartog's background, check there's no links between Hartog and Blue Square, or for that matter any eco groups.'

The church clock struck midnight.

'I'm off home,' said Shaw.

Valentine stretched out his legs. 'I'll stick with it for ten.'

'Keeble?' he asked as a parting shot.

'Yeah. Progress, thanks to smart work by PCC Jan Clay no less. There was a Keeble family bash down on the Fisher Fleet a month ago. She's a Salt, right? Big family – fishing, boats, the lot. Anyway, the wet-fish warehouse is rat-free thanks to industrial supplies of strychnine. Still doesn't tell us why she did it, though, does it?'

'Maybe we'll never know.'

TWENTY

Lena sat alone in front of *Surf!*, the café windows dark, a single light showing in the cottage on the dunes. Shaw, running the last hundred yards in the moonlight, collapsed on to the seat beside her. Two glasses stood next to an ice bucket, inside it a bottle of Prosecco clouded with condensation.

Shaw checked his watch. 'Bit late for a celebration, isn't it? What's the occasion?'

'An exciting trip to a foreign country where there's loads of sun, good music, and a silver sea. Problem is, I don't think you can come, Peter. Which is why this isn't strictly a celebration. More a consolation.' She poured the drinks. 'Fran's asleep. I checked a few minutes ago,' she said, noting Shaw's glance back into the shadows where their cottage lay in the dunes. A sudden wave broke in the dark, drawing a white line across the night, the water sparkling with phosphorescence.

'It's Mum,' she said. 'They read the will. Marcus was there. I talked to her a lot, you know, towards the end. About coming here, about the beach, how we could make a flat above the shop, so she could be with us. This could be her place too. Her final place. I thought then she liked the look of our lives, but she wasn't really listening.' She took a sudden gulp of wine. 'She wanted her ashes scattered in Jamaica. Some village I've never heard of, off the track, in the west. Seriously – sixty miles from Kingston, a town called Black River. Fran looked it up online; the water's black because of the rotting vegetation on the riverbed, so that's something to look forward to.'

Shaw just sipped his wine. He'd learnt that the best way to deal with Lena's family issues was to listen.

'Marcus says we should ignore the will. She left a little cash, and I think he's got his eyes on it. The flat's gone to Jessie, which is sensible, and it means Marcus can't get his hands on that, at least. He's willing to compromise – his word – with a cremation, but he wants the ashes buried at the crem. So that's big of him. She wants her ashes taken to the Caribbean, and he's prepared to have them stay inside the M25. How did he end up so . . . *venal*? How can he be my brother?'

Shaw stared into the dark, waiting for her to say what she wanted to say.

'I thought about what Mum always said, that if someone asks you for a loan, then you give them the money and don't ask for it back, but you never do it again. Life's not about debts. It's about gifts. So that's what I want to do for her, Peter. I want to give her what she wanted. And I want to do it now. This way, Fran can come too. It's summer, I can organize cover here; we could go for a month. And Jessie says she'll come with me if money's not an issue. She's got nothing of her own. So I bought the tickets. And I've paid for the cremation, at Tooting, the day before we fly. There's regulations, but I'm sure we can get by.'

'You've been busy.'

'I wish we could all go. There's no way?'

Shaw smiled. 'Murder inquiry. It's a mess. I can't.'

'I know.'

'But you should go; you're right. Find out why she chose it. And Fran needs to see the place. It'll make a mark.'

'Maybe. But it makes no sense to me. She said she wanted to go home. It's about the only thing she said at the end that made sense. She was nineteen when she came over on the boat. The family lived in Kingston, a place called Half Way Tree, which was a slum then, but it's posh now. That was home. So why this dead-end township, Black River? Marcus has no idea, but he's not curious. I am.'

TWENTY-ONE

Valentine was back where he didn't want to be: on the beach, his black slip-ons skating uncertainly on the pebbles, his eyes watering in the salty breeze off the sea. A hundred yards out, beyond the breakers, a school of blue swim caps bobbed: the Leander Club was afloat, heading out to round a buoy which marked the theoretical extension of the old Victorian pier, before returning to the beach on a wide, lazy oval course. Behind Valentine came DCs Birley and Twine, hauling a trestle table, clipboards, and evidence bags down to the sands.

Tad Atkins was there to meet them, his teenage assistant further out on the water's edge, where he busied himself preparing hot drinks, towels, and folding chairs for the returning swimmers. The cherubic athlete was a study in dutiful concentration, partly, Valentine sensed, in order to avoid any further conversation with a detective sergeant of the West Norfolk Constabulary.

Atkins helped them set up the table, ready to log in each of the swimmer's Leander Club watches as they staggered ashore.

'You've said nothing, I trust,' offered Valentine.

'Not a word,' said Atkins.

'While we've a moment, Mr Atkins, I have a few questions.'

'Everyone calls me Tad.'

'We've checked every club member with our central criminal files. These go back several decades, of course. We included Flume! staff.'

Atkins seemed to visibly deflate, his shoulders sagging, head down. That curious buoyancy he seemed to affect was gone in a heartbeat.

Valentine's voice softened. 'Mr Atkins – Tad. We're not interested in past convictions that are not relevant to the inquiry. But I do need to ask some questions.'

Atkins' answers were curt but delivered without delay. On leaving prison, he had applied for a job with the council as part of a prison rehabilitation scheme. The original contract had been for just six months. He'd been lucky, but he'd worked hard too, and he hadn't taken an alcoholic drink in the intervening years. He never drove. The memory of the accident would live with him for ever.

'I guess it's not something you can just forget,' said Valentine.

Atkins filled his chest with sea air. 'It's not something I *want* to forget, Sergeant. The boy's buried at Wells; I go to the cemetery every week.'

Valentine wanted to ask other questions. Did he visit at night, at dusk, at dawn? Did he sit close by, or just on a bench in the distance? But he knew any more questions were simply intrusive.

'If that's all you need, Sergeant,' said Atkins, 'I'll be getting back to the pool. Theo will look after the club members, and provide any help you need.'

'Tell me about Theo first,' said Valentine. 'He keeps his head down.'

Atkins offered a brief biography: the surname, it transpired, was Kersk. The young man was a twenty-one-year-old Romanian citizen, with up-to-date EU migrant papers, who had arrived in the UK eighteen months previously. Before being taken on, he had passed, under council supervision, all the necessary safety certificates and a CRB check.

'We're lucky to have him,' said Atkins. 'Great swimmer. He's magic with the kids, the OAPs – everyone. Language isn't a problem, either. He set the Leander Club up, you know – that's his thing really: wild swimming.'

With that, Atkins trudged off towards Flume! while Valentine headed out towards Kersk, who looked up at his approach, manufacturing a smile.

'They're brave,' said Valentine, nodding towards the blue caps, which had begun to stretch out into an arrow-head formation, the leaders rounding the distant buoy.

'A challenge. But all safe.'

'Tad said it was your idea – the club. Why Leander? Your choice?' he asked, subsiding into one of the folding chairs the teenager had set out to welcome the swimmers back to dry land.

Kersk knelt on the pebbles, pulling the ring on a can of Red Bull.

'A romance,' said the teenager. 'Leander, he is on one side of the sea.' He gestured at the waves. 'The Hellespont – yes? You say the Dardanelles. I live on the Black Sea – we say Hellespont still. Each night Leander swims to his special one – Hero. She is priestess of Aphrodite. He swims the Hellespont, to her bed.' The cherub face broke into an accomplished leer. 'In summer – no problem. Then the year ends. Hero must hang a light from the tower of her house to be a guide. A storm comes and blows out the light.' Kersk blew a kiss as if extinguishing a candle.

Out at sea, those in the arrow's head were just a hundred yards off the sands. Atkins had insisted the club was non-competitive, but it looked like a race to Valentine.

'Four miles, this Hellespont, and the water is rough. He drown in the dark, and body she sees on the beach from her high tower at dawn. She throws herself from this tower in her grief.' Kersk placed both hands over his heart.

'Four miles,' said Valentine.

'This,' said Kersk, looking out to sea, 'just two and a half.'

'You could tackle the Hellespont then?'

For the first time Kersk held Valentine's eyes. 'I have. We take the boat to Stanboul. Yes – I swim this. Not alone. A club too.'

In one movement he was on his feet, running down the beach to help the first swimmers out of the surf; both were women, with full figures, in their sixties perhaps, one revealing white hair as she pulled off her blue cap.

While Kersk sat them down and gave them coffee and towels, Valentine introduced himself, explained why CID were interested in the club, and asked them to check in with the two officers at the trestle table on the pebbled beach above.

'Just routine, nothing to worry about,' said Valentine, promising that the watches would be returned at the next Leander Club meeting – a 'wild swim' in the moat of Hunstanton Hall on the following morning.

Within twenty minutes all the swimmers were back and being processed by Twine and Birley.

After dispensing hot drinks and towels, Kersk sat on the sands with a girl in a one-piece swimsuit and a Leander Club blue cap. They whispered into each other's ears as lovers do. Valentine caught her voice on the breeze and noted the crisp clear English vowels.

Of the fifty-one watches manufactured by WaveCrest, forty-six were collected in forensic evidence bags, labelled, and laid out on the trestle table. Two club members had called in sick, and so uniformed branch had dispatched motorbike officers to pick up their watches from home.

The three club members issued with watches who were unable to produce them fell into three distinct categories. Bill Cartwright, a forty-nine-year-old butcher, said he'd lost his watch on holiday in Madeira on the beach in December the previous year. He'd made an insurance claim on their holiday policy, and Birley had been furnished with the details after a quick mobile conversation with Cartwright's wife.

Sian James, a thirty-year-old PE teacher, had lost her watch from the lockers at the swimming pool in Peterborough just after Christmas. She was able to show Valentine an email on her phone from Peterborough police confirming that she'd reported the theft and giving her a crime number for insurance purposes. She'd made no claim, due to a £200 excess on the policy.

Finally, Lester Finn, a sixty-eight-year-old pensioner, had given his watch to his fifteen-year-old grandson, Ethan, because he found the weight of it distracting as he swam. Twine phoned Ethan's parents who reported, reluctantly, that the teenager had sold the watch on Lynn's Tuesday market to a dealer to provide some spending money for a school skiing trip.

Given that WaveCrest had confirmed the original delivery of fifty-one watches, Valentine had now tracked each one down: forty-six here on the beach, two to be collected, one stolen, one lost, one given away and sold. It was, in some ways, a dispiriting outcome. The watch left on the rig had to be one of the three separated from their original owners. It was unlikely to be the lost one, but it might be the one stolen from the public baths in Peterborough. The third had been sold locally. If they could find the market trader, they might get a lead, but it didn't look promising. Nothing looked promising.

Valentine sat for a moment, sipping his coffee, as Kersk and his girlfriend returned to the water, holding hands, until the final wave – a wall of tumbling water perhaps six foot high – reared up like a window, and they simultaneously arrowed their bodies through, to emerge on the other side, clutching each other, shocked at the impact of the icy sea.

For the first time Valentine thought what a morbid choice it had been: to name a swimming club after the classical Leander, lost at sea, washed ashore, dead.

TWENTY-TWO

The details of Dirk Hartog's last days were beginning to emerge into sharper focus. A string of witnesses had responded to newspaper, radio, and TV appeals and come forward with information to help track down his killer. Besides his evening drink in the Wash and Tope, the Dutchman had been a regular in the Copper Kettle tearooms. He'd mingled with the holiday crowds, and entered his name in the visitors' book at the lifeboat station on three separate occasions. RNLI volunteers said he'd seemed interested in books on local history, sold in the shop, and always took time to climb the staircase to the observation deck above the lifeboat, as well as checking out the hovercraft through the glass 'ports' built into the sides of its hangar.

A woman in Hunstanton Marine had sold the Dutchman the scuba gear with which he'd made his last, fatal dive. Hartog was no stranger in the store, having previously hired several items, including a small, hand-held underwater camera (which, Shaw noted, had never been recovered) and an underwater GPS unit. His English, she said, was near perfect, if obscured by a heavy accent which mashed vowels in a thick sibilance.

Asked why he was on the Norfolk coast, he'd offered 'walking and swimming' in search of a break from a busy life back in Holland. She'd judged his mood as buoyant, which Shaw found grimly humorous in the circumstances. Diving enthusiasts who used the shop said he'd been seen on several occasions emerging from the sea at various points along the coast, from Shepherd's Port in the south to Holme in the north, a stretch of beach nearly six miles long.

He'd bought the telescope the police had found in his room – a Gali 13 – from Birdwatchers' World in the town, explaining that he wanted to track seabirds on the sands at low tide, and that binoculars made him go cross-eyed. The shop assistant, a keen twitcher, told Shaw he doubted Hartog's credentials as he'd been unable to name any breeds he'd seen so far. The Gali provided a modest magnification of x22 and cost Hartog £146.99, including tripod and cover.

Perhaps, most significantly, Hartog had hired a small sea-going motorboat at Wells harbour on three occasions. A fourth voyage had been booked and paid for, but he had never appeared at the yard to pick up his boat. The owner of the fleet of inshore motor boats, usually hired to fishing clubs, said he'd paid in cash in advance each time, and shown a Dutch marine navigation certificate. In the box on the hire form marked *Purpose of trip*, he'd filled in *Sightseeing*. Given the fuel-tank capacity, and the boat's GPS and radar, the owner had stipulated a maximum range of forty nautical miles. When asked his planned destination or route – standard safety practice with all such hirings – he'd answered Roaring Island, an area of sand banks out on the edge of the deep water channel, popular with fishing trips and parties trying to get close to the Wash's resident seal colonies. Shaw had pulled Hartog's charts from storage at the Ark, and found the sandbanks marked Roaring Island – the oiled paper slightly smudged by a persistent fingertip.

Was this where Hartog hoped to find the elusive *Cala*?

Their final witness had telephoned St James' and offered to speak to a member of CID, explaining that he had become a 'friend' of the deceased. And he'd provided an address of sorts: *Beachcomber*. Hut 1314, South Beach.

Valentine looked at his black slip-ons, partly submerged in the white sand. 'Is this really necessary?' he asked, noting Shaw's bare feet.

The coast stretched ahead into a noonday heatwave, the long line of huts and beach houses flexing in a mirage. From the promenade the tinny soundtrack of an ice-cream van rode the breeze.

Shaw walked on, counting off the house and hut numbers along South Beach. This stretch of the coast of the Wash, leading away from the open sea but towards the estuary that narrowed into Lynn, provided a bleak prospect even on a blazing blue summer's day. For a few hours it could pass for the seaside at high tide, but for most of any twenty-four-hour cycle it overlooked a desert of black mud and the exposed sands that clogged the heart of the great inlet.

The shoreline itself was an almost continuous necklace of houses, ranging along a spectrum from glass-and-concrete second homes to shacks built of driftwood and corrugated iron, boarded up against spring tides.

'That's thirteen hundred; we're close,' called Shaw, waiting as Valentine trudged the high water mark. The sea was high, but still unnaturally calm, as it had been all summer after the storm-wracked winter. For Shaw, the temptation to simply run into the water was almost as strong as the one that was propelling Valentine up the beach, to the safety of dry land.

Shaw knew something of *Beachcomber*, thanks to Lena's business diligence. That winter, sitting outside one evening by the firepit, she'd floated the idea of opening up part of the restaurant as a gallery. If they added images to the website, they could attract new customers, and by rotating artists they could have a series of 'private view' evenings, invitation only, when they could offer a deal on food and wine. She said there was already a string of galleries on the coast going east towards the Chelsea-on-Sea villages of the Burn Valley – but nothing local, except *Beachcomber,* which she'd checked out, and officially classified as 'eccentric', if not 'wacky' – with no food, and a coffee offering she typified as 'sub-Nescafé'.

The sign, when Shaw glimpsed it, was neon, unlit, in the style of *American Graffiti*, the hut itself an old diner – nearly fifty feet of gleaming steel and sleek Greyhound Bus windows. Valentine noted a Stop the Pier poster, and a trailing flag from a radio mast which bore the campaign logo of STP. Inside, the whole length of the unit was a gallery, with a few pictures hung, but mostly accommodating sculptures made of driftwood or found objects from the beach. The old counter had a red bell, which, when Shaw hit it, seemed to echo round the metallic cigar case of the café/ gallery.

Valentine examined a work entitled *Littoral 6* which appeared to be constructed from broken plastic bottles and a fishing buoy. 'People pay for this rubbish?' he asked, unaware of the clever play on words, while examining the price tag and whistling in appreciation.

A man appeared, and it was immediately apparent he was also the artist; paint-spattered dungarees hung from bony shoulders, on a frame which could have been driftwood itself, beneath a weathered face, eroded by sea and sun. His exact age was as difficult to calculate as most flotsam: possibly sixty, but probably a decade more, with silver hair cut close to his skull.

The introductions were curt: his name was Joe Lester, owner of hut 1314, aka *Beachcomber.*

'It was the website,' he said, without further preamble, hardly glancing at the proffered warrant cards. 'I put up photographs – mine, other local artists. This guy posted on the site, said he was looking at Hunstanton online and saw a link for the gallery. He said it was the word that caught his attention: beachcomber. As a kid he'd spent a lot of time walking beaches. He wrote about the word – I guess you'd say he was eloquent on the subject – so we had that in common, an interest in the shoreline . . .' Looking out the long diner window at the sea, his eyes narrowed, the tanned face creasing in dark lines. 'He said *strandloper* was better – that's the South African, right? For the tribes on the coast who lived off what they could find. Apparently, their rubbish dumps were full of shells and whalebone – that's what Hartog reckoned. That's what sets us apart, Homo sapiens, from the uncouth lot – the Homo erectus. We scavenged on the beach. Salvaged stuff. That's smart . . .' He searched for the right word. 'Adaptive. So that's a kind of pure vision of the beachcomber as one with nature, an eco-warrior. I tweeted the text, and loads of people joined in – hashtag beachcomber.'

Valentine, bemused, pointed at a coffee machine and asked if he could have a cup. Wordlessly, Lester gave him a metal token for the slot, and as his arm extended from his shirt sleeve, Shaw noted a tattoo, faded, but reading *The Rock.* The interruption seemed to derail his thoughts, so that he had to look out to sea again, trying to reconnect with the thread of the narrative.

'Anyway, we had a good chat online, then he turns up, walked through that door one day, what – three weeks ago, more? Sat right there, drinking coffee. I had to tell him then that the English version isn't so starry-eyed. Beachcombers. One up from tramps, just runaway sailors who lived off the land. Vagabonds. Riff-raff. I have to say I feel kind of more at home with that . . .'

Shaw nodded, distracted by a mural on the wall which advertised *Beachcomber*'s food, with a telephone number for booking, replete with bulbous, graffiti-like numbers, including a pair of Continental sevens.

'Did he say why he'd made the trip?' asked Shaw.

'Well. Sort of. On the website he saw something he wanted, so he'd come to buy it.'

Lester had a laptop on the old diner counter which he flipped up. The *Beachcomber* website had a gallery feature which allowed him to arrow through the images until he reached a photograph of several items of flotsam scattered artfully amongst glistening rocks. There was a long blue float, some rope, a seal's skull, and a piece of wood bearing the letters *Cala*.

'He wanted to know if I still had this piece and where I'd found it. It was round the back on the grass bank. I said he could have it – I found it a year ago – but he gave me fifty pounds, which was good of him. I asked why it was precious and he just said, "Long story" – which in my book is shorthand for don't ask.'

'And where did you find it?' asked Valentine, pulling a face as he sipped the coffee from a paper cup marked with the STP logo.

'About half a mile north of the old pier. I walk the line . . .' Lester smiled at the Johnny Cash. 'With a torch in winter if I need it.' Lester examined the grain in the wooden bar top. 'It's odd, it's been gone thirty-five years, but when I walk this beach, my beach, I still see it, the old pier. Graceful – that's the word. The one they're putting up looks like the conveyor belt on *The Generation Game*. Bloody eyesore.'

Shaw spun the laptop so he could see the picture that had enticed Dirk Hartog across the North Sea. 'It's a ship's name board, right?' he asked.

'Yes. Certainly. He said he was thinking of some scuba diving off the beach, thought he might find the rest. I said he'd be better off out on the sandbanks. This is just flotsam. The wrecks tend to be out near the deep channel.'

A detail still troubled Shaw. 'You walk the beach after dark?'

'Yes. I don't sleep nights – well, not much. And I don't sleep indoors much either.' His eyes narrowed. 'You're with the lifeboat right, the hovercraft?' Shaw nodded. 'Thought I knew the face. Next time you're in the lifeboat house, have a look at the rescue board: the night of thirty-first January 1953. My name's up there. Joseph Lester, aged four.'

'The North Sea floods?'

'We lost my sis. Mind you, wasn't for the lifeboat, we'd have all gone.'

Shaw held up both hands. 'Sorry. Didn't mean to open old wounds . . .'

'No, no. S'fine. Here, I'll show you.'

He led the way out the back of the diner and up the grassy seawall to the grit road, beyond which stretched the reclaimed land, marred by a caravan site, a mobile home park, a sandy track linking a line of post-war prefabs, and a field of rough grass dotted with the kind of tents that have picture windows and a canvas veranda. Every tent had a tethered car, as if they were on leads.

'We were over there . . . beyond that line of chalets. Dad worked on the roads, navvying, so it was all we could afford. A Sunday, of course, which didn't help, so there was no warning. These days – radio, internet, TV, radar – we'd have been evacuated. Back then, nothing.'

Valentine reached the top of the bank, his narrow chest heaving.

'The water came over the bank along at Heacham, then back up here. About one in the morning. First thing we knew, there was three feet of it in the house, and no electric. So Mum lit a candle. We had to get on the top bunks and wait. Me and my sister thought it was an adventure. When the water got to the door handle, Dad went out, wading – trying to, anyway. There was no moon and no lights. Mum got up with us on the bunks, and then the candle went, and we got cold – really cold.'

Lester fumbled in his pocket for cigarette papers and tobacco, his fingers shaking. Shaw looked away, embarrassed by the intimacy.

'That's the thing about the sea: it comes at you, in waves, and I've never had a problem with that. But the water that night, it just rose, so it felt like we were just sinking, and it seemed to crush the air so it was hard to breathe. Others – we could hear loads of people talking, and shouting out for help – they had to sit tight too. I held on to sis but in the end she was colder than the sea. We ended up sitting on the rafters under the roof. Light came, Mum knew she was gone. Still don't like it – the moment of dawn, the first light. Never know what you're going to see.

'The TA got to us first – just the local lads, but they did a great job, and some of the US servicemen from up in town. The lifeboat crew had got some small boats out and they brought Dad. He tried to bring her back – that was the worst bit really, the effort, because in the end he just got angry – with her, but really with himself.' Again, the eyes narrowed as he considered Shaw. 'He never got over it. Simple thing to say, hear it a lot, but it's true. Most of us, it's a slow realization – that life's been a failure. Dad, he knew that morning. He was thirty-one.'

Shaw wondered if Lester's support for the STP stemmed from that night in 1953, whether it was an attempt to restore the landscape, and the seascape, to what it had been before the tragedy had over-taken his family, with its graceful arrow's-flight pier: a bid, in short, to wind back the clock.

'Between here and Lynn, they lost sixty people,' said Lester. 'Difficult to believe. Three hundred and more on the East Coast. Up in town, they didn't even know. Thought it was a winter storm, end of story. They call it a *tempest* on the memorial, but most people thought it was just a gale. They laid in bed thinking, *I'm glad I'm not out in that.* Holland – three thousand dead. They don't forget. The sea can kill you. That's what I see when I sit on the beach: a killer. People spend their holidays in the water. Me? I give it a miss.'

Shaw looked back out to sea, thinking about Dirk Hartog.

'To be fair,' said Lester, 'and I am a fair man, the government didn't want anyone to remember about us. Eight years after the war, morale shaky, trying to rebuild the cities, last thing they wanted was a national emergency. So we just got on with clearing it all up. And burying the dead. Sis is at Heacham: *Safely in harbour* – Mum chose it, it's from *The Tempest*. Most of those who died lived in one-storey housing on reclaimed land. Today we'd be white trash.'

Out beyond the mobile homes a child flew a red kite.

'So I don't sleep nights,' said Lester, smiling. 'I walk the beach. Sorry – that's a bloody long answer to a short question. I'm looking for anything really. Dad said I'm watching the sea, to make sure it doesn't happen again, but that's just imagination. I just can't abide a roof.'

TWENTY-THREE

Robbie Ross had worked a double shift in the underwater caisson, the damp cold of the concrete chamber getting to his joints, so that his left elbow, left knee, and the finger joints on both hands had swollen up, making his body feel bloated and arthritic. In the cacophony of noise within the box he had to flash his torch three times at the foreman to mark the end of his shift, heading for the cage. This moment, the jolt of the lift cable and the giddy rise, always set his spirit free, so that he could almost smell the open sea above and envisage the stretched blue wire of the horizon.

The cage clattered between its iron-clad walls, coming to rest at the decompression chamber entrance, marked in red capitals: *MANLOCK*. Through the observation porthole he could see two men were in the airtight chamber, but the attendant was already spinning the airlock wheels and Robbie's ears registered the sudden, sharp hiss of decompression. As they trooped out the far end of the womb-like chamber, he took their place, discarding his overalls, boots, and socks in the cradle provided, and sitting in his shorts.

As the attendant programmed the computer control panel with Robbie's details – time in the caisson, age, and medical profile – he took a picture through the porthole to send to Marc. The boy hankered for the life of a tunnel tiger, and Robbie, with Donald's blessing, was thrilled to be a role model. One day he'd have to have a heart-to-heart, man to man, painting perhaps a more realistic picture of life underground. The money was good, but the working conditions were often brutal, and the death rate – particularly in China and the Far East – was eye-wateringly high. Robbie had promised himself retirement at forty, if he lived that long.

Adding a text line – *Coming up for air!* – he sent the image to Marc's phone.

The attendant was a man called Royle, an outsider in Robbie's world, because he worked for the company that manufactured the manlock, and maintained a studied air of superiority, literally setting himself above the world of the caisson, with its realities of sand, and rock, and muscle.

Royle always had a book at his workstation, which consisted of a narrow metal pull-down seat by the observation port, and a small desk top. His world was scientific, spotless, set against the civilized hum of electronics.

Robbie, following the manual instructions laid down in the contractual code, made eye contact with Royle and put both thumbs up. The LED display in the manlock wall showed *28 MINS*, the time period for his decompression, without which he would be exposed to the risk of the bends – the potentially lethal condition suffered by divers returning from the depths – although no tunnel tiger would ever call it such, preferring its historically accurate forerunner, caisson's disease.

As an apprentice, digging a road tunnel under water on the outskirts of Manila, he'd seen a victim of the bends, a man who'd skipped the manlock to find a bookie and put his month's wages on a horse running in Singapore. They'd all been hauled up from the caisson by the warning bells and they'd had to file past the body, twisted and distorted like a victim of medieval torture, finally released from the rack.

It had been Marc, a studious boy, who had discovered the origins of that strange short form – the bends. US engineers had used caissons to build the East Bridge in St Louis, and twelve men had died in agony. The Brooklyn Bridge, Marc gravely informed his uncle, had cost 110 lives. One of the symptoms was seizures and cramps which made the sufferers stoop forward, a posture reminiscent at the time of the latest dance fad in New York – the Grecian Bend, in which women, in corsets and bustles, bent forward at the waist in a posture that seemed to mimic the graceful figures of an Athenian frieze. Ross thought it was a macabre metaphor, the cramps of death mirrored in the dainty steps of a dancehall craze.

Scrolling through the pictures on his smartphone, he flashed past images of little Eric in bed at the hospital, clutching the plywood kit Robbie had bought him of the Empire State Building. Glancing up at the attendant's porthole, he noted that Royle was not at his station. Despite his aloof good manners, Royle was a smoker, and they all knew that beyond the manlock exit a gantry led to one of the outside platforms, where a blind eye was turned to the half-dozen addicts who found the rig's smoking ban intolerable.

Robbie took a deep breath. His T-shirt stopped above the elbows, exposing the skin, and he felt a minute skitter of legs, so that he went to brush away the insect that must have sneaked in through the airlock. But there was nothing there. Taking another deep breath, he was vaguely aware that something about that unseen insect was significant. He felt another, above his ankle, and scratched vigorously. The first insect had somehow switched his mood from joy to a numb sadness, but the second flipped him back on to a high, and his face, stupidly, broke into a broad smile.

On his phone he found an album of pictures of his girlfriend, Jantine. She worked for the company at its worldwide headquarters in Rotterdam. The pictures showed a white beach, with Jantine on a raffia rug. She had long legs, which were very thin, and angular arms, so that there was something brittle about her that made Robbie anxious. Astonished, he found himself wiping a tear off the screen of the smartphone. Guiltily, he looked up at the porthole, but Royle was still freighting his bloodstream with nicotine.

Robbie's double shift had been seven hours long, and he promised himself now that he wouldn't do it again, even if they did pay treble time. Fatigue was making his limbs twitch, and he couldn't shift an image from his mind of his bunk bed in the accommodation block. As a foreman's mate, he had a single room, so he could close the door, open the window, and sleep. His body, ahead of his mind, seemed to subside into an imaginary mattress, a subtle nausea seeping through his nervous system. When he looked up again, Royle was back at his post, but – briefly – the image doubled up so that he saw two metal portholes, in twin orbits, trying to meld.

At this point, in retrospect, he was close to death. His skin crawled with insects, but he was too tired to activate the necessary muscular response. His shallow breathing left a bead of sweat disfiguring the T-shirt. A series of vignettes from his life did not so much flash past as appear in a stately series, as if someone was showing a slide show on the inside of his head. The idea of God, as a disembodied projectionist, made him laugh out loud. He had no energy left to fight his way out of the coma that was drugging his brain, as its blood supply began to fizz with oxygen.

There was no order to the images, but they were all so vibrant they made his heart race. Images of childhood, fragments from his travels, a woman he'd met in Piraeus who'd given him a pomegranate, a previously unremembered image of his mother standing at a kitchen sink.

And then the final image.

The family flat on a stillborn winter's day, looking out at the estate, the 1930s stucco facades blotched with damp like gunshot wounds. The ground floor, but the fifteen above pressing down. The smell of Christmas dinner clogged his nose and mouth like a gas mask, especially the gamey edge to the turkey juice, and the hot steam from the Brussels sprouts. Alone, but surrounded by family voices, he was waiting for something, someone. Outside, snow fell in feathery cartwheels, and when a car crept past, all he heard was the baseline creak of snow compacting under the tyres. Opposite, in the living room of a council house, the lights of a Christmas tree winked on and off. Pressing his face against the window, he could feel the cold, while his breath misted the glass. A doorbell rang.

The bell became a buzzer, the buzzer became an alarm. Air, rushing in through the manlock exit, failed to fill Robbie's lungs. The first seizure struck, his body snapping at the waist like a mouse-trap, so that he fell to the floor.

TWENTY-FOUR

S haw and Valentine picked their way through the rocks below the town's emblematic multicoloured cliffs: the white chalk and the red chalk, lying in neat layers over the terracotta ironstone. The beach echoed with the chatter of birds, their calls amplified by the concave amphitheatre of the rock face above. Shaw, unable to resist a childhood habit, clapped his hands and counted to three before the sharp echo bounced back. With the sea flat, the humid summer air seemed trapped against the cliff face, creating a sense that they weren't outside at all, but on a wide outdoor stage, in a limitless auditorium, full of still air. When Shaw spoke, the words seemed to have the resonance of an actor's, bouncing off the seats in the circle, reaching up to the gods.

'You OK?'

Valentine, a hundred yards to the rear, struggled on, stopping briefly to disentangle a frond of seaweed from his shoe. The way ahead lay through a maze of smooth ironstone rocks, like the wet backs of a vast herd of hippopotami, each with its head down, drinking at a waterhole. Many were covered in a slimy green algae which made it precarious to try to step from one to the next, although Shaw managed, leaving Valentine to zigzag on the sand, stepping over the myriad pools that lay between the wave-sculpted rocks.

'Peter!'

Looking back, he saw Valentine, his hands cupped in a living megaphone, then pointing out to sea, where a bright yellow air ambulance helicopter was approaching the rig. It circled once, before dropping down to the heliport deck. Checking his phone, he found he had no signal. Valentine shrugged too, holding out his own in a despairing gesture. Something had happened on the rig, but they'd have to wait for a clifftop signal to find out more.

Ahead, amongst the green-backed rocks, they could see Anna Roos, clutching a clipboard to her chest, surrounded by a dozen school kids of varying ages in shorts and T-shirts. Shaw recalled that one of the many eccentric innovations of Winterhill was that all ages were part of one class, and that all were invited to stay at school throughout the holidays if they wished.

Roos sported the same rimless reflective sunglasses she'd worn in the STP offices, shielding her eyes as she looked up at the sound of approaching voices. Shaw had often asked witnesses to remove dark glasses during interviews so that he could watch their eyes. He was unsure if this was a breach of anyone's basic human rights, but he somehow felt that the attempt to hide the eyes was an infringement of his. They might not be windows to the soul, but they provided a spectrum of clues to the keen observer. One of the many positive side effects of his disability was an almost unnatural fascination with the eyes of others.

Roos crouched down, and so did her audience, as Shaw vaulted the final line of ironstone boulders. He couldn't be sure if she'd done it deliberately, a snub to his arrival. In the unnatural calm below the cliff he heard her voice: 'We can think of each rock pool – every single one – as a little world of its own. An ecosystem – who remembers that word?' A series of small hands rose tentatively.

Shaw found himself a rock to sit on and waited for Valentine. Roos told her pupils about the rock pool, how it was linked to other ecosystems – like the sea – and how it was really two ecosystems – one at low tide, when it was a world apart, and one at high tide, when it was reduced to a shallow depression on the heaving floor of the sea. So each day, twice a day, the ecosystem was transformed, and that affected the fish, and the plankton, and the weed. The tides, she told them, also brought energy to the pool – to go alongside the heat and light of the sun. What kind of energy was this?

Shaw heard the word 'kinetic' whispered, followed by a round of applause.

Roos stood, her knees caked with sand, and pretended to see the detectives for the first time. Shaw pointed at his watch, and she nodded, clutching the clipboard again. 'Now,' she said, in that tone of voice perfected by teachers, 'in your pack are the first few pages of the book we discussed in class – *The Shrimp and the Anemone*. It tells you how two children played on this beach a hundred years ago. Right here, in these rock pools. So – let's go up on the sand and read, and then we can have our picnics.'

As the children fled up the beach, she sauntered over, and for a moment Shaw thought she was going to reveal her eyes, but the hand dropped from the metal arm of the frame and brushed instead at the salt and sand on her knees.

'Inspector. I hear there may be other bombs in the sand.' She nodded south, where metal barriers now kept the public off nearly a mile of prime holiday beach. 'I'm surprised, given the dangers, that they're still working out there on the rig . . .'

On cue, the helicopter rose from its pad out at sea, swinging over their heads inland.

Shaw waited for the noise to fade before asking the question that had brought him to the rock pools. 'I don't have a lot of time, Ms Roos. When we last spoke, you denied any knowledge of the email threat posted on Blue Square's website.'

'STP issued a press release. We said our campaign was a non-violent one. We issued it again after they found that man in the water.' She glanced along the shore to a police launch that was still anchored over the spot where Dirk Hartog's body had been recovered.

'It's a skill, tracking a digital post like that back to the account of the sender,' said Shaw. 'Especially if they know the tricks of the trade. A message can be broken up into separate digital packages, you see, each one a nonsense of numbers or letters, before being sent through a series of different mainframe servers to the same target site. At that point they can be programmed to reconstitute themselves into the original message. Fiendishly clever, my sergeant here is on top of the detail obviously, but I'm just fine with the big picture.'

'Fascinating,' said Roos, flicking a stray hair out of the corner of her mouth.

'Indeed. I have a young DC who's into this stuff. She's just spent fifty hours without sleep tracking back through the servers to the sender of the Blue Square threat. The sender's account is aroos@winterhill. co.uk. That's your work email address, isn't it?'

'I leave my laptop in the staff room at school, and at STP's offices for that matter. Neither is a secure environment.'

'That's a very rapid response,' said Shaw. 'No time for a direct denial, I note. You've leapfrogged my implied question, Ms Roos. Did you send the message?'

'No. Of course not. We're running an ecological campaign – an ethical campaign. Mindless threats of violence are counterproductive.'

'Where is your laptop now?'

'At home.'

Shaw consulted his notebook. 'At forty-one Lancaster Buildings? DS Valentine here has a warrant. He's going to go back there now with you and secure the laptop, and then we're going to review the emails sent. I'm sorry about this. In the meantime, I'd like you to stay in the town. No unexpected trips. Is that clear?'

Both fists balled into white knuckles, she didn't move.

'Do you have something to hide, Ms Roos?'

'No.' She waited ten seconds, and then removed the dark glasses. 'What am I supposed to do with the class?'

'I'd give them some licence to freedom, Ms Roos. That's the motto, surely? Several are teenagers, so perhaps a lesson in leadership would be timely. I think they can survive in downtown Hunstanton unchaperoned, don't you? But if we walk them back to the esplanade, I have a police constable ready to make sure they get back to school safely.'

'Am I being charged?'

'Not unless you want to be. But we are in a hurry. We need that laptop. I'm afraid we have to ask that you don't use your phone until we've signed over the computer to our forensic unit. Sorry. Rules.' He held out his hand.

Looking out to sea, she eventually gave Shaw the phone. 'I have a right to care about this place, you know. Just because my name doesn't fit, it doesn't mean I can't invest in the landscape. The beach. The beauty of it.'

'I don't doubt that. Sorry – I don't really understand. You have a mildly exotic name. It never crossed my mind that you *don't fit*. Do you encounter prejudice? Has anyone ever questioned your right to be here? I doubt that very much.'

'It's unsaid. That's a very English vice. It's the surname, of course. It does mark me out as an outsider. The immigrant. I'm not allowed to be angry, I don't have the birthright.'

'Ms Roos,' said Shaw. 'I don't know—'

'I think, sometimes, that I'm seen as a newcomer, trying just a little too hard to be accepted. Patronizing, isn't it?'

'That's not the issue here. The issue's the law. We need access to your laptop.'

She told the children to finish their packed lunches and collect their things, then she turned back to Shaw. 'My father was Dutch. An *Engelandvaarder* – you know of this?'

Did Shaw detect the slightest of Dutch rhythms within the sentence? Had it gone undetected before, or had she consciously switched the cadence?

Shaw shook his head, checking his diver's watch, watching her pack up her books and clipboards.

'A broad term, but a group – I suppose – all Dutchmen, who wanted to go on fighting after the Germans invaded in 1939. Some walked to Spain, or Switzerland, or got to Norway in time. Thirty of them – very brave – crossed the North Sea in kayaks. Crazy, I know. Now I think about it, very British. Eccentric perhaps. It's more than a hundred miles and it took the few who made it more than fifty hours. There's a memorial down the coast to the ones who failed. My father was one of the lucky ones. He came ashore at Sizewell – a bleak place. Not a pretty spot. Not picturesque. He settled here. But he always told the same story. How they landed at dusk, with the sun going down, and how he felt in that moment that he had arrived home, because it was – you see – so much like home. The marshes, the sands, the silence. The cliffs here are an aberration. It's a flat coast for a hundred miles – more. The pier, if it opens, will destroy all this.'

'Is that a confession?' asked Shaw, as Roos prepared to gather the children into line.

'No. I'm just saying I have a right, like everyone else, to resist. I belong. This is my home, as it was his. Adopted homes are precious.'

Shaw found the little speech preachy and unconvincing, and now that he saw Roos's eyes, he noted they were an oddly lifeless grey.

'The dead man, Hartog, was Dutch,' noted Shaw, testing connections. 'A tourist only. Did you meet?'

Roos's natural colour had bled away. Did she regret her little lecture on family history? 'No. Never.'

Valentine's mobile buzzed once, cut out, and then buzzed again. He scrambled on top of one of the boulders and held the phone up above his head, trying to recapture the signal. 'Text,' he said, reading. 'Twine says there's been an incident out on the rig. He says the army's got an inflatable we can use down on the beach. Thirty-two ill – two in the 'copter. No details, but he says sabotage. No fatalities – yet.'

TWENTY-FIVE

Seen from the beach, the pier-head construction resembled a steel city, a suspended chaos of girders, cranes, and platforms; up close, as Shaw navigated the army dinghy along a channel marked by yellow-and-green buoys, the site divided neatly between three separate structures: the support tug riding at anchor; the crane, towering nearly eighty feet above the sea, supported on four legs sunk to the sea floor; and finally the rig itself, the work platform, supported over the sunken caisson by a series of metal pillars. This too, it seemed, lived part of its life as a ship; its name – *MV Telamon* – ran vertically down one of the supporting legs. At the base of one of these legs a floating landing stage led to a switchback flight of metal stairs, leading up to the deck – a work area the size of a football pitch, holding a two-storey accommodation block, the platform control room, and the entry/exit shafts for the manlock and the mudlock.

Valentine, who'd felt sick in the boat, stood to get his breath back at the top of the stairs, framed against a *No Smoking* sign ten feet long and six feet high.

'Dry land, at last,' he said, tracking the crane as it lifted a bucket from the mudlock chute, swinging it out over the sea and down to a floating barge, where the claw-like hand opened, spilling out sand and gravel.

Half a dozen men in shorts and trainers stood around talking on a marked-out basketball pitch, cradling mugs. A cook in a white smock trundled bins behind a Portakabin.

'Christ. Imagine if this was home,' said Valentine.

Shaw looked back at Hunstanton, a view once available for the price of a ride on the old pier's miniature railway. While the beach was still closed, the fun fair and rides were all working on the South Beach, the big dipper plunging from its heights as he watched, the accompanying wave of mock screams reaching his ears a few seconds after the cars splashed down in the crocodile-infested river provided. His good eye tracked north until he saw

the sun glinting on the windows of *Surf!*, the blue dolphin flag
flying from the Old Boathouse. Shaw appreciated for the first
time this unheralded virtue of piers, that they allowed you to look
back on your own life, as it were, framing the everyday from a
fresh angle.

A yellow line on the concrete deck, made up of arrows, pointed
them towards *Bridge*.

Captain John Ring, commander of the *MV Telamon*, sat in a
swivel chair in front of a panel of gauges and digital computer
screens. Observation windows surrounded him at all four compass
points. A bank of CCTV screens showed men working in the
caisson below with that same shadow-like lack of 3D reality that
reminded Shaw of the Apollo moon landings.

Shaw knew Ring: born and based in the town, he travelled the
world with a master's ticket, captaining supertankers and long-
distance freighters, but always made a point of contacting the
lifeboat crew when he was home on leave, as he was listed on the
station's back-up crew. One Christmas he'd joined Shaw's crew on
the hovercraft to rescue a family of three marooned on a sandbank
after trying to rescue a runaway dog.

'Peter,' he said, shaking hands but not getting up. 'Sickbay first?
It's your shout.'

'Just run us through security, Captain. The basics.'

Ring manipulated the CCTV screens by remote, showing them
a complete set of live images of the exterior of the *Telamon*, a
second bank of interior images, including the view inside the caisson.
A further display panel controlled an emergency automatic lock
system with which he could close bulkhead doors throughout the
structure in the face of fire, flood, or unspecified threat.

'Standard kit now to deal with pirates,' said Ring. 'You don't
want to be on one of these things in the Indian Ocean without the
ability to lock it down.'

'She's run as a ship?' asked Valentine, sensing for the first time
a slight shudder in the structure.

'Part ship, part rig. When she floats, she's not exactly graceful.
But that's not her job. Her job's to stay afloat until the tugs get her
into the right spot, and then drop her legs to the seabed, hauling
herself up out of the water. Which is not a bad trick when you think
about it.' Suddenly embarrassed by his enthusiasm for his command,

Ring jumped down from the captain's chair. 'Sorry. That's not why you're here, is it? Follow me.'

A short man, and slight with it, he compensated with a smart, rapid pace, as he led them out across the deck towards the accommodation block, a one-storey prefab belching steam from an aluminium chimney.

As Ring punched in a security code to release the door lock, Shaw recalled that a telamon was a male caryatid – a figure in stone, supporting a roof, as might be seen on a Greek temple. In his mind's eye, he saw the rig as a giant, its feet on the seabed, the platform held high above the water by upturned hands.

Inside, down a corridor that smelt of bathwater, they found the sickbay. All the beds were full. Two men provided a soundtrack of groans, their bodies jackknifed at the waist. The air-conditioned interior was laced with the unmistakable aromas of vomit and urine. One patient sat up, coughing drily into a wad of tissue paper.

'We flew in a couple of doctors from Lynn. Everyone's fine – well, everyone's recovering. Ross and Cheetham have been flown back out. They'll be all right, but they'd both worked double shifts, so they need a blood transfusion and monitoring in intensive care. But they'll live.'

'Robbie Ross?' asked Shaw, recalling the scene around young Eric's bed the day after the bomb explosion on the beach.

'Indeed. He passed out inside the manlock itself, the last man through. Everyone from the previous shift was back in the accommodation block, or in the TV lounge, when the symptoms hit. It's all a bit random. Take Joey there.' Ring pointed at one of the jackknifed patients, lying on top of his sheets, scratching at his legs and arms. 'He was fine. In fact, I reckon he was the first through the chamber after the second shift. He watched *Top Gear*, had a plate of chilli con carne, then couldn't remember where his room was: total blank-out. One of his mates found him wandering the corridor. Memory loss – plus some double vision. The rest have got joint pains, and the itching, of course – that's classic.'

'We need to see this manlock chamber,' said Shaw. 'Is it up here, or down there?'

'Up here. I've told Pete Royle to stand by; he's the operator.'

The decompression chamber lay at the end of a long corridor with blue lino and no windows. Royle, the attendant, swung the door out, revealing the four-inch-thick metal width of the chamber's skin and the spotless interior. Shaw took a seat, but Valentine held back, watching Royle take his seat outside by the control panel.

'So – the science, please,' said Shaw. 'Or as much as we need to know.'

Ring joined him inside the chamber and nodded to Royle, who shut the door and swung the circular lock. Shaw felt his ears flutter, his heart beat responding to the claustrophobic interior.

'Working underwater for long periods of time means the blood absorbs gases,' said Ring, his voice echoless. 'If you come up too quickly, the gas comes out in the blood as bubbles. These can kill you. So the chamber slows that process down. The men come up in the cage and then spend anything up to an hour in here – the pressure at first matches that below, then slowly recalibrates to match atmospheric pressure at sea level. The process is computer-controlled, but monitored manually by the attendant. It's on a standard setting. All Pete does is make sure the timing is right. And he maintains a visual watch.'

Shaw felt a single drop of sweat slide down his scalp. 'Can he hear us?' he asked.

'Not at the moment. He can switch on a two-way mike – but if he does, this light comes on,' said Ring, touching a small green LED set in the pale cream metal wall.

'You trust Royle?'

'First thing I did was call up his file with head office. Eighteen years' experience, unblemished record. We conduct police checks in nearly twenty jurisdictions before offering anyone a job. Technically, he's a consultant, not an employee – but the checks stand. Crew think he's a bit standoffish, bookish, keeps himself to himself. But that's not a crime.'

'OK. Let's ask him what happened.'

Ring nodded to Royle and the locks sprung open with a faint hiss.

'Talk us through it,' said Shaw, noting the strong smell of disinfectant on the air of the corridor, compared with the dead air of the chamber. There was something else too – a faint aroma of nicotine.

'Someone reset the chamber overnight,' said Royle. 'I didn't touch it. I hardly ever do. There's no need because the pressure of the caisson and its depth are constant – and so is our height. So the variable is the *time* spent inside the chamber – that's what I set, and the name of the occupant, which brings with it their medical record. Ross's time chart indicated that he'd been down for a double shift, so I just punched in his personal code and set the clock at twenty-eight minutes. Then I went outside for some fresh air.' Royle put his hands in his pockets before Shaw could ask to see his fingers.

Ring examined his boots. 'She's a non-smoking vessel, Peter. There's clearly a bit of give and take I didn't know about. It won't happen again.'

Royle licked his lips. 'I just went out because twenty-eight minutes is a long time, and nothing can go wrong. Ross is an old hand, and he looked fine – cheery even. When I got back, he was just about to pass out. He's OK, Captain?'

Ring nodded but didn't take his eyes off Shaw, who raised a hand and asked, 'The control room – is the chamber not monitored from there?'

'Yup. The night shift didn't spot the recalibration,' said Ring. 'We'll change procedure; it won't happen again.' He took a deep breath. 'That's two things that won't happen again.'

'Question is, how did it happen this time? Any ideas?'

'Well, like Pete says, someone reset the computer.'

'And you can do that at this panel?'

'Yup. Or in the control room,' said Ring. 'But it's more likely here because this area's open to the crew unless the control room shuts the doors.'

'So we're talking know-how here,' said Valentine. 'This isn't an alarm clock, is it? It's a bit of high-tech kit. I bet you're not on a deckhand's wages, right?' he asked Royle. 'This is a professional job.'

'That's right,' said Ring. 'It's complex. I'm employed by Red Chamber, a subsidiary of Blue Square, which makes and maintains this kind of equipment all over the world, not just on Blue Square projects. But I need the expertise to deal with problems. Actually setting the chamber time is easy. If you were here on a mobile phone, and I was on the other end, I could talk you through it – the recalibration. It's effectively been knocked back to the default setting of sea level. In fact, if someone tried to tamper with it, *and failed*, the computer would react by going back to that default setting. That may well be what happened.'

'Could it be an accident?' asked Shaw.

Royle looked at Ring, then Shaw. 'One in a million. Less. You've got to *try* to do this. Accidental resetting can't happen.'

Ring produced a printout from the pocket of his high-vis jacket. 'I got this from Rotterdam an hour ago. We're closing down the caisson at noon until further notice. All operations are at stop from then. They'll review that in forty-eight hours. This incident is classified as an accident and as such will have to be the subject of a health and safety investigation. We don't have a choice. The work stops – if we're lucky, a few hours; unlucky, weeks.'

'What about the crew in the meantime?' asked Shaw.

'You're in charge, Peter. We're a mile offshore, not fifteen; if I was in international waters, of course, I could tell *you* what we're doing. But if you're still thinking this might be an inside job, there's one other person you should see – a guy called Abel DeSouza, one of the mop-up crew. It was his job to check the corridor was clean this morning at dawn. It was spotless, as he'd left it six hours earlier, except for two sets of wet footprints, one set in, one set out. Footprints – that's bare feet, not boots.'

TWENTY-SIX

B lue Square Inc. issued a statement to the London Stock Exchange at noon precisely, announcing that work on the new Hunstanton Pier would cease while investigations continued into an incident on the site rig, which might, or might not, be the result of sabotage. The share price fell 2.4 per cent, wiping £210 million off the value of the company. The *Financial Times* ran a short item on their website quoting a source at Blue Square who estimated the daily cost of the shutdown to be in excess of £1.2 million. In Brussels, a spokesman for the development fund, the principal backers of the project, told the press that delays were a concern and the project would be monitored closely. The company, which retained the services of three MPs as consultants on infrastructure policy, pressed them to lobby the Cabinet Office, insisting on a quick and efficient investigation by the police in the interests of protecting local jobs and public investment in the scheme. A Home Office civil servant was summoned to Downing Street and briefed, resulting in a telephone call to the chief constable of the West Norfolk at six fifteen p.m.

Shaw got the call ten minutes later, and responded by calling the serious crime unit's eight officers to a meeting at *Surf!* They sat outside at the picnic tables, the rig silent on the horizon, the summer crowds already drifting back towards town, dragging pushchairs and cool boxes, children and wetsuits.

'Sabotage is an ugly word,' Shaw told them. 'It just got uglier. This latest attack signals a degree of premeditation and organization, so we need to drill down into that, and at the very least disrupt any plans for further attacks. The pressure's on from the top down. It's pretty clear someone is reckless enough to risk human life; in fact, it may be that Dirk Hartog was their first victim. So, all leave is cancelled – we're on this until we crack it.'

They would reinterview Anna Roos, and double the team sifting through her email account, which had turned out to be extensive. A warrant had also been obtained to search Winterhill, and Roos's family home, further along the coast. Peterborough CID was making some effort to track down the Leander Club watch stolen from the city baths, while uniformed branch was trawling the Tuesday market in Lynn, in the hope of finding some trace of the shopper who'd picked up a similar watch at a cut price.

'The wet footprints point to a swimmer. Maybe they point a little too conveniently to a swimmer – but we can't ignore the obvious. We'll get Atkins and Kersk into St James' for a formal session too.'

A liaison officer from the Met's animal rights squad was travelling up to brief them on links between known activists and the anti-pier campaign. A warrant had been obtained for a raid on the offices of STP, which would be conducted while most of the organization's members were at a rally, to be held in the town's Princess Theatre the following day, at which a vote would be taken on plans for a major public demonstration calling for the rig close-down to be permanent.

Each member of the team was given a set of duties and deadlines. DC Twine would coordinate data and circulate anything relevant.

Shaw took Valentine in the Porsche to check on the army's progress clearing the beach, before using a Skype link from Captain Wharram's four-by-four to talk to Captain Ring, organizing interviews with all crew members aboard the *MV Telamon*. In the interim, they were all to remain offshore.

The chief constable wanted a face-to-face briefing from Shaw at his office in St James', so Shaw offered Valentine a lift back to Lynn.

'Sorry, house-hunting to do,' said Valentine. 'Jan's seen one she likes, wants me to check it out on the way home. Which means I'll need to catch the T45. Good job Keeble's in the cells.'

'How long can it take?' asked Shaw, in no hurry to endure the chief constable's cross-examination. 'If you can stand slumming it in the Porsche, you're welcome to a lift.'

Shaw pointed the car south on the Lynn Road, the night rising in the east, closing like a lid over a cloudless blue sky. Valentine gave him a postcode and they let the talking voice guide them down a back lane, into Heacham, and then on towards the marshes. A field, which Shaw recalled had once corralled wild horses, now held a small estate of executive homes: six houses, with double garages, but postage-stamp-sized gardens behind rustic walls. A *For Sale* sign stood outside one, the house lights blazing, a family sitting at a kitchen table clearly visible.

'They said to just call by,' said Valentine, unmoved in the passenger seat.

'Price?'

'Two forty-nine nine-nine-nine. Daft, isn't it – the way they shave a quid off, like it's going to make you jump at it. A quarter of a million. We got Greenland Street for nineteen thousand.'

'Got to move on,' said Shaw.

'Not here, I don't.'

'Gonna give it a miss, then?'

'Yup.'

Valentine's mobile buzzed, and Shaw noted the screen had lit up with Jan's name.

Shaw listened to Valentine's half of a conversation which consisted of three 'yups' and one 'will do' before a perfunctory 'bye'.

'As we're here, Probationary PC Clay has a job for us,' he said, stashing the mobile in the glove compartment. 'We need to walk, apparently. Down that lane, past the bus stop. We're looking for the Willows Rest Home.'

TWENTY-SEVEN

'**K**eeble's sister-in-law,' explained Valentine, pressing an intercom buzzer and giving their names and ranks. 'Jan's been trying to get her for days. She tried turning up on the doorstep but got the bum's rush. Appointment only. She just rang her back. Now's good. Maybe she knows why the wonderful Esther has taken up a career as a random killer. Nobody else does.'

Bach played in the reception area of the Willows, the tinkling notes following them as they were led into the heart of the Georgian building and then down into a spa area in the basement.

Several elderly women swam in stately, metronomic lengths in a pool illuminated by underwater lights. Alice Banks, George Keeble's sister, was in a large jacuzzi, floating in a metal cradle, the water bubbling and swirling around her. She wore a green swimming cap dotted with sunflowers, and a matching one-piece swimsuit. Her narrow limbs floated and bobbed in the artificial currents, the painful narrowness of her ankles and wrists exposed to forces which Valentine imagined might at any moment tear her apart.

'Ah, good,' she said by way of welcome. 'This is such a bore. It's therapy, you see. I have to lie here for hours. I welcome any distraction, even a discussion of my saintly sister-in-law.'

She had small nail-head eyes and a wide mouth, which was oddly marked out by a crude slash of red lipstick.

'Esther visited, I understand?' offered Valentine, faintly unsettled by the fact that he seemed to be spending a great deal of his time beside water, as if it offered some fatal attraction.

Banks floated in her metal cage. Shaw judged her to be eighty years old, wiry, slightly bird-like. There was something predatory, even cruel, in those unblinking black eyes.

Valentine realized she was waiting for a specific question. 'Had you noticed any changes in her character, her behaviour? Did she talk about any particular anxieties?' he asked.

Shaw looked up at the ceiling, mottled with reflective light. 'Who – for example – did she hate?'

'She hated herself,' said Banks, and lay back in the water, apparently satisfied with this summation. 'That's why she's so *good.*' She laid a peculiar emphasis on the word, indicating a level of disdain for the concept of good and evil. 'Strange, tortured woman. Before my husband died, eight years ago, she promised *him* she'd visit me every week. No one asked me if I liked the bloody woman. I've been a paraplegic for nearly a decade. She took on this duty of care with some alacrity. For a while I suspected she wanted my money, but I told George years ago it was all going to my children. I have three, although you'd never guess by the visitor's book.' She reached over to the side of the pool where a glass of orange juice stood on a linen napkin.

Valentine hauled some chlorinated air into his lungs to ask a fresh question, but Banks hadn't finished.

'George wasted his life, of course. He had opportunities – not least a decent education. Ended up running a corner shop, for heaven's sake, selling grubby newspapers to grubby people. And wasting the rest of his time playing boats with the RNLI. But that's all right, because it's a *charity.*'

'I guess they have each other,' offered Shaw, feeling the need to fight the absent Esther's corner.

For a moment they saw it then, in the dead-nail eyes: a sudden angry void too bitter to label loneliness. The recovery was almost instant, the wide mouth parting to reveal small, beautifully white teeth.

'You know George is dying? Lung cancer. Still manages twenty a day. That's a considerable reduction by the way: he was once proud of smoking sixty on occasion. A failing heart has put him in that wheelchair, but his lungs will kill him. From my perspective, I've always seen them as the perfect couple: I can't see what she sees in him, or what he sees in her. The idea of them cooped up in that dingy prefab is pure hell.

'They never *asked* for money of course, although George specialized in heavy hints. But as I said, I have responsibilities, family responsibilities. The last time she visited, she said George had been given six months, possibly less. She'll live for ever, of course; she's the type. And she's *so* proud of walking without a stick, despite the new hip.

'As for a motive for what she did, your guess is as good as mine.

She had her – what can I call them? – *targets*. The health service
for letting George down. The doctors for taking so long to get her
in for her hip. The bus company for making it *so* difficult to get
his wheelchair on board. The City of London for frittering away
their little nest egg of shares. The people at Swansea for insisting
she take her driving test again – which she failed, of course. That's
what she couldn't abide, you see. She thinks the world owes her
something because she's been so conspicuously good.' She stretched
her arms out and Shaw noted a gold wedding ring, a diamond
ring, and a bracelet of silver charms. 'Well, the world doesn't owe
her anything. Maybe, in the end, that was just too much to take.'
She altered her position in the water, setting up a series of concen-
tric waves that creased the oily surface of the pool. 'Frankly, and
I mean this, it's probably the most interesting thing Esther's ever
done. And it brings with it the untold joy associated with the
knowledge that, with luck, I'll never see her again.'

She smiled then, to indicate that this was perhaps her idea of a
joke, and the thin scarlet lipstick formed a zigzag across her face,
and Shaw knew the precise word he'd been searching for to describe
her later to Lena.

Poisonous.

TWENTY-EIGHT

S top the Pier supporters filled every seat of the town's Princess Theatre for their rally, with children on laps and playing in the aisles. The local paper had done the campaign no harm by printing an artist's impression of the new pier-head fun park, the highlight of which was a seventy-foot death-plunge ride called Moon Shot. The foreground of the illustration showed crowds of thousands on the beach, and coaches parked across the town's trademark 'village green' opposite the pier entrance.

This public relations disaster had been compounded by news that an application had also been filed with the council and the Home Office for a casino licence. 'Up in arms' was a tabloid cliché, but the crowd bristled with a genuine sense of outrage and anger, while party balloons – in the campaign colours of blue and white – bobbed randomly from row to row. Two TV crews were on site – one inside and one outside the theatre.

The stage was stark, empty, but for a trestle table supporting a huge campaign sign:

STOP THE PIER
WHY WASTE £77m?

The on-stage theatre scenery was in disarray, caught between a production of *Peter Pan Goes Wrong* and the backdrop for an Elvis Presley tribute band. The old theatre, a 1930s gem, looked odd in the white TV lights, the colour scheme of raspberry and silver hard on the eye.

Tom Coram climbed on to the stage, the fluid, relaxed body language a counterpoint to the white hair and the reading glasses slung round his neck on a cord. To 'clear the air', as he put it, he read a short prepared statement condemning the sabotage on the *MV Telamon* which had affected more than a dozen workers, two of whom were still in a hyperbaric facility at Peterborough City Hospital. BBC Radio had already broken the news that work at the pier head was suspended while an inquiry was held into the failure of decompression procedures. A Blue Square team from Rotterdam was due on site later that day. A government health inspector would follow.

'We condemn such sabotage unequivocally,' said Coram. 'But the suspension of work is nonetheless welcome, as it provides all sides with that most precious of commodities: time.' A wave of dutiful applause followed this artfully balanced summary of the situation.

Coram introduced a barrister hired by the campaign to try to reverse the allocation of EU funds to the pier project.

Shaw, standing at the back, saw Valentine at one of the side exits, beckoning with a slight inclination of his hatchet-like skull. A strange, tawdry corridor led them to the rear of the stage, the scenery suspended above their heads, and then on, through a door Valentine unlocked, so that they could ascend a steep wooden staircase. Shaw lit his iPhone to bathe the way ahead in a lurid light. Distantly, they heard applause, and a muffled, unintelligible PA system.

'Best seats in the house,' said Valentine, opening a door which until the moment it swung out had been perfectly secreted within the panelling. Beyond lay a box, twenty feet above the stalls, crammed with six seats covered in worn red velvet. As they sat, Valentine pointed out the CCTV camera fixed to the wall, just out of reach.

'I've told Mark. He's monitoring the crowd. The Met's animal rights expert's sitting in beside him in case any of the real nutters have joined up.'

On stage, Coram was back on his feet. 'This is our big chance,' he said, holding up a council poster with the slogan *Big Bang Day*.

The army bomb disposal unit had dug down on the beach and uncovered the three anomalies identified on the electromagnetic sweep. Each turned out to be a 1,100-pound bomb of the type delivered to the Zeppelin factory at Friedrichshafen in 1915, manu-factured – ironically – at Vickers Armstrong's armament complex on the Tyne. Rust had reduced the casings to fragile shells; the interior chemicals were almost certainly now a harmless soup of degraded chemicals. However, a small risk remained that one or more of the devices might still be dangerous if moved. The decision had been taken to blow the bombs up *in situ* rather than attempt to raise them, and defuse them, on the spot. Charges would be attached, then set off by remote control, in two days' time.

The council, keen to regain the tourist initiative, had decided to promote the Big Bang. A public lottery would be run, with the winner picking up £1,000 and the chance to push the button to set off the charges. The original suggestion, that little Eric Ross should have this honour, had been quietly dropped due to the mysterious provenance of the original 'bomb'. Crowds would be allowed on the green, the clifftop, and the South Beach esplanade. The *Daily Mail* had already predicted 10,000 sightseers.

That was before a British company which specialized in airships for advertising and TV work contacted the council and offered to fly its latest 'blimp' – christened *Free Spirit* – over the town after the bombs had been destroyed. It was also offering sightseeing passenger seats for the event – and by way of compensation, a special seat to Donald Ross, to mark the role inadvertently played by his three boys in uncovering the history of the 1915 raid. There was no doubt the proposed fly-past would be a sight to see. The *Daily Mail* had more than doubled its crowd prediction to 25,000 for Big Bang Day, and set off to try to find relatives of the Germans who'd flown the Zeppelin that day in 1915, offering to pay for them to take the passenger seats on offer for the flight. It had labelled this gesture a 'token of reconciliation'.

'This is our big chance,' repeated Coram. 'There will be TV and national newspaper coverage. International coverage. We need to put pressure on our local MPs, and our MEPs, to get a public inquiry into the pier underway. We've got clear grounds: nobody who voted the project through in 2010 would recognize what they're planning to build now . . .'

Applause swept the auditorium, energized now, even angry.

'So we need to make ourselves felt. They need to know that this is a protest they can't ignore. So how can we make a real splash? We need to use the Big Bang to our own advantage. We've had several suggestions and they're all on this ballot paper . . .' Coram waved a piece of yellow card. 'Anyone here can vote. The decision will be taken by the STP committee, but we want to know what you think first.'

Coram outlined the four options.

A. A human chain encircling the town, crossing the main roads.

B. A floating demo off the beach with protestors and banners in local boats.

C. Five hundred specially made STP placards to be held up during the Big Bang and for the airship fly-past.

D. A 50-foot square STP banner to be laid out on the green – clearly visible from the airship, which had already offered a window seat to the BBC.

Ballot papers were handed out, and a deafening buzz of discussion filled the theatre.

Shaw rested his chin on the velvet edge of the box. 'We're missing something, George. Missing the most important thing of all: motive. Someone wants to stop the pier so desperately they'll kill to do it. Maybe they've killed already. But why? It's not this lot, is it? These are middle-class bleeding hearts. Or grasping shopkeepers afraid they'll lose a few quid? Eco-warriors? They don't fit either. All right, if the Met finds us a real extremist group, then maybe. But otherwise this is about something much deeper, George. Something corrosive. We're just too close to see it.'

Coram was ready with the votes: B was the winner – a floating demo, right where the cameras would be pointing on the big day. An open debate began on organizing the fleet of little ships required. A police representative was invited on stage to advise on safety.

The box door creaked open and DC Birley's belligerent face filled the gap. 'Sir. Jackie's been on. They've finally wrung some sense from Roos's email account. A lot of it was encrypted, apparently. Plenty of stuff, all incriminating, most of it copied to Beachcomber@btinternet.com.'

TWENTY-NINE

S haw and Valentine took a table outside *Beachcomber.*
A small clue had been there from the very start. The standard
Arabic numerals – 0, 1, 2, 3, 4, 5, 6, 7, 8, 9 – are so much a
part of modern life that they are hardly seen at all – the neural
message containing their inherent meaning speeding, sub-atomically,
through the brain on the pathways of calculation. Except for the 7.
That strange Continental affectation of the cross-stroke always
caught Shaw's eye. He checked his own notebook and noted the
carefully crossed sevens he had used since a teenager.

Why had he started? The stylish tick was mildly nerdy, a habit
to set him apart, suggesting an easy familiarity with sophisticated
French artists, radical thinkers, and liberal ideas. If challenged,
especially by teachers, he'd been happy to trundle out the usual
explanation: with the added stroke, a ticked number one could look
like a seven. But in reality it had all been about ego and proclaiming
difference. It had quickly become part of his hieroglyphic baggage
– as personal as his signature.

Shaw considered the cheese toastie on the menu (with
Worcestershire sauce) listed at a price of £1.70 – the seven neatly
crossed. Lower down, the soup of the day (potato and scallop),
with freshly baked bread, was £7.50, the seven cross-beamed again.
On the façade of the diner, the number was listed to phone in a
reservation for food, the two sevens crossed, as he should have
noticed on their first visit.

Lester brought their coffee, and a large glass of white wine for
himself, pulling out a chair at an angle which suggested he was
only interested in the sea.

Shaw switched the menu round and held his finger over one of
the Continental sevens. 'Interesting affectation,' he said.

'Common amongst artists, actually. It's far more stylish – needs
a flourish, don't you think?'

Shaw opened his phone and showed Lester a picture of the largest
anti-pier graffito on the A10 railway bridge – huge bulbous letters

in a spectrum of colours, and the numbers indicating the money wasted on the pier.

'Snap,' said Valentine.

Lester had the wine at his lips, but his hand held steady, only pausing a half second before he poured it down his open throat.

'It's only a number,' he said. 'Like the ones in two and two makes five. If that's it, I've got some work to do out back.'

'This morning we arrested Anna Roos, Mr Lester,' said Shaw. 'She's a member of STP, as you'll know. Her laptop was used to post a threatening note on the website of the company building the pier, which implied that following the explosion on the beach there would be further direct action if the work was not suspended. This further implied that she was in some way responsible for the explosion, and possibly the arson attack last week, and that lives would be put at greater risk.'

'I know Anna,' said Lester, crossing one leg flat across the other: 'She's spirited, passionate. She walks the beach too, so we're not strangers. She's about as capable of organizing an arson attack as one of the shrimps in her rock pools.'

'Not strangers?' asked Shaw. 'Interesting choice of words. Her laptop held records of twelve thousand emails, Mr Lester, many of them digitally encrypted. You're copied into nearly four hundred of them. Take this one: dated twenty-fourth June at three thirty-five – this is last year . . . Joe. Targets at PE36 6BL.'

Lester's eyes played over the seascape.

Shaw waited ten seconds. 'That evening a fleet of lorries carrying construction equipment was vandalized – sand in the petrol tanks, tyres slashed, cabs broken into. They were parked overnight at the council lay-by on South Beach. That's the postcode for the spot: PE36 6BL.'

'This is dull,' said Lester. 'Why don't I ring my solicitor? I'll come down the station. It's a waste of my time and yours, but if you want to carry on . . .'

'You could share Anna Roos's lawyer,' said Valentine. 'She's been charged, by the way, and bailed. So he'll have a free hour . . .'

Lester went for the wine again, but this time it was a lunge, and he spilt some in the sand.

'What about this?' said Shaw. 'From ten days ago. "Joe. We need to talk. This wasn't what we planned. I'm worried. Scared. Call."

That was the day after the arson attack on the rig. We'll ask her what she meant, but you might like to get in first. Given the current tariff for arson, she may well like us to see that as a denouncement of you, and a defence of her reluctance to risk human life.'

Lester didn't blink. 'I'm a beach-bum artist, Inspector. Not a commando.'

'As I said. We've done our homework. Not a commando certainly, but hardly a peacenik either. Did it start that night in 1953? When dawn broke, you saw soldiers – Territorial Army volunteers. They must have been a welcoming sight, admirable certainly. Is that why you joined up?' Valentine produced a file from his raincoat and handed it to Shaw. 'This says you spent nearly eleven years in the TA. Rank of sergeant. Home defence, of course, but a short period on Gibraltar in the seventies. The Rock. Plenty of training too – my sergeant here's read the file, but I seem to recall a course on radio communications, weapons, and a placement with the sappers. That was three months, at Norwich. We'll make further inquiries of course, but presumably this included explosives.'

A police squad car came into view, creeping along the bank top.

'And one detail.' Shaw shook his mobile. 'I just rang an old mate at the MoD, who traced your unit in Gibraltar, and found the name of your commanding officer: Major Pryce Simms. He's behind a desk now, in Whitehall, but it means he lives by a phone. He remembered you – or, more precisely, something *about* you.'

Lester started texting on his phone. 'Carry on – you seem to be enjoying yourself. I'm just getting that lawyer . . .'

'Swim2Africa, they called it. Nine miles, from the Spanish coast, to the other side. Four hours in the water. Not easy, according to Simms – fog, shipping, currents, water temperature, waves. Three of you tried, but only one made it. So congratulations on that. Quite an achievement really, swimming between continents. It's odd, but when you told us all about that night in 1953 – and I've checked the details, and it was all true – you gave us the impression, deliberately perhaps, that you hated the sea. No – more, that you feared it. Thalassophobia, by the way – a phobia of the sea. Not aquaphobia – that's fear of water. Why did you want us to think that, Mr Lester?'

THIRTY

Lena touched his arm. 'It's all right,' she said. 'Peter, Peter. It's the nightmare again.'

But it wasn't, not entirely, because there was a noise outside.

'It's the sea,' he said, putting a foot on the wooden floor.

They'd built a short corridor between the old cottage and the café, and his feet scuffed the sand which was always caught in the grain of the floorboards. He had to squeeze between the suitcases they'd got out for the flight to Jamaica, and the piles of laundry.

The plate-glass windows of *Surf!* were hinged, so that he could swing one out, revealing a moonlit seascape.

The sound wasn't a sound at all. It was the absence of a sound. The sea had gone.

Lena religiously pinned up tide tables in the entrance to the café. Shaw noted that the highest tide of the year was due the following day; and so this was its ghostly counterpart, the lowest tide of the year. The sea, syphoned out of the shallows of the Wash, had left an eerie landscape of sand hills and creeks, ribbons of black water threaded between white, moonlit miniature cliffs. The illusion that he could simply walk the thirty miles west to the unseen Lincolnshire coast was magnetic.

He grabbed jeans and a jumper, hauled them on, unable to take his eye off the view. Outside, his feet sinking in the cold sand, his ears searched for the familiar swish and swash of the sea, but there was nothing but the echo of a trickle, a distant bubble of percolating water, as the last of the salt water decanted itself from pool to pool, the great moon drawing it north. Using the telescope on the stoop, his good eye swept the vista, finding two or three of the great green-and-red navigation buoys high and dry, lying on their sides like discarded toys.

The shattered reflection of a flare caught his eye, a second before the thud of the maroon shook his ear drums; then came the triple echo, first bouncing off the distant cliffs, then the side of *Surf!*, and finally the Old Boathouse. Instinctively, he turned south towards the lifeboat station, in time to catch the trailing light of the falling firework, its elegant downward trajectory unbroken by the slightest of atmospheric winds.

Running back indoors, he grabbed a pre-packed rucksack from the corridor and his running shoes. Sitting on the wooden steps, pulling on his socks, he felt the pager on his belt vibrate: the code 111, indicating a 'shout', followed by 222, indicating that the hovercraft was needed, not the boat. *His* hovercraft.

By the time he reached the slip-way at Old Hunstanton, three crew members had folded back the doors on the *Flyer*'s hangar, and switched on the floodlights which illuminated the runway – a twenty-metre-wide gap in the dunes from the boathouse down to the water's edge.

Shaw, in the pilot's seat, edged the hovercraft out into the night, using the ailerons to swing her down the narrow pathway past the beach huts, the headlamps catching the sands ahead. *Flyer* had searchlights mounted on her cabin roof, and Shaw switched them all on, revealing the sand-dune landscape through which they were picking up speed, the exposed sea floor ribbed and patterned, burnished, it seemed, by the retreating sea.

Findlay, the communications officer, gave them a summary of the incoming data over their helmet radio links: the vessel in distress was a thirty-eight-foot yacht called *Germinal*, registered in the port of Dunkirk. The crew was five strong, although two of them were teenagers on their first trip. The captain – a fully qualified ship's master – had tried to make Lynn with a following wind but had misjudged the depth of the tide, running aground on Roaring Island, the five-acre sickle-shaped sandbar eight miles off Hunstanton, marked by an automatic anchored lightship.

Given that *Germinal* was beached on dry ground, the lifeboat was useless; *Flyer*, in contrast, was perfectly suited to the terrain, and once free of the shoreline's dips and berms, hit a steady forty knots, skimming over a series of low sandbars before encountering a wide lake, a mere inch deep, which held a perfect reflection of the full moon, a light so bright that Shaw was forced to pull down a tinted shade as he peered ahead through *Flyer*'s windscreen.

Heading directly for the winking light of the lightship, *Flyer* came within sight of the deep water channel six miles out from the beach, cutting across their path, forming the umbilical cord that linked the North Sea to the Port of Lynn. Shaw slowed the hover-craft, swung her a few points to starboard, and hit the deep water at thirty knots, mist rising as they raced to the far bank, and the leading cliff edge of Roaring Island, a gentle ten-foot bank, which *Flyer* breasted with ease.

Shaw would never forget the sight that greeted them as they made the high ground. *Germinal* lay a mile distant, on her port side, high and dry, the mast broken. The automatic lightship stood on the horizon in a shallow trench, its light winking on a ten-second cycle: once after two, twice after four, and for a third time on ten. What was extraordinary was that these two vessels were far from being alone on Roaring Island, for the flat sands were littered with wreckage: a Bermuda Triangle of lost things, thought Shaw, revealed perhaps just once or twice a year at the lowest of tides.

The marooned crew of the *Germinal* had built a fire, gathering driftwood from around them and adding paraffin from the hold. Silhouettes waved wildly in welcome as *Flyer* edged forward, finally sinking into her skirts a hundred yards from the blazing beacon. Even here, the surface was scattered with debris: ship's timbers, rope, broken hold cases, buoys, plastic bottles, a holed dinghy, a ripped sail still attached to a splinter of mast.

Only the owner seemed reluctant to abandon the yacht, until Shaw suggested a plan. Roaring Island's crescent shape sheltered a lake to the south-east. This stretch of water, even at high tide, seemed to offer an anchorage of sorts, the shallow water dampening down high seas in winter. Local fishermen called it Holme Lake, although the maps never carried the name, perhaps chary at charting a lake in the middle of the sea. A large green navigation buoy lay beached in the lake, and Shaw suggested the crew of the *Germinal* ran an anchor line to it, so that when the tide washed in, the ship could ride safely until they were able to return. Given the benign forecast, there was every chance she'd survive the night intact, despite the broken mast.

As the crew worked on running the line out by hand, Shaw walked away half a mile, surveying the flotsam and jetsam littering the sand. The twinkling lights of the rig lay directly south-east by six miles, the wind-farm navigation lights off Skegness directly north-west by fifteen. If the pier *was* built as planned, the ferry service would skirt Roaring Island twice daily on its scheduled route. Was there something here? Was there something that *might* be here, that someone wished to remain a secret? Hartog had made the trip several times according to the boatyard in Wells, and only his murder had prevented a return.

By the time Shaw returned to the *Flyer*, the rescued crew was crowded into the rear recovery cabin. Wrapped in silver heat retention sheets, they looked cold and scared – the bravado of the fireside extinguished. Shaw took them back across the Wash at thirty-five knots, and they were back on dry land in less than twenty minutes. A medical check-up was standard practice, so an ambulance waited by the floodlit hangar as the *Flyer* crept back into the windless interior.

The hovercraft crew took refuge in the mess on the second floor of the lifeboat house. A wood-burning stove provided a burst of heat, and a bay window gave a fifty-mile vista of the Wash – its channels and creeks still bleeding out into the North Sea. It would be long after dawn before the tide turned, bringing a flood into the Wash.

Shaw's second in command, Joe Paul, used a laptop to log details of the rescue and post them on the station's website: crew names, the vessel assisted, those rescued, the weather and sea conditions. This was the digital record. In the quiet winter months one of the crew – an old navy hand – would transfer the key facts to the old-fashioned rescue boards in the boathouse, with their copperplate golden lettering, showing shouts going back to the mid-nineteenth century.

A detail from the file on Dirk Hartog returned to Shaw: the Dutchman had visited the RNLI station *three* times in the period before his disappearance, taking a keen interest in the boat. Could his interest be entirely explained by a passion for marine engineering?

The boathouse itself, below the mess room, was in darkness, but the idea had taken hold, so Shaw used his smartphone torch to light up the stairwell, and then the view from the observation platform above the boat itself – an inshore rigid inflatable – and the sand tractor designed to haul it down to the sea.

The copperplate lettering on the boards caught the light. The nearest covered the period from 1945 to the present day. His good eye, always sharp, saw it immediately, the painted letters magically clear against the polished mahogany.

> 31st January 1953
> 18.30 hours. *Le Strange* launched to assist *Calabria* eight miles SW off Holme Point. Sea state tempest. Ship lost with crew of three.
> 23.00 hours. *Le Strange* proceeds to South Beach to assist evacuation from inundated homes. Eighteen hours in attendance. Total rescued 128.

The golden paint on the word *Calabria* seemed to shimmer with an inner light, as it did on the date: 31st January 1953. The night of the *tempest*: the night Joe Lester lost his sister to the cold North Sea.

THIRTY-ONE

That morning, shortly after dawn, light had fallen on their faces for the first time in more than half a century, leaving shadows in the eye sockets, catching the gold of a filling, and the silver of a signet ring on an exposed, extended finger bone, which lay in the sand, as if pointing to the refracted, shimmering light that dappled the wreck.

The dogfish circled their grave, its dead eyes searching for the riveted plates of the hold, the patterned surface of the deck, which had held them in the dark for so long, but the jolt of the explosion on the beach had shook the wreck's fragile hull, popping rivets, the rusted plates finally collapsing into the hold, to create a cloud of silt which had hung over the scene for days. The triple explosions that followed had rocked the dead in their steel cradle.

Now the silt and sand had finally settled, like phantom snow clearing from a nightmare paperweight, revealing the lost ship's cargo of bones. Two victims lay together, the skulls touching, in a bed of sand which had drifted over the pelvic bones, but left their legs lying clear, impossibly fragile, the feet a collection of disarticulated fragments, still roughly splayed. The right wrist of one was crossed with the left wrist of the other, the shattered bones held together by a leather bond.

Around this couple, who lay at the centre of the hold, a shoal of fish now flashed in iridescent colours.

Their companion lay apart, beside a brass porthole, the glass still in place but obscured by weed and barnacles. This victim's bones were almost dust, except for the skull, although the point where the ankles crossed was marked by the third, and final, leather bond.

The grizzled dogfish nosed at the skull of the skeleton by the porthole, releasing a thread of weed from the jaw bone, creating a miniature whirlpool of sand, which rose in the vortex left as the fish's spine flexed, powering it upwards and out, in a sudden retreat.

It circled twice, then returned, attracted by the glint of light in the skull's dark eye sockets. But it fled at last, spooked by its own double image, held in the two unbroken lenses of the spectacles that lay still either side of the gaping nose.

THIRTY-TWO

As the mobile rang, Shaw imagined it lying on Jack Gosling's desk, the sound rising up through the great glass atrium of Lloyd's of London, as his old friend tried to end a conversation on a landline perhaps, or on one of his three other mobile phones. Gosling had been a fellow student at Southampton, an artist, with dreams of a studio in Amsterdam (his then girlfriend, now his wife, was Dutch). But the Gosling family had all been *Names* – the individuals whose collective wealth underwrote the world's greatest insurance market. It's difficult not to follow in the family footsteps, especially when they lead to a pot of gold.

'Peter?' Behind the voice, Shaw could hear the strange spacious echo of the great room, the stairways and lifts in tubular steel, and at its centre the wooden Gothic podium on which hung the Lutine Bell: rung once to signal the loss of a ship, twice for its return.

'Peter – two seconds.' With a thud, the mobile was thrown to the desktop.

Shaw looked out at the beach beyond the panoramic window of *Surf!*. The incoming high tide had flooded the visible world. Not a single square yard of sand was above water level. The Wash was full, a bottleneck of salt water, brimming over. A coaster ran in towards Lynn on the horizon, following a path which a few hours earlier would have embedded it in a sandy grave.

Lena brought him a fresh double espresso. 'You should sleep,' she said.

He shook his head. 'I'll run you and Fran to the shops. Then I'll crash.'

Out at sea, the coaster had inched perceptively further south.

Its progress reminded Shaw of Jack Gosling's favourite story, of a great ship and a sandy grave. He'd taken Lena to meet his friend before they were married, and Gosling, proud of the family tradition, had insisted on a tour of the new Lloyd's building. He had the story of the *Lutine* off pat: lost in 1799, it had foundered amongst the twisting channels of the Frisian Islands, a sandy maze of treacherous currents and shallows.

The ship was never forgotten, for the simple fact that it was carrying gold bars, held in fragile wooden barrels. A persistent rumour suggested it had also taken on board – at a time of war – the Dutch crown jewels. Lloyds paid up in full – an estimated £1.2 million at eighteenth-century prices, and then claimed the gold cargo under the rule of abandonment – a sub-clause of that great ephemeral legal tome, the laws of salvage. The Dutch said it was theirs by right too, under the sub-clause of 'prize of war'. But the sea won, claiming it on the basis that the gold, and indeed the wreck, were swiftly entombed in sand. Very little of the precious metal had ever been recovered. But Lloyd's had paid up in full on the policy, securing a reputation for reliable honesty.

The mobile clattered. 'Peter. Sorry. Everyone OK – Lena, Fran? Sorry, sorry. I got your email. You asked for some help on that ship name. I've been running from pillar to post; I'll make it a priority. Sorry. What was it? The *Cala*? Nothing came up when I did a digital search . . .'

Gosling's desk was out on the main floor of the market, and Shaw imagined him now, slumped back in his chair, looking up into the guts of the twelve-storey building, around which occasional sparrows circled on invisible gyres.

'It's all right, Jack. I've got more info. But I still need help. In fact, it's pretty urgent. I gave you a fragment of the name. Now I've got it in full: the *Calabria*. She went down on thirty-first January 1953, eight miles off Holme Point – so that's in the Wash.'

Shaw explained that he had already used Lloyd's register online to trace ships lost within fifty miles of Hunstanton and had found none with a name starting *Cala*. So how could this be true?

Gosling, walking now, said he'd check the written register for that date. Shaw heard a tannoy announcement of a Caribbean hurricane warning, then the sound of a lift rising, followed by the sudden hush of a small room: a library perhaps, or an archive.

'Here we go,' said Gosling. 'I've got you on the earphone, Peter. If I disappear, just hang on. Right. Here we are: Feb first. Hell of a night, Peter. This was the North Sea surge, hundreds killed, ships lost . . .'

'I know, I know. But the *Calabria*?'

Shaw actually heard his friend turn the page on the ledger – the tiny flick of aged paper between fingers.

'Ah. OK. On that night, in that position, we have listed the loss of a Dutch coaster – the *Marlberg* – *formerly* the *Calabria*. A five-hundred-ton coaster – I'm guessing here, but from that size I'd say she was an old wooden ship. Steel ships, modern vessels, are larger. But there's your mystery, Peter – name changed. Not as rare as you think, and almost always bad news. You pick a name for a fresh start. That implies you need a fresh start. I guess that's why people think it's bad luck.'

'Why does it appear as the *Calabria* on our rescue board at the boathouse?'

'Crew often go on using the old name, especially if there's been a change of ownership. So if your guys asked the crew the name of the ship, they'd have said *Calabria*. If it was its first voyage under the new name, then they might not even have got round to a fresh nameplate. A name change often means the last owners went out of business. If the crew didn't like the new owners, that's another good reason to stick with the old name. I'm guessing here, but you see my point?'

'Anything else?'

'Yup. Loss of crew. Three dead. You want the names? I can send you a digital version. Surnames are Beck – listed as captain – with Spaans and an engineer, Hartog.'

Gosling filled up the silence on Shaw's end of the line with a description of the cargo: a hundred tonnes of Scandinavian timber bound for the Lincolnshire port of Boston, plus fifty tonnes of dried fish meal, and eighty tonnes of sea salt.

But Shaw was transfixed by the idea that Dirk Hartog, aged sixty-three, had come to Hunstanton in search of the wreckage of the *Calabria*, a vessel on which he'd lost – surely – his own father, sixty-three years earlier. Shaw bitterly saw his error in not pursuing the father's story. Hartog must have been a babe in arms. Did the father ever hold the son? Why had Hartog returned to the coast? Did he plan to scatter his mother's ashes out on Roaring Island, close to the spot where the *Calabria* had sunk? Why had that simple ambition cost him his life? Did the son simply wish to mark the spot, or did he suspect the wreck held other secrets?

THIRTY-THREE

Valentine's text message pinged on Shaw's mobile: *999 call at 22 Empire Bank. George Keeble. Can you?*

Shaw ran to the Porsche along the beach, then, checking the distance with the map app on his phone, carried on running, along the cliff edge, down past the still cordoned-off beach, and out along the seawall to the south.

Empire Bank was a row of pre-war prefabs clinging to the seawall, which at this point comprised an earth embankment nearly thirty feet above the marsh on the landward side. Lester's *Beachcomber* café stood a mile further, just visible on the tapering sands. High tide washed against the seaward bank, churning its way up the beach in coffee-coloured waves.

The ambulance stood on the dirt road, its light flashing silently. The houses were neat, whitewashed, with faux Tudor beams; the whole row bungalow-style, with pebble-dashed walls and corrugated iron roofs.

The Keebles' door stood open, and Shaw met a paramedic coming out. 'Family?' she asked, a sudden sweep of sunlight making her high-vis jacket glare orange.

'There's just the wife – she's away,' said Shaw, offering his warrant card.

'I know. He said.'

'How is he?'

'See for yourself. Heart's erratic. He's elected to stay put. No resus. Otherwise, I'd take him in, which would start the whole process off again – tests, and check-ups, and scans. He blacked out, so maybe a small stroke. Home help found him. It's happened before. He's a dying man, but he knows that, so there's no need to labour the point.'

Shaw found the home help in the kitchen making a cup of tea. A teenager, despite proudly calling herself Hilda, she took her time examining Shaw's warrant card. She explained that she worked for the council social services and that she had delivered Mr Keeble's breakfast, before cleaning the kitchen and toilet. She'd found him lying on the living-room floor.

'It's sad, isn't it?' she asked. 'When people give up.' They stood awkwardly in the tiny galley kitchen. 'I'll take him this,' she said, escaping with the cup.

Shaw took a quick look in each room: a double bedroom, a box room full of tea crates, a WC and hip bath. Dampness, he'd expected, and he noted the disfiguring blotches in the corners of the bedroom, but there was something else too: a sense of precarious survival, a home perched on a flood bank, the rear windows looking out across a thousand square miles of seawater.

From the double bedroom he could see the slope down to the sea's edge, a family already encamped behind a windbreak, three children trailing spades.

There was a single wedding picture over the bed, in which Esther looked timid and scared, and George held her arm as if he was on parade. A cat, a long-haired specimen with pink eyes, watched Shaw dubiously from the pillow.

He knocked once on the door to the living room and found Keeble in an armchair, flicking through a box file. He was deathly white, his skin glistening with sweat.

'Ah. DI Shaw? Yes – I knew your father. You're on the hovercraft, right? Very good. I was on the boat. Thirty years . . .' He shook his head, surprised at his own life story.

'You should take it easy, Mr Keeble.'

He shrugged. 'The next time I go out that door, I'll be in a box, Inspector.' It was the kind of thing people said, but it made Shaw feel cold, despite the sun on the sea outside the window.

'They need Esther's medical card. She's at Bedford now – in the prison, on remand – and they want to see her NHS records.' Losing patience, he tipped the contents of the file on to his lap. 'They hanged Hanratty there, of course, at Bedford – bit before your time . . .'

The arm of his wheelchair held an ashtray, attached by elastic bands and full of butts. His hand wandered towards a pack on a handily positioned shelf, and he deftly selected a cigarette, perhaps distracted by the idea of his wife, in another age, paying the ultimate price for murder.

The acrid stench of the lit cigarette was a shock, concentrated in the small room. It propelled Shaw back into the decades in which smoking indoors was simply part of everyday British life, like holding a smartphone. The wallpaper in the living room was stippled and magnolia, but vertical lines of nicotine ran from the picture rail to the floor, as if the house, like some discarded tin cooking pot, had boiled over on the hob.

They'd interviewed George Keeble under caution at St James', but he had insisted he knew nothing about his wife's aberrant behaviour. Shaw felt that here, in his home, he might be enticed to speculate. According to the file, they'd been married for fifty-one years. It was an almost inconceivable period of time to live beside another human being. He must, surely, have an insight into what Shaw could only term his wife's pathology: what had been the course of her disease, where had it begun?

But at the mention of her crime George Keeble seemed to retreat, at least psychologically if not physically, immersing himself in his pile of documents and old photographs. Of his wife's motive he knew no more now than he had done on the day she'd been arrested, he said, indicating that he'd like that particular conversation to end there.

Shaw felt obliged to stay with him a little longer while he drank his tea. He stood at the window, noting with approval the absence of the otherwise ubiquitous bungalow net curtains, and was looking out to sea when it occurred to him for the first time that George Keeble might have been a witness to the sinking of the *Calabria*.

'The tempest, Mr Keeble. The great flood. You were on the boat that night?'

For the first time Keeble looked up. 'God, yes. Won't forget it. I was living in the village then, at Old Hunstanton, so when the maroon went up, I ran for the boathouse. I hadn't met Esther – she was here, in this house, with her mother and the small boys. Four brothers. So you can imagine.'

It gave Shaw a moment to reimagine the house: not one set of footfalls running in from the beach, but a whole tribe, bouncing off the walls, clattering through the doors.

'Esther's dad had died the winter before, so her mum had to cope alone. Fine woman, Annie. We all had to cope. Forty-four dead here, Inspector. But you'll know.'

'So you were on the boat which stood off the *Calabria*? Out beyond Roaring Island?'

'Yes, indeed. Another sad loss. No chance to help there; she was under at the stern when we saw her. I was the lookout. Won't forget it. Dreadful sight. But we had to move on, because by then we knew the water had got through the seawall. Frustrating, of course, because we couldn't get the old boat on to the marshes, where people were stranded. We dropped anchor and took some small boats out, dragged them over the seawall, did what we could.' Keeble glanced up at a framed picture over the fireplace of the lifeboat cutting through a stormy sea. The old man's eyes were rheumy and tired. 'A lot of the prefabs on the marsh were swept away. This lot were high and dry, so they left them. Bit battered, but they stood the storm. They gave 'em a lick of paint and said get on with it. When Annie died, we moved in. Seemed to make sense. The shop was shut, so no reason to stay in the flat, you see. That was in 1990. Sixteen years . . . incredible really. It's flown past,' he added, but something about the grey skin and the rheumy eyes made Shaw think that might be a lie.

Despite the packet of Marlboro and the lighter on the table beside his chair, Keeble didn't light up a second time, stubbing out his first with a look of self-disgust. His large head, like a bowling ball, nodded until he spoke. 'The bus queue's the thing that's been on my mind,' he said.

'In what sense?' asked Shaw, taking the other chair.

'I don't think Esther's well,' he said, and some extravagant tears began to squeeze themselves out of the corner of his left eye. 'I'm sorry,' he said. 'It's just that without her . . .'

The empty room, the damp house, seemed to finish the sentence for him.

'But the queue,' prompted Shaw.

'Sorry. It's just our life has turned into a queue. The post office for the pension – OK, we get it now in the bank, but we did queue for years. The queue for the hospital. The queue for benefits. I worked for half a century – more. I'm not a scrounger. Not like a lot of 'em who come over here . . .' His resolve broke and he lit the second cigarette. 'Sorry. I shouldn't have said that. Esther wouldn't have let that go by, you see. I'm a better person when she's here.' He tried to fill his lungs. 'This summer, in those first weeks, when it was really hot, she pushed me along the esplanade, and we just sat and watched. Kids on the beach. We never had any, not because we didn't want them, but because we weren't blessed. And we tried, you know . . . Anyway, I said she should have an ice cream if she wanted one. I can't – the sugar – but she's got a sweet tooth, Esther. Thinks everyone else has too. So she gets the money and I watched her, in the queue for the ice-cream van. She was right at the back. She let some kids push in – and then it was a scrum, and she gave up. Said she'd gone off the idea. Maybe she just got the idea that it wasn't fair . . .' He pulled a face. 'I sound like a kid meself. It's not fair!' He tapped his temple. 'The bus, right – there was always a queue. Especially in summer, she'd have to wait for the next bus sometimes. I know she's trim, but still, you'd think, wouldn't you, that someone would say she could just get on first. Especially with her hip. And we gave up trying to get my chair on. Forget it. So I thought that perhaps it had weighed on her mind and she'd decided to let the anger out.' Keeble's voice had suddenly risen, as if acting out his wife's frustrations. 'She couldn't have picked someone, singled them out. Not Esther. So perhaps she thought this was the answer, to let fate choose. I don't understand, of course. But it might make sense.'

He looked out the window then, his eyes welling up, his left hand holding the burning cigarette. Patting his chest, he began to sort through the papers on his lap, his lips forming a bow to produce a sibilant whistle. Shaw thought that, despite appearances, and his imprisonment in a chair, his enforced passivity, George Keeble was oddly in control of what was left of his life.

THIRTY-FOUR

The darkened room shimmered with martial music booming on the soundtrack, as a white bordered 'blackboard' carried the title *The Great Tempest* and the *Pathé News* reel logo. The narrator's voice, in epic American tones, overlaid an aerial shot of a devastated landscape, a drowned world, within which only an outline of civilization was left – tree-lined lanes, the rooftops of a village, a church tower, the water sweeping south. It looked like an ocean on the move, which made the caption all the more chilling: *Lelystad: 42 miles inland.*

'Six nations have already come to the aid of the stricken Dutch,' boomed the commentary. 'One sixth of the country, so recently devastated by the world war, now lies beneath the waves . . .'

Shaw consulted a note he'd been given by the curator and used the remote control to pause the digital projector, then fast-forwarded it two minutes and thirty seconds. Once the picture was frozen, he stood as close as he could without obscuring the beam of light, then pressed the restart.

'They died at sea, as well as on the land. The *Marlberg*, pictured here leaving Antwerp on her maiden voyage just three days earlier, was lost with all hands in a sea torn apart by a storm of biblical proportions. Little did these men know that this would be their final voyage . . .'

Who had shot the film? The new owners of the ship perhaps, marking her return to service and a new beginning. Captain Beck, a distant figure in cap and spectacles, waved briskly from the bridge as she slid past a set of dockside cranes. A crewman stood at the forward rail, hauling in rope. Hartog, reasoned Shaw, would be below, tending the ship's old engines. What looked like a lick of fresh paint could not disguise the ship's dilapidated condition: rust dripped from the davits and the bridge rivets; the smooth marine curve of the wooden hull dented by decades of collisions with docksides and tugs; the smoke billowing from the single funnel, sooty and dense.

The door opened and a wedge of white light redefined the room. Radley Tombs, the curator of the county archives, pushed in a trolley carrying a large bound volume and a cardboard record box. 'These might do the trick,' he said, his voice slightly reedy with the physical effort of hauling them on to one of the desks.

The rest of the building – by day, Lynn's central library – was silent and closed.

'And you don't need these anymore,' he added, unleashing a set of blinds which rolled up to reveal the night outside, the town-centre lights harsh beyond the gardens of Greyfriars Tower.

'Thanks for this,' said Shaw, pointing at the frozen image of the *Marlberg*.

'Glad to help,' said Tombs, his hand fluttering at his forehead. 'We often show it to school parties – so I remembered the name, the *Marlberg*. Not much information, however; these should be better, although you'll appreciate that local news coverage of the loss of the ship was very limited, given that the papers were full of what had happened on the coast itself. Forty-four dead, the heroes who'd saved so many, the public inquiry – it went on for years. By comparison, the loss of a foreign ship nearly ten miles out to sea didn't rate a fuss. Anyway, I've marked the entries: three press cuttings from the *Eastern Daily Press* for 1953, and the documents box from the inquest. Enjoy.'

Shaw left the image on the screen and used a downlighter to illuminate the bound editions of the *EDP*.

The first cutting was for 2nd February 1953. It simply listed the ship – giving its former name, the *Calabria* – as 'lost', quoting the coxswain of the lifeboat:

> She was in the eye of the storm, showing navigation lights, and lights from the bridge, but we couldn't see the crew, who must have been below. She rose on her beams in a few minutes, almost vertical, then sank. It was a dreadful sight. We felt the boilers blow a few moments later, and we circled the spot for thirty minutes, but there was very little debris except oil and some wooden duckboards. Our thoughts are with the bereaved.

The second cutting was a news brief from April 1953, which simply stated that the consul from the Dutch Embassy would attend an inquest into the deaths of three mariners on the night of the great tempest. The consul, while in the town, would lay a wreath for those who had lost their lives on the South Beach at the memorial by the pier. The Lord Lieutenant of Norfolk would present the consul with a book of remembrance for those lost in the Netherlands, which had been opened at the town hall and had collected 12,000 signatures.

The third cutting recorded the inquests on the crew in less than 200 words, although it did note that several relatives had made the journey to Norfolk from the Netherlands for the court appearance. The coroner heard that radio messages to the owners in Bremen had reported that the ship had begun to take on water forty miles out from the Dutch coast heading north. Captain Beck had taken the decision to try to reach Lynn before the storm reached the Wash. But the failure of the three electric bilge pumps had fatally slowed the ship's traverse of the North Sea. The verdict in each case was left open, due to the absence of the bodies. But the coroner said he was confident the men had drowned at sea.

The coroner issued a rider to his verdict, pointing up design faults in the ship that had contributed to her loss. The radio messages to Bremen made it clear that the ship had taken on water because the transom – the rear deck – had proved too low in the water, allowing the sea to flood the hold. The subsequent failure of the pumps had sealed the ship's fate. The coroner added that the actions of the captain had further contributed to the loss of his own life, and that of the crew, in that he had turned down a radio message from the tug *Lagan*, which had offered assistance.

Shaw knew this was the turning point, the moment when the truth began to unravel, but he forced himself to calmly write the name in his notebook with the addition: *Coram's boat.*

Opening the inquest document box, he found a typed statement from the master of the *Lagan*, William Edward Coram, presumably Tom Coram's father, a laconic narrative which had been signed into the official evidence by the coroner, but not read in court. It contained one final surprise.

We accepted a contract to stand by at the Alexandra Dock in Lynn by telephone at 16.30 hours that afternoon. Several vessels had sought safe harbour after a brief warning had been broadcast at 15.00 hours. We were to assist on the full tide. We left Wells and at 18.45 hours, approximately 18 miles off Holme, we made visual contact with a ship, lifeless in heavy seas. The captain identified her as the *Calabria*, a Dutch coaster. We offered a tow to port. This offer was declined. We stood off for 20 minutes and observed, from a distance of 300 yards, a severe forward list. We repeated the offer, and were declined. By just after 19.15 hours the storm had reached force 9. The sea state was chaotic.

We ran for cover at Lynn, but at a speed of thirty knots we met a wave on the port side which drove a railway sleeper through the starboard plates, a foot below the waterline. At 19.25 we abandoned ship, and took to our dinghy, which we allowed to run before the storm south-west. We beached a mile north of Hunstanton. The next day we searched for the wreck of the *Lagan*, but despite making visual contact in shallow water, plans to salvage the vessel were abandoned. The wreck was not visible again.

So the *Lagan* and the *Calabria* had sunk on the same night.

Which seemed to bring the investigation back to the Coram family. Coram's father had skippered the tug that had tried to save the *Calabria*. Was he still alive? Now his son led the campaign to stop the rebuilding of the old pier. Hartog's body had been found between the piles of the old pier. What possible connection could there be between the pier and the loss of the *Calabria*?

THIRTY-FIVE

S haw had never appreciated the extent to which the pier – or, more accurately, the precise east–west line of the old pier – was in fact a boundary, a border, between two very different worlds. The view from the rail of the roof café on top of Marine World gave him this new perspective. To the south lay the town's Sea Life Sanctuary, then the dodgems and helter-skelters of the fun park, and the Big One – a 150-foot-high junior version of Blackpool's towering white-knuckle ride. Beyond that, the seawall protected caravan sites, chalet homes, camping sites, and the distant holiday camp at Heacham. A collection of sometimes ramshackle homes jostled for a sea view along the grassy seawall, including the fragile line of prefabs comprising Empire Bank. In the far distance lay the cranes of Lynn Docks, a stubby flourmill, the lone pinnacle of the Campbell's soup factory tower.

The view north offered an aesthetic opposite. The planning rules, so freely interpreted south of the pier, were here rigorously applied. Within a few hundred yards, the concrete front petered out into the wave-cut platform below the toothpaste-striped cliffs. This was the last point of any height before the coast became a nearly contin-uous beach, leaving behind the rock-pool coast, stretching in a sinuous golden line past Holme and Brancaster, Wells and Morston, Blakeney Point, and on to Sheringham and Cromer: the hundred-mile beach, backed by dunes and marshes, sandy inlets and hidden harbours. The beach formed a linear wilderness, a littoral desert, stretching the eye to breaking point.

Now, out on the sands, Shaw could see the army bomb disposal crews preparing the three sites where they planned to blow up the First World War 1,100-pounders the next day. At each pit a tent had been set up, and cables ran to a 'trigger point' on the green above. Here the winner of the special lottery would press the button and set off a series of controlled explosions. All along the clifftop and esplanade Shaw could see council workers setting out crash barriers to keep back the crowds. Offshore, a few boats were already anchored in a line 200 yards from the high-tide mark – the outliers of the small fleet that would carry protestors from STP, ready to feature in every TV and newspaper shot of the triple explosion.

Anna Roos, when she arrived, was clearly an inhabitant of the world to the north of the pier, her face in shadow under a straw hat, her long, bare legs leading to bare, sandy feet. When he'd first seen her, amongst the rock pools with her young students, she'd seemed a natural, as one with the ecosystem she was trying to reveal. Given what Shaw now knew, this studied free-spirit image seemed disturbingly fraudulent.

'Inspector,' she said, taking a plastic bottle of mineral water from her bag, pulling out one of the café's metal seats, the legs screeching on concrete. 'Odd place to choose for breakfast. Given that I'm on bail, my solicitor informs me that I don't have to answer any questions. And I hate *this place*. So the auguries aren't good, are they?' She'd almost spat out the words 'this place'. Marine World was a glitzy tourist dive, with performing seals and sharks, a 'casino' of one-armed bandits, and a 3D cinema; a stark contrast to the Sea Life Sanctuary with its eco-friendly habitats.

Shaw refused to be hurried. Out on the beach a small inquisitive crowd was forming behind the safety cordon 200 yards from the bomb pits.

A text rang on his phone, incoming from Valentine: *Coram Senior alive. Up at the Old Lookout. Hospital today. He'll see us 9 tomorrow.*

Shaw took his time with a reply, before turning back to Roos. 'How do you feel about fish in tanks?' he asked.

Below them, within Marine World, sea creatures lived in a dingy twilight environment beneath dimmed artificial lighting, in tanks of decanted, salinated water. The blue-green light, refracted by the water, played little captured rainbows on the drab concrete walls. It was one of the saddest places Shaw knew.

Climbing up to the café through the central observation stairwell, separated from the attractions by a plate-glass window, Shaw had glimpsed a single grey seal on its artificial beach, gloomily staring at a party of Italian language students, one of whom had pronounced gravely: *Gli occhi tristi* – What sad eyes!

Roos slung a pair of sunglasses on to the table.

'Coffee?' offered Shaw.

'Can we get on? I've been summoned here for a philosophical debate on the concept of the zoo, on freedom and imprisonment?'

'Your email inbox has proved illuminating,' said Shaw. 'I'm not quite sure where to start. I've a young DC called Paul Twine who dabbled with a career in finance. He's at home, to some extent, in the world of offshore trusts, inheritance tax, investment vehicles. What used to be covered by that slippery euphemism, *personal finance*. He took an interest in your digital savings account – and particularly the regular payments from the Anchorstone Trust. Nice touch that – the nod to Hartley and the rock-pool coast. Nice touch or deliberate blind-sider?'

She took off the sun hat and seemed to make an effort to sit up straight. 'Go on.'

'I don't need to tell you this story, do I? Brave Dutch freedom fighter kayaks across North Sea. Then peace breaks out. His parents – your grandparents – didn't survive the occupation in Amsterdam, which left him the sole heir to the family's lucrative diamond brokerage. He sold up, and, taking the money, he bought a parcel of land. This land, Ms Roos . . .' Shaw pointed down below their feet. 'The operators of Marine World rent off the Anchorstone Trust; still do. And when your father died – tragically young, I'm sorry for that – he left you and your mother the income from the fund. Every time I hear a one-armed bandit chug out a few coins for the dopey gamblers downstairs, I'll think of you, Ms Roos, and your cut of the takings. My DS saw your modest flat when we picked up the laptop. But that's not really home, is it? There's a Jacobean quayside house at Cley, and of course your mother's house near Aix-en-Provence. I'm only guessing, but it sounds stunning – all that painterly light.'

Below, a bell marked feeding time, and they heard a chorus of seal barks.

'You're a bit of a fraud, Ms Roos,' said Shaw lightheartedly. 'An environmental campaigner bankrolled by the unacceptable face of the seaside resort.'

'There's a dynamic equilibrium between the two,' she said, but the easy smile was forced.

'Is that what you tell yourself? I'm not really interested in self-justification. I'm intrigued to discover that you have two reasons to stop the pier being built: to protect your precious rock-pool coast and to safeguard the future of your income, and your mother's income, because the new pier includes plans for a Water Wonderland – direct competition for Marine World. That makes you my prime suspect, Ms Roos. No wonder you wanted to help run the STP campaign. Does Mr Coram know about your interests?'

'Ask him,' she said, almost spitting out the words.

They were enveloped in the smell of frying onions and the sweet cloying scent of candyfloss.

'All of that amounts to a very sharp motive to try to stop the pier. The question is how far were you prepared to go – and how far was Joe Lester prepared to go? Graffiti, vandalism, criminal damage, arson, *murder*?'

She laughed, but the smile slid off her face too quickly.

'He doesn't know, does he, Ms Roos? About all this? Was he the cat's paw? Egged on by one of his heroes, I suppose – the campaigning Ms Roos. Defender of the rock-pool coast. Or did you pay him? I'm sure the resources are available. Perhaps you paid others. It's been dirty work – why soil your own hands?'

Roos replaced her dark glasses. 'Resources buy lawyers, too, Inspector. I think I should call mine.' The crisp, clear voice told Shaw the answer to one question: that there was no sense in which this young woman was conflicted within herself between the two worlds she sought to inhabit.

'Good idea. We have your fingerprints; we'd like a saliva test too. There's indications that we might have skin fragments on the control panel of the decompression chamber out on the rig.' This was largely fictitious, but Shaw was thrilled to see the blood drain from her face. 'Are you a good swimmer, Ms Roos?'

'Adequate.'

'Also, I'd like to ask you a few questions, under caution at St James', about the two emails you exchanged with Dirk Hartog. That's the Dutchman you professed never to have met.'

She stood, neatly folding down the material of her shorts, 'The Dutchman? I remember now. He wanted to know if I'd ever seen wreckage from a ship – the *Caledonian*? Something like that. Or maybe not. Joe told him I walk the beach too. I couldn't help. I forgot.'

'You agreed to meet him on the beach the day before he disappeared. We have the email.'

'He was persistent. I'm polite. You'll hear from my lawyers.'

'Did he tell you why he was looking for the ship?'

'No,' she said, and for the first time in the entire interview he was sure she was lying.

'Did he mention another ship? A tug, called the *Lagan*?'

'Never.' She'd said it too quickly. Her lips struggled to rework her answer, but then she gave the effort up and turned on her bare heels.

THIRTY-SIX

t was Paul Twine, fittingly, who returned to the mystery of the Leander Club watches. Within the tight-knit squad that was the serious crime unit, Twine had a reputation as Mr Accessorize; there was the Mont Blanc pen, the latest iPhone with personalized case, the Gucci glasses, the Ask the Missus leather shoes with red soles, and his own watch, a stylish Italian Fila. So when he saw Tom Hadden with the watches laid out in the forensic suite, he gave the problem some thought, turning one of the timepieces in his hand, admiring the elegant script.

Twine's easy familiarity with accessories came from an aborted career in retailing. He'd left university and joined the graduate training scheme at John Lewis. Crisp, clean-cut, smart, he'd thrived, if underwhelmed privately by the generally gormless inquiries of the great British public. He'd quickly advanced from the retail frontline to head office. His degree had been in maths, so he'd particularly enjoyed the complex, free-flow world of buying and selling in wholesale quantities, because his brain was fast enough to spot a lucrative margin. His employer reference, when called in by the West Norfolk Constabulary, described him as a born salesman.

So he rang WaveCrest and asked for the name and number of the rep who'd sold Tad Atkins the fifty-one watches, and then he rang him, pretending to be from the council, interested in ordering a hundred watches for the sports staff of the local authority's fifteen secondary schools, with the council's own brand image – a seagull – included on the face. Twine said twice he knew Tad Atkins and that the Leander Club watches had been a big hit.

Darren Forbes, the salesman, was quick with numbers too. 'Right. So if we go for the sports model, with the local authority logo, I can do that at eighty-eight fifty a go. That's for the hundred. No returns, I'm afraid.'

'Right. Well, it's not my call, of course,' said Twine. 'I have to put it to the committee chairman, although I know he'll take my advice on this. It's still fairly pricey. Like, I love the look of it – the online image – but I'd think twice about laying that much out just for a watch. My wife says nobody needs a watch anymore, what with the phone and stuff.'

Twine let the silence stretch.

'Yeah, yeah. You want a hundred, right?'

Twine heard pages being turned, a muffled conversation off stage.

'Here's the thing,' said Forbes. 'I can do seventy-nine ninety-nine – final price. And as you've been so helpful, I'm happy to send you a free one, complete with the logo, just as a way of showing our appreciation for the business. Nothing on paper – that's just between you and me. How does that work?'

'Oh. That works just fine, Mr Forbes. I'll be right back to you.'

THIRTY-SEVEN

Valentine had been planning Esther Keeble's first – and possibly only – appearance in court for some days. A prison van would collect her from Bedford Prison at noon and transport her the ninety-two miles to King's Lynn Magistrates' Court. The van, with a single frosted window, slowing down for the last fifty yards before entering the secure underground entry, would afford enterprising newspaper and TV photographers the chance to grab a flashlight picture before she disappeared from sight. BBC Look East and ITV Anglia had both indicated they would have live reports from the scene. The 'sweetie killer' tag had secured Keeble a national profile.

She would be held in an underground cell, one of ten in a Victorian suite of cold, whitewashed cubicles, each with a grilled basement window, again in frosted glass. It occurred to Valentine that this was how she might well see out the rest of her life: through opaque glass, occasionally reinforced with wire. Her appearance at Lynn would be to confirm her details, extend her custody, and deny bail, but principally to set a date for her trial at Crown Court. She had not uttered a single word in explanation of her crimes but had indicated – to her allocated defence solicitor – on several occasions that she intended to plead guilty.

By three o'clock she was in her cell. A lowering sun was shining down Queen Street, and straight in through the sub-basement window, so that the box-like white room was radiant with light. Valentine took her a cup of tea. In a strangely intimate sense he'd got to like Esther Keeble, possibly as a subconscious compensation for the life she'd had to lead, caring for a wheelchair-bound husband, surviving only as a shadowy presence on the edge of a bustling, burgeoning family.

He leant his back against the cell door as she sipped her tea. 'I'd understand it if you'd tried to kill Alice,' he said.

She shook her head, a mannerism he'd come to recognize, and checked the clock on the wall. In Bedford, during her first twenty-four hours in custody, the woman PC assigned to provide surveillance had remarked on the number of times she consulted watches and clocks, and her habit of double-checking the date with her jailers each morning.

'What are you waiting for, Esther?' asked Valentine.

'To go up,' she said, and used a paper napkin to dry her bottom lip.

'It's a formality,' said Valentine. 'Even the Crown Court case will be over in hours. Pleading guilty tends to take the wind out of the legal process. Not speaking – not explaining – won't help with the sentence. They've explained that? They'll not be in the mood to sympathize. After all, there's Roach's family to consider – they don't know, do they, why he died, why he had to end his life like that.'

She nodded.

'You said, that first time we interviewed you, that you were sorry – that you *didn't want it to end like this.* What did you mean, Esther? What's ended like this?'

Valentine thought then that she looked impossibly alone: a frail, old woman, sitting on a cell bed, cradling a pea-green cup of lukewarm tea. It was as if she had decided to leave this world – the real world of the cell – and place herself in some kind of *purgatory*. As soon as Valentine formed the word, he knew the meaning was precisely right, in the sense that she was in a state of waiting, of subservience to some outside force. And the room's vibrant, celestial light seemed to chime with this sense that, thrillingly, paradise might be close.

'It's George, really,' she said. 'I worry. He needs to take pills, in the right order, at the right time. Confusion can reign,' she added, and again Valentine noted the spark of life that seemed to revitalize her eyes.

'I think a nurse is calling, twice a day now,' offered Valentine. 'It was a scare, the stroke, but apparently there have been others?' She nodded. 'But he's confused. Stressed. We all are. Perhaps he's waiting for you to explain, Esther. What do you reckon?'

He put a hand on the whitewashed wall and the damp paint came away on his skin. Outside, at pavement level, they heard a mobile phone tone, and a playful voice in answer.

And footsteps in the corridor.

Looking out through the observation portal, Valentine recognized DC Lau. She asked for a minute of his time at the far end of the corridor, her voice light and informal, so they left Esther Keeble with her cup of tea.

'The judge wants to postpone,' said Lau. 'Or go later today, maybe last thing . . .' Even as she said it, her eyes slid back down the corridor towards Keeble's cell.

'Why?'

'It's the husband. He's dead; looks like suicide. Defence wanted to try to get him to appear – maybe secure bail? Duty solicitor paid a call first thing, couldn't get an answer, so they rang us. Anyway, he's dead. Looks like pills. In his wheelchair, apparently; no suspicious circumstances.'

'A note? Letter – anything?'

'I'm heading out there now to check, but the constable on the scene says he was pretty careful to check, and there's nothing obvious in the room, by the bed, or by the chair. Looks like he just wanted to go.'

Valentine looked back down the corridor towards the cell. 'He might have said goodbye.'

'And a message from the boss,' said Lau. 'Two things. Twine's made some kind of breakthrough on the Leander Club watches. They're bringing the pool manager – Atkins – in for a formal interview tomorrow afternoon. Looks like he might be our swimmer.'

'And tonight, a CID briefing on Big Bang Day – half six at the Red House. Three line whip.' Lau consulted a notebook. 'Boss says we need to get our ducks in a row. Traffic are reporting roads busy already, and the campsites are bursting. Media's gone mad; one commercial radio report predicted fifty thousand plus. The airship company needs a flight path – apparently, that's our job too, but we'll need to liaise with RAF and Civil Aviation. Uniformed branch is on top of crowd control, but they've just cancelled all leave. Chief constable wants to check we're across keeping the floating demo safely out of the way of bomb disposal; boss is on to that now with the RNLI. Army reports that triggers will be live by eleven tomorrow. Detonation is noon.'

'What could possibly go wrong?' said Valentine.

THIRTY-EIGHT

Shaw woke early on Big Bang Day to the sound of a distant engine, the rhythmic shock waves pulsing over a sea as flat as mercury. Standing at the café window, swinging it out open wide, he noted the time – one minute past six – and, through the mounted telescope on the stoop, the sight of the jack-up crane hoisting dripping mud and sand from the mudlock on the rig into its waiting flat barge. Blue Square Inc. was clearly back in business.

Lena's Italian coffee machine produced a double espresso, which he took outside with a glass of juice and a bowl of cereal. Then he punched Captain Ring's number into his mobile, and imagined the airborne signal flying out to the *Telamon* over the creaseless water.

'Shaw. Morning. How can I help?'

Shaw detected a note of brisk evasion. 'Busy, I see.'

'Yeah. I guess the owners put some pressure on. We've had to up security – metal gates on the landing stages, some CCTV – but it's all in place. We got the green light an hour ago. Health and safety executive have completed an on-the-spot check. Chief exec of Blue Square's flying in from Schiphol by helicopter at one, so that's going to make my day.'

'They couldn't wait twenty-four hours? It's provocative, to say the least. There'll be a hundred boats in this protest off the beach, and you're making it pretty clear Blue Square's back in business. Is that smart?'

'Smart. Stupid. What do I know? It's costing them more than a million a day, Shaw. I don't think considerations of community relations come into it. I'm a marine engineer. My opinion, for what it's worth, is that it's designed to be provocative, to show they won't be scared off. If Brussels puts a stop to this project, Blue Square takes a hit – a billion-euro hit. That's not acceptable to them. This is a statement of intent. Sorry. I know it doesn't make your job any easier. I have to go.'

Shaw sat watching the crane swing its next load over the sea, then sent DC Twine an email telling him to make sure that everyone who should know the rig was back in business did know. Then he checked through the dispositions agreed at the Red House meeting the night before. Big Bang Day was an infuriating diversion, but he had no choice but to apply maximum manpower to the problem to make sure there were no disasters.

Satisfied he'd done all he could, given the early hour, he ran to the lifeboat at Old Hunstanton, changed, and then walked along the clifftops to Marine Court, where the STP's giant thermometer had nearly reached its target red bulb. Valentine sat on the whitewashed wall, watching a small crowd of early risers claim their positions at the crash barriers. Below on the sands, three large flags bearing army insignia flew from the pits in which the unexploded Zeppelin bombs lay, wired for destruction. A BBC outside broadcast van had taken pole position on the green, bristling with satellite dishes.

'Let's do it,' said Shaw.

Although Big Bang Day would demand their attention in the hours to come, Shaw's number-one priority was interviewing Edward Coram, the skipper of the *Lagan*, the tug that had offered the ill-fated *Calabria* a line on the night of the 1953 flood. Having slept on the series of discoveries he'd made concerning the last hours of the *Calabria*, Shaw was more than ever convinced that here lay the heart of the mystery of the murder of Dirk Hartog.

Leading the way up a steep banistered alleyway, they climbed to the low ridge behind the town on which the Victorians had built Hunstanton's trademark villas: stately brick mansions adorned with Gothic trinkets – towers and cupolas, grand bay windows with lead roofs, stone friezes depicting shells and tridents, mermaids and whales. It was in one such house, Shaw recalled, that Eustace and Hilda had lived, the protagonists in Hartley's classic of an Edwardian seaside childhood.

The Old Lookout, which Tom Coram had pointed out to them from the balcony of Marine Court as the family home, was perhaps the finest of the villas: four floors, each with double balconied bays, and a flagpole rising from the roof, flying – Shaw noted with surprise – the starred insignia of the European Union.

Coram junior was sitting on the doorstep, behind him a clear view into the house and a dark interior of polished wood.

'This isn't necessary,' he said, by way of welcome. 'I demand to know why you want to interview my father; he's in his eighties, for God's sake. He's not well – in fact, he's in pain. If this goes ahead, I'm telling you now I'll make a formal complaint to the chief constable. In writing.' He held up a white envelope.

'If we're unable to interview Mr Coram here, we will require him to report to St James',' said Shaw, taking the time to turn his back on Coram and take in the sea view. 'Your call.'

Coram's eyes flitted beyond Shaw to the distant rig, the jack-up crane's engine grating through the gears.

'You'll regret this,' he said, hauling himself up and leading the way into the cool hall. 'And today of all days. Couldn't it have waited?' he asked over his shoulder.

The interior ticked: two grandmother clocks stood by the staircase, and in one of the living rooms a chime marked the half hour. A lift had been installed in the kitchen, which took them up into what looked like the attic.

Edward Coram was outside on the balcony. Valentine knew immediately that he'd caught sight of the old man that first morning they'd called at Marine Court, the flash of binoculars glimpsed from the high turreted tower.

The room itself, which was spacious, was entirely orientated to the view: even the bed, set back, with banked pillows, would have afforded anyone an instant panorama of the Wash, and – over the last few months – Blue Square's construction rig.

A wide desk stood cluttered with maps, and Shaw noted a detailed naval architect's plan of what looked like the *MV Telamon*. A set of sea charts lay spilt on the floor, and a montage of old photographs had been laid out showing the front at Hunstanton in the 1950s.

A mounted telescope on the balcony was a reminder of Dirk Hartog's lonely guesthouse bedroom. Just inside the room, partially hidden by a heavy set of drapes, stood a camera tripod. Shaw felt as if they'd stepped into a great eye – the bay, the iris; the wood-panelled back wall, the nerve-stitched cornea. Light flooded in, reflected, refracted, filling the space with random shards of colour.

Edward Coram showed them his back, broad and muscular, supporting a round head, the neck lost in the collar of a crisp white shirt.

'Father. I tried, but the inspector has insisted. DS Valentine is here too, no doubt on hand in case you try to outrun DI Shaw.'

It was a strangely literal, patronizing introduction, and apparently superfluous until Coram half-turned, to reveal a right eye entirely obscured by a milky white cataract, the left still its original blue, although this too was glimpsed through a film of new, blinding tissue.

The contrast between the eye-like room, staring out over the sea, and these cruelly disfigured irises actually took Shaw's breath away.

'You're not needed, Thomas,' he said, revealing a voice possibly three decades younger than his weather-beaten face.

The son went to answer his father but bit back the thought before he could vocalize it, pausing only to give Shaw a murderous stare, the lift gates crashing closed as he fled as instructed.

'A seat, Inspector . . .' Coram directed his voice at Shaw, but selected an orientation for his head a few degrees from true. Looking back at the desk, Shaw noted a large magnifying glass, and a Cook's glass for map reading.

'Has this always been the family home?' asked Shaw, as Coram took a seat at the table, and Valentine walked to the balcony edge, looking out to sea, where the floating protest was beginning to muster its miniature armada.

'Not at all. I bought it in 1972 – after the property crash, when the price was right. I was born in a two-up two-down in Wells, Mr Shaw. There are no silver spoons in this family. I knew your father, by the way – Jack. Bit of a tearaway, but then we both were. I was on the council back then – police committee. So our paths crossed.'

Shaw ignored the attempt to subtly edge the interview on to a more convivial footing. 'I wanted to ask you about the night you took the *Lagan* out and tried to assist a Dutch coaster – the *Calabria*, although you might remember it as the *Marlberg*. January thirty-first, 1953. The night of the great flood.'

The flesh on Coram's face had long ago succumbed to the force of gravity, but the bone structure was still strong beneath, and Shaw thought he detected a stiffening of the jaw.

'Not a night I could forget,' Coram said, half smiling. 'I lost a lot of friends, Inspector, out on the South Beach. And I lost the *Lagan*, of course. My first boat. We've a fleet now: six tugs – deep water, not little pond-skaters like the *Lagan*. I . . .'

'A night to remember for the families of the crew of the *Calabria*, too. Three dead.'

Coram's eyes turned seawards, searching. 'Sixty-three years ago. Time passes, and we can say now what should have been said then. If they'd taken a line, they'd have lived to see the next day – all of them. Money talks. It did that night. They had a radio link to Bremen. I think the owners said no, although it was never clear. She was in a bad way, the ship, but we'd have secured a decent percentage of her scrap value and the cargo. And they'd have all got to see their families again.'

He gestured to a chair so that Shaw could sit close. 'But a captain's got the final word. What was it – Captain Beck?' Coram looked suddenly vulnerable, as if he'd forgotten his own name.

'Beck, yes,' said Shaw. 'Arjen. You saw her sink?'

Coram covered his mouth with a hand the size of a rudder. 'No. We left her, although we got close.' He held his hands apart. 'What – a hundred yards? The radio link failed in the end, so I got Ring to use the lamp – to signal. We offered to take *them* off – sod the ship. No answer. So we took her clear. Worse sea I'd ever seen, that night – no waves, no pattern, just like she was boiling, but flattened out by the wind.'

'Tell me what you could see on board the *Calabria*. The crew?' It was a question to buy time. So one of Coram's crew was called *Ring*?

Coram shook his head. 'Lights. And maybe some shadows on the bridge. But no crew. I don't think we saw anyone. They must have been below decks trying to fix the pumps.' He sat back, apparently exhausted. 'What's this about, Inspector?' The old man's hands seemed incapable of staying still, constantly moving over the objects on the desktop.

'The man murdered in the sea, just off the coast, the diver – he was the son of the *Calabria*'s engineer.'

'Good God,' said Coram, blinking sightless eyes. He licked his dry, cracked lips, and Shaw wondered if, in his bluff overconfidence, Coram felt he'd said too much.

'How did the *Lagan* sink?' asked Shaw.

'Flotsam in the sea – that's how we lost her. We didn't know then, of course, the extent of the damage along the coast. All sorts of stuff had been blown offshore. The wind ripped up homes, roads, took out the railway line to Lynn, and that's what we hit, a sleeper. Solid pine, like a torpedo, right through the port plates. Worst

moment of my life, bar none. I heard it . . . I hear it now in my
sleep.

'We had a wooden dinghy, pretty thing, a slip of a boat. That's
what saved us, of course; she was so light she just skipped with the
wind, which was from the north, driving us on to the sands. I've
still got her, up at Wells on the quay. She's not been in the water
for half a century, but she saved my life that night.'

'And the *Calabria* was over Roaring Island when she went down?'

'Yes. A full tide, so there was plenty of depth, and she was
drifting badly. Mind you, don't forget this is 1953 – no GPS on
board. But she'll be in the sand somewhere. One day we'll see her
again – or her timbers.'

Out at sea they heard a foghorn call.

'Something's up out at the rig,' said Valentine, already keying a
message into his phone.

They could see hoses playing a series of curved watery rainbows
out from the rig and down to the sea. In response, a water canon
seemed to be firing back from a skidoo weaving between the legs
of the *Telamon*. The jack-up crane seemed transfixed, its latest load
of mud and gravel held motionless in mid-air.

'Ring?' said Shaw, trying to regain Coram's attention as he struggled to his feet. 'You said you got Ring to signal. The captain of
the rig is Peter Ring – a local man. Same family?'

Coram affected a shrug, walking stiffly out on to the balcony.
'Probably. You know what this coast's like. This was a Peter too
– a good man. I spoke at his funeral. Family man, and you're right:
there may have been a boy.'

Out at sea the protestors on the ships offshore were cheering
wildly, banners high, as the skidoo made another high-speed pass
beneath the rig. The foghorn boomed again, and Coram gripped a
pair of binoculars from his desk and pressed them to his blinded
eyes.

THIRTY-NINE

For a long time the boy had lain under Tad Atkins' desk in his poolside office. At first he didn't *see* him, not as an everyday, conscious incarnation, but he felt his presence, and, as the hallucinations continued, he heard him, whispering those final words: *Is the bike broken?*

Of course, the words themselves were real, in an historical sense, in that the boy Tad Atkins had killed that day in the van had asked him that very question. The answer had been no – the bike was untouched, the back wheel spinning still, as Atkins held the boy's broken body. The inquest had listed a litany of clean fractures, which had been stylized by the newspapers as 'every bone in his body'. This had been unfair, even libellous, but Atkins' lawyer had advised silence, given the circumstances.

The mental health counsellor had told him that, while the images and the sounds continued, he should never consciously conjure up the boy's name, which was bad advice, because there was no doubt that the effort of keeping the words at a distance from his conscious mind simply imprinted the letters indelibly on his subconscious. As a result, Josh Ridding, aged nineteen, was haunting Tad Atkins.

The boy was there now, and he knew that if he looked under the desk, he would see him; instead, he poured himself some more vodka, stood up, and went to the window of his office. The pool outside was deserted, despite the sunshine which seemed to fill the space with a sense of a suspended solid, a great rectangular block of golden energy. It was beautiful, and might have redeemed him in another life, on another day. Today, it wasn't beautiful enough.

He pressed the message button on his phone and listened once again to the constable's voice, asking him if he could attend at St James', Kings Lynn, for interview with DI Shaw and DS Valentine, who were conducting inquiries into members of the Leander Club. He knew the game was up, not because they might have evidence of his complicity, but because he couldn't stop his hands shaking.

It had been relatively easy to contrive the evacuation of the building: he'd poured a plastic bottle full of his own urine into the water filter monitor in the basement, and the three red lights had come up on the control panel. Knocking them back to green, he'd repeated the exercise three times and the programmed computer protocol had overridden the pump, locking in the red lights. Making the necessary calls to the maintenance crew, he used the public address system to clear the pool. The health and safety executive's regulations were not open to debate. The pool was closed until at least five o'clock. A notice on reopening would be posted on the Flume! website.

Pouring himself another shot of the strangely sweet alcohol, he considered the poster on the wall. At home, in the bedsit, he had this same image over his bed. *Boy on a High Dive*, by Norman Rockwell, was a painting of preternatural reality; the crisp lines of the diving board and the metal steps seemed to invite a dive. A boy lay on the board, peering over the edge, looking down with wide eyes at the plunge beneath. The image spoke of fear, but it also implied bravery, in that Atkins could imagine this boy struggling to his feet, controlling his breathing, taking the heart-stopping plunge. He'd dived as a boy, developing that peculiar self-control that stemmed from constant, mind-numbing practice, so that finally he could take to the air without fear.

It took courage, and he'd had that then. Now, when he looked at the image of the boy – which he'd read once was actually the painter's son – he saw the face of Josh Ridding, the eyes wide in fear, not at the drop below, but at the approaching white van, with Tad Atkins at the wheel, his eyesight fatally distorted by alcohol.

'So no excuse,' he said now, out loud, because the simple fact was that he'd started drinking years before he'd killed Josh Ridding.

If they'd sent him to prison for the full term for killing the boy, he'd have been torn apart, but – perhaps – rebuilt. But they hadn't sent him to prison for long, and even then it had been an open facility on the south coast. Old friends paid off old favours, and the parole board – told that he'd have a job, that he'd have support, and that he'd be a force for good – had decided that he could go back to his home town and undertake community service, while accepting a lifetime ban from driving.

What they didn't know – the great and the good of the parole board – was that there would be an appalling payback for all those favours that had secured Tad Atkins' early release into a secure job. They didn't know, and could never have guessed, what he'd have to do *in return*. And – and this is where the concept of evil really first emerged – what he'd have to make others do, because, of course, he had very quickly realized how powerful favours were, and that if he extended them to others, he too would one day be in a position to collect.

Trying to pick up his mobile, it fell from his uncertain fingers. Pathetically, he had to lean forward to check the screen and confirm that there were no messages or calls. He'd asked Kersk, cherub-faced Theo, for a final favour, and now it looked as if he'd never know if the young man had done the job. But this wasn't really about honour; it was blackmail. It was all blackmail really, dressed up as other things, with which it had been easier to live.

Why he'd put on his swimming shorts would be an enduring mystery, because he didn't really need them. Leaving his tracksuit top on his chair, he went out and padded down the side of the pool, feeling the strange stipples beneath his skin, and recognizing that they were part of his life too, along with the chlorine and the hurtling plummet of the dive itself: the free fall, the sense of escape and *otherness* – as if he could transform himself in flight. At one time he'd hoped that in the moments of the dive he'd be free of the boy with the broken body, but even those brief, blurred seconds were haunted now. A sudden insight made him shiver: as a small boy, he'd dreamt of being Peter Pan, and in some ways diving had been a way to fly. Now he saw Peter's elusive shadow in a different light, as a haunting too.

As Atkins climbed the steps to the diving board, he tried to distract himself from reconsidering his purpose: he counted the steps – twelve to a tier, zig-zagging up, in eight switchback floors. It had been Atkins' idea, during the redevelopment of Flume!, to push for the installation of the thirty-three-foot board: the top actually stuck out, above the roofline, just like the pinnacle of the flume tube itself, both encased in stylish glass domes. The pool far beneath was twenty feet deep – often appearing as a blue oasis, slightly inky at its heart, which reminded Atkins of the burial pits of Maya, in which they flung the murdered sacrificial youths. Those pits were seen as gate-ways to heaven.

Climbing the final tier, he breasted the roofline and through the thick glass glimpsed the sea: a sudden vista he had not anticipated, which opened out with each step – the protest boats in a line offshore, the distant rig, tourists packed along the top of the esplanade. A helicopter swooped overhead, making the metal staircase beneath his feet hum with vibration.

Eight steps got him to the end of the board.

Never look down: the golden rule.

The blue pool beneath, the blue-inky heart of the deep well into which he could fall, had always been waiting for him when he stepped off into the air. But not today: he had carefully monitored the pumps for the twenty minutes it had taken to drain the pool, 110,000 gallons of water gushing out, so that all that lay beneath him now was a damp tile floor, pump grids, and the blue lines separating the arid lanes.

In the end, he fell: his knees giving way, his eyesight blurred.

It was a blessing he never counted that there was no one to hear the sound.

FORTY

'FIFTY, FORTY-NINE, FORTY-EIGHT . . .'

Shaw had always found the sound of voices in concert to be rather moving, an affirmation perhaps of community, of a common purpose. Even from a distance of a mile, the crowd on the esplanade – 8,000-strong according to AA and RAC reports on the radio, well short of the more hysterical predictions of the media – was still clearly, crisply audible.

Lena, never slow to spot a business opportunity, had put picnic tables out on the sands in front of *Surf!*. The day's special offer was a cocktail for £9.99, with a gourmet burger, cooked on the barbecue, toasted wholemeal bun, and salad. She'd judged her clientele perfectly, attracting families and couples who were keen to witness the Big Bang, but not too bothered about *going* to see it, content to sit back, away from the crowds, with an iced drink, some classy food, and a clear, if distant, view of the action.

Besides, the real highlight of the event was likely to be the noise. The army experts predicted that the small detonators, when triggered, would ignite the original explosives within the corroded shells. The result would be a distinct double blast: a discrete cough, followed by an earth-shaking rumble. Three seconds after the first blast, the second would automatically follow, with the third another three seconds later: a triple bang of double bangs. The local paper, which had brought out a special supplement for the day, had described the noise with characteristic journalistic restraint as *BA-BOOM! BA-BOOM! BA-BOOM!*

Lena, bar towel over her shoulder, stood looking south. 'Radio says there's still plenty of people crowding into town, so maybe ten thousand in the end, when the counting's done. If you believe the promoters, that's what it will be like *every day*, Peter, once the pier's open.'

She didn't look displeased at the prospect. Shaw knew that while he had doubts about an ugly conveyor-belt pier blocking the view from *his* beach, Lena saw discerning holidaymakers heading north,

away from the crowds, the muzak, and the amusement arcades, to
the peace and quiet of *Surf!*. For Shaw, though, there had to be a
point when the popularity of peace and quiet became a self-defeating
attraction.

'THIRTY-NINE, THIRTY-EIGHT, THIRTY-SEVEN . . .'

'All packed?' he asked. Lena and Fran's flight left that evening
from East Midlands Airport. As soon as the triple blast was over,
they were on the road, hoping to get ahead of the retreating crowds.

'Ready to go.'

'Just in case.' He kissed her. 'Let me know when you land. And
tell me what you find. Your mum did this for a reason, Lena. She
wants you to know something. Keep your eyes open. I've said
goodbye to Fran. She's so excited she can't stand still. You'd never
think you were off to a funeral.'

Down at the water's edge it was low tide, so there was plenty of
room for two uniformed constables to arrange a set of bollards
around an area the size of a football pitch, at the centre of which
they'd placed a large fluorescent yellow sheet marked H.

As soon as the army signalled the all-clear after the blasts, the
West Norfolk's police helicopter was due to touch down, picking
up Shaw and Valentine, and executing a short hop to the *Telamon*'s
helipad. Access by sea was still restricted, thanks to the STP
supporters in the skidoo armed with a water cannon, who had been
cheered on by the floating flotilla of their fellow protestors in their
armada of little boats. A Dunkirk spirit had gripped the crowds,
with STP banners sprinkled along the clifftop.

'NINETEEN, EIGHTEEN, SEVENTEEN . . .'

Shaw was keen to interview Captain Ring about his father's
recollections of the night the *Calabria* sank. Coram's version had
seemed flat and self-serving. Ring was due back on the *Telamon* at
any moment, having descended to the caisson to monitor the impact
of the triple explosion, before sending down the first full shift to
restart work on the pier footings.

'TEN, NINE, EIGHT . . .'

The sound of the crowd, which had dimmed with the tedium
of the long countdown, now rose with each digit.

'THREE, TWO, ONE!'

Shaw felt his eardrum flutter in the second of silence before he
saw the sand rise in a vertical plume. Then the distinctive double

blast hit them, shaking the glasses and bottles behind the bar in *Surf!*, and setting off a hundred distant car alarms. Thousands of birds rose off the dunes and marshes like a visible shock wave. Then a new sound, a wave breaking, shimmered in the air like radio interference, before Shaw recognized it for what it was: applause.

The second and third explosions followed, each one throwing up a shaft of sand into the sunlight. Louder cheers and applause swept along the shoreline. A band on the South Beach began to play the theme from *The Dam Busters*.

'All we need now is the all-clear,' said Shaw, setting off down the beach.

An army Land Rover stood on the sand above the high water mark, its rear doors swung open, revealing an interior dominated by two banks of gauges and computer screens, a swivel chair between. Captain H. Wharram, bomb disposal expert, held one hand lightly to a set of earphones pressed to his ear.

'Verdict?' asked Shaw.

'On the money – see?' Swinging a monitor round, he showed Shaw a seismograph reading, a horizontal line suddenly forming three sets of double peaks, before returning to the horizontal.

'The second peak is nearly five times the amplitude of the first in each case, which means that the detonators did their job. The size of the explosion ensures any fissile material has been burnt up. I've just signalled the all-clear to your people on the front.'

The council, keen to enhance the wartime spirit, had announced that Hunstanton's old police station still had a working air-raid siren. It would signal the success of the triple explosions, the first time it had been used for nearly thirty years to sound the all-clear.

Standing, listening, Shaw heard a seagull call, a car alarm, and then, just on the edge of hearing, a low, dismal note. It began to waver, almost fading out, before gaining energy, winding itself up, in a series of cyclical, mournful notes. Shaw felt the hair on his neck bristle. The siren played for a minute, then died away.

Valentine, who had been up on the dunes trying to pick up a decent mobile signal, came down the beach, holding out his phone for Shaw to see a fuzzy picture, which looked as if it had been lifted from CCTV footage.

The image showed the cockpit of a skidoo at sea; the pilot was a woman in shorts, while the water canon off the prow was aimed by a tall man. Anna Roos and Joe Lester.

'They clearly don't mind breaking bail conditions,' said Valentine. 'Magistrate'll throw the key away. Nobody likes being made a fool of, especially on prime-time TV.'

'True,' said Shaw. 'Have to kind of admire their chutzpah. But ask yourself this, George: if they knew who'd killed Hartog, if they'd been behind the arson attack, and the rest, would they really be ready to see the inside of a cell so quickly? I'd say they were keen to end a campaign of protest on a high note. But my guess is that's all it was.'

The siren fell silent and then, out of the sky, they heard the approaching police helicopter, cleared to enter airspace over the beach, creating a choppy circle of water as it skimmed the sea. Looking west, Shaw's eye was caught by something else: a single white dot, which appeared stationary, suspended over the distant horizon. At first he thought it might be a scrap of cloud, a flock of birds in tight formation, a single puff of smoke.

Captain Wharram was out of his Land Rover, one of Lena's cocktails in hand, face wreathed in smiles.

'Can I?' said Shaw, pointing at the binoculars round the captain's thick neck.

For a moment, Shaw's single eye struggled to accommodate the focus, but then it was there, a single arresting image at x50 magnification: an airship, a miniature Zeppelin, a silver, pillowy cigar with a blue logo, en route for the beach and its historic fly-past over the crowds.

FORTY-ONE

W ithin the caisson, deep below the surface, few exterior sounds ever penetrated an almost primordial silence. Devoid of workmen, the open space projected a strange acoustic landscape in which any noise seemed simultaneously to be swallowed whole, as if wrapped in cotton wool, only to return within a heartbeat as a ping-like echo. The white noise of the air pump and the power supply lay like a blanket on the seabed.

A small seismograph, beside the spiral staircase that led up to the manlock, had recorded the triple blast in slightly panic-stricken peaks. Captain Ring, despite complete confidence in the rigid strength of the caisson, had struggled to keep his heartbeat flat as the power cut out, the emergency lighting flickering on half-heartedly. Then he heard the *Telamon*'s generator powering itself back on line, and the floodlights had ignited, driving the shadows back into the concrete chamber's deepest corners.

Satisfied that the caisson had survived the impact of the triple explosion, Ring went to the control panel mounted at the foot of the mudlock stairs and switched on the twin hot-air blowers designed to moderate the ten-degree chill. Standing in the centre of the caisson, Ring discerned distinctly the rhythmic vibration of a ship's screw and concluded it must be the *Titan*, the rig's attendant tug, edging closer to the rig, perhaps to confront the protestors' skidoo. Of the sea itself he could hear nothing, although he sensed its presence, massed beyond the concrete walls, responsible for the pressure that made his eardrums creak.

Armed with a clipboard, he began a safety check, but less than a minute into the procedure he heard a distant, high-pitched hiss. He held his breath, tuning his ears to the sound, as if surfing some distant marine waveband, until he'd isolated it, set it aside, and confirmed its existence beyond imagination or fear: a *whisper*, no more, but unmistakably the sound of air escaping the pressurized, inverted hull of the caisson.

Within thirty seconds, the rate of air loss indicated by the whisper doubled, then doubled again. The caisson had air vents in the north-east corner. These had been locked, on the outside, by Blue Square divers after the caisson had been lowered into position, flooded with seawater. Once closed, air was pumped in, driving out the sea. Upon the security of the vents rested the lives of those inside.

Ring climbed an interior ladder to the vents. Up close, he could actually feel the buffeting air flow as it rushed from the caisson out through the filters, a gill-like structure of flutes, which buzzed slightly with the velocity of the gases seeping out into the sea. A gifted amateur marine engineer, as well as a qualified ship's master, Ring could see in his mind's eye what lay beyond the caisson's three-foot-thick concrete shell: a diver, poised, turning the airlock spigot, the air escaping in gouts and bubbles, a shimmering, vertical silver river, twisting up to the surface.

When he looked down from the top of the stairwell that led to the vents, he knew what he'd see, but its glistening, mirror-like surface nonetheless made his mouth go dry: a lake of water had seeped under the caisson wall along the western perimeter, to take the place of the escaping air. Nature, abhorring a vacuum, was trying to kill him.

Escape was now his only priority. Returning to the seabed, he splashed through the fast-widening pool and climbed back to the manlock: the spiral staircase leading to a circular doorway, above his head, which was raised by an electric motor. Pushing a green-lit button marked *Exit*, he heard the sound of the motor firing, but the portal didn't move, or rather it seemed to try to move, vibrating slightly at the edges. A slither of water seeped down the metalwork wall from one edge. It took him five seconds to work out what that meant – that the thirty-five feet of tube above the doorway was probably full of water – so he hit the red button *Lock*, and the engine died.

Looking down, he saw that the floor of the caisson was now a shallow lake, with its own wave pattern. A painted gauge on the concrete wall indicated that the depth was one foot eight inches at the eastern perimeter, although the rate at which the sea level was rising was visible. Ring, a scientist by nature as well as training, could not prevent his brain making a rough estimation of the time he had left: if the flow didn't alter, he calculated he had approxi-mately three minutes. If it did, it might be much less.

Wading across the seabed, he went to the caisson office, a prefab box, and, lifting the landline, waited one buzz, two buzzes, three . . .

'Captain?' It was his second in command in the control room aloft, and he felt a small surge of hope, because of all the surface engineers this one had the sharpest brain.

'Listen. Someone's opened the air vents – from the outside. The water's rising. The manlock won't open. I think the tube's flooded. Check it – now. If there's any way of opening it, open it. I've got three minutes – less.'

Two seconds of silence followed, and the second in command said, 'Check the stores: the sink crew may have left suits. Oxygen – maybe.'

Ring cut the line and headed out, the water at his waist now, towards the metal container that served as the caisson stores. The sink crew was the team that had been inside the caisson when it had been lowered to the seabed, before the water had been pumped out. Regulations stipulated that their diving gear be returned to the deckside stores. For once he hoped they'd been lazy, slipshod, or just forgetful.

How long would the lights last? It had to be *less than* three minutes, because the wall-mounted lights were six feet below the ceiling. So he swam to the store, shuddering as the icy water percolated through his overalls. The store was a doorless metal box, so he floated into the interior, which was lit by a neon wall light, and executed a 360-degree pivot, surveying the scene.

The relief at what he saw was like an injection of adrenaline. A bright orange dive suit hung from a hook; above it, on the shelf, was a single oxygen cylinder and mask. A foot away from getting his hand on the kit, he heard a buzz of short-circuiting; the neon blinked and cut out.

If he panicked now, he'd die here. Outside in the caisson, the blue emergency lighting provided a ghostly glimmer.

Floating, he kept his body rigid, flat in the water, his arms stretched forward until they made contact with the corrugated metal wall. Discarding a hard hat, a hand-drill, and a set of boots, his fingers clamped on the face mask, then the tank. A sixth sense, maybe survival, made him search one foot further along the shelf, and there it was: a diver's torch – standard, waterproof. When he pressed the button, the full beam dazzled. He set it down for a moment, gathered his kit, and then fixed the torch to his belt, before swimming on his back out into the open caisson.

Climbing aboard one of the earth-movers, he stood on the cab roof and stepped into the suit, strapping the tank to his back, clipping the mask and mouthpiece into position. How much air was in the tank? Was there *any* air in the tank? A brave man, he still couldn't bring himself to test the valve.

Climbing the spiral staircase to the manlock, he sat on the top step and waited. Nothing flashed before his eyes. His childhood, his family, his home, all seemed to inhabit the life of another. Instead, he watched the water rising, until it touched his toes. He zipped up the suit, pulling the fasteners tight at the throat, ankles, and wrists. If he was trapped in the manlock, if the manlock didn't open, he'd need to survive, maybe for hours if the air lasted, so he had to keep his body heat close, warming his skin.

Thirty seconds later the water lifted him off the seat, so that he floated beneath the manlock hatch. The exit and lock buttons were no longer lit, so he took hold of the circular hatch wheel and waited, waited, for the water to rise, rise, to the roof itself.

The emergency lighting failed, the water rose past his chin, and at that moment he turned the valve on the oxygen tank and felt the glorious relief of the gas entering his lungs, inflating them, dousing the red panic that had been glowing, like an ember, behind his eyelids.

It was black now, lightless, and he forced himself to wait one more ticking minute. Then he turned the hatch lock and it flipped open with breathtaking ease, the pressure pop audible. Kicking, he rose up the tubular stairwell, circling the lift, his neck back at a vicious angle, his eyes locked on what lay above: a circle of dim orange luminescence, which grew wider and larger, until – with his arms outstretched – he burst out into the neon-lit entry lobby to the decompression chamber. Arms reached forwards, faces crowding round, but he ignored them all and looked instead beyond to the circle of blue sky visible through the nearest porthole.

FORTY-TWO

PPC Jan Clay pulled the handbrake on the squad car, parking neatly in the forecourt of the Willows. The marsh, manicured here with clumps of cypress and willow, with cattle grazing, ran to the seawall, on top of which a single-file crowd faced out to sea, tracking the approach of the still-distant airship. A voice, amplified by the esplanade PA system, came to her on the breeze.

Standing by the car, she filled her lungs with the salty air, the oxygen reinvigorating her blood. How had George described the spot? *A windswept acre of damp grass.* Which was a pity, because she'd liked the house, and they could have had a dog and walked it along the seawall. That morning, at ten, they'd had an appointment to view a property down by Shepherd's Port, a ramshackle beachside township a further mile south. Clapboard, whitewashed, with a second-storey balcony, she'd been desperate to show George, because inside it had the snug, urban predictability of the house in Greenland Street, until you got to the first landing and the picture window opened out, revealing a world of mudflats and racing tides.

But when she woke, she'd felt immediately the coldness on the left side of the bed. George Valentine still left notes, punctiliously avoiding the digital world, and this one had been pinioned under the kettle: *Early start at beach. Sorry. X*

Straightening her blouse, pulling down the edge of the tunic, she gave the Willows a brief visual interrogation: eight bay windows reflected the lawns, the upper stories no doubt rewarded with a view of the seascape beyond the dyke. The house gave nothing away, so all she had to go on was the call, relayed through the St James' control room, from Shaw's landline at *Surf!*. Alice Banks, sister-in-law of Esther, wished to see DI Shaw and DS Valentine. Subject – unspecified. Status – urgent.

Clay knew the case inside out, not because she'd been assigned to it, but because it had constituted what passed for pillow talk at 32 Greenland Street.

Clay marched up to the front door and pressed a button, prompting a discrete buzz from within the bowels of the building. She checked her hair in the glass of the door, a mannerism she could never slough off, despite the fact that, neat and blonde, it had the happy knack of always falling into position. A buddleia bloomed over the doorway and a shower of butterflies, shed by her arrival, seemed to sprinkle her with a sickly, funereal scent.

Three minutes later she was in Alice Banks's 'drawing room', behind one of the bay windows, a bedroom glimpsed through a half-open door. Clay's mother had spent two weeks in a private care home before she died, the bill neatly wiping out her entire estate. Clay always recalled her sitting in one of the wing-backed high chairs, her legs too short to reach the ground.

Banks was in a wheelchair, but she didn't offer Clay a seat.

'This came in the post this morning. Frankly, the second-class stamp says it all. It's from George, a posthumous epistle from the scribe of Empire Bank,' she said, smirking at her own wit, until she saw that Jan's face was a non-reflective mask of polite inquiry.

Clay took the letter, flipping it over to check if it had been opened, which it had. 'A précis?' she asked.

Banks retrieved a handkerchief from the sleeve of her cardigan; it was a mannerism so suited to her surroundings that Clay suspected, for the first time, that the whole image was a façade, a carefully reprised role. She thought there was something inherently brittle in Banks's cold, clipped style. She seemed to have shrugged off the death of her brother with indecent haste.

'Well – it's a confession. Yes. George laced the chocolates with rat poison and gave them to Esther, who unwittingly delivered them to the bus queue. She's entirely innocent of the crimes. The poison's hidden behind the electric fire, in the old flue. George stole a packet at a family party at Salt's warehouse. It's all there – dates and times. What do they say? *It'll stand up in court* – that's it.'

'Motive?'

'Ah. How pedantic of you. George never really forgave the world for what happened, for what became his life. Esther is good, you see; George wants to be good. Vital difference. He doesn't articulate a motive, I'm afraid – simply a desire to take revenge on the world before he leaves it. But he does mention the inherent poor manners of those in the queue – although that seems like a rather thin justification for murder. Overall, I'd say the tone was slightly unhinged and self-pitying.'

A knock at the door brought coffee.

'I didn't order this,' said Banks, examining a plate of biscuits with mild disgust. 'Help yourself,' she said, pouring a cup of black coffee for herself.

Throwing open the balcony door, Clay went outside and read George Keeble's last letter. His sister-in-law had gutted it for its factual content, but entirely deleted the note of emotional sadness. The detective in Clay thought there was something slick and superficial about the 'confession' – and she asked herself the pointed question: Why send it to his sister, and not his wife, as it was designed to secure *her* freedom?

The last line, above a surprisingly forceful signature, read simply: *In memory of the affection we once shared.*

Clay read the line out loud, and Banks put her cup down, unable to disguise the shake of the hand. Turning away, she pointed to the airship, now a distinct cigar-shaped silhouette in a cloudless sky, its attendant gliding shadow turning a patch of sea a deep marine blue.

'Taxpayers' money, no doubt,' she said.

Something in her seemed to snap then, and she briskly wheeled her chair away, into the bedroom, returning with a large box of Milk Tray which she set on the table.

'I can have one. Just one: doctor's orders. Diabetes – recently diagnosed. I'm working my way through the box.'

Her hand hung over the selection, her tongue emerging from her narrow mouth to lick her upper lip.

Clay looked at the chocolates. 'Who gave you this box?'

'Esther. She always brought chocolates, from George. Not always Milk Tray, but always cheap. I told her when she brought these not to bother anymore. They hardly had money to waste. It's unkind of me, but when I heard what she'd done, I thought, she didn't tell George, she wanted the chocolates so that she could make friends on the bus.'

Clay picked up the box, noting that the second layer was untouched. 'When she visited, she came by bus?'

'Yes. As I said. Once a week.' Banks's hands, which often fidgeted, were suddenly still.

Clay took the top layer off and held the tray up to the light. One of the chocolates, an orange truffle, seemed to be slightly smudged with a fingerprint. She had a good sense of smell, and noted that, despite the presence of a hazelnut cluster, the box gave off quite a strong smell of almonds.

FORTY-THREE

When Captain Ring finally spoke, he was close enough to the observation porthole to fog the glass, the blemish of his breath coming and going like a visible heartbeat. The decompression chamber's neon-lit interior seemed to swallow his words in its soundproofed walls, so that when they did emerge through the intercom above the hatch, each syllable was dull, flat, and nasal. Shaw, perched on the chamber operator's metal seat, struggled to dispel the illusion that Ring was still underwater, trapped beyond the watertight door, and that a fish might idly glide between them.

The captain sat slumped on the bench, his black hair hanging in rat's tails, like a piece of human flotsam, washed up, shipwrecked. His skin seemed to soak up the white light, reminiscent of a piece of cod on a marble slab, the muscles on his narrow legs hanging loose, still occasionally twitching as his nerves shot inaccurate, desperate signals around his body. The fingers of the left hand were bandaged, bloodstains marking the point where his flailing hand had hit the steel rim of the manlock tube as he'd swum towards the surface.

In shorts and a T-shirt, Ring cradled a flask of hot, sweet tea, and a thermal cup. Shaw felt that he had acquired the aura of the survivor; stripped down, he seemed younger, the hero who'd risen from the sea.

'The diver?' asked Ring.

'Nothing yet,' said Shaw. 'My sergeant's up aloft on deck. There's a thin trail of oxygen still escaping to the surface from the caisson. But no sign as yet of a diver, a boat, or anything marking the spot. We've got men checking the beach. But remember: this was Big Bang Day; apart from the protest boats, which were held within a tightly patrolled area, there was nothing moving on the water, and certainly nothing on the shoreline. You're sure there was someone *outside*?'

'No question. Once I located the vent, I could hear the lock turning. There was someone outside, someone trying to flood the caisson.' He took in a long, calm lungful of air, but a judder of the ribcage betrayed the strain.

Shaw splayed a hand on the glass, 'Look: this is all about a ship called the *Calabria*. It sank in 1953, on the night of the great flood. I think your father was on board Coram's tug, the *Lagan*. It stood off the ship, waiting to put on a line, but the crew refused help. Did he ever talk about what happened that night?'

Ring tipped his head back, a sigh causing the glass to blush again. 'Christ. This isn't about something that happened half a century ago, Shaw. This is about some bunch of nutters trying to stop this construction project.'

'We'll come to that,' said Shaw. 'But first: the *Calabria*. You shared a love of the sea. You must have talked. Just tell me what you know.'

Ring held the warm flask to his cheek. 'What makes you think it was a subject that we could talk about? The loss of a ship, and on *that* night? Mum and Dad lost friends, the town was devastated, so the anniversary – January thirty-first – was to be endured. I don't think Dad ever got over what happened to him; he certainly quit the boats. Old Coram got him a job at Wells in the back office, on the radio, like he was running a taxi firm at sea. Demeaning really, but he was never bitter. He knew the sea, loved it, but he couldn't go back out. Ever. So, no. We didn't talk about it. Not for years.' Ring closed his eyes, and for a moment Shaw thought he'd passed out. Reopened, they scanned the interior of the chamber, widening to clear the focus. 'But Coram talked about it. You couldn't shut him up. It was part of the narrative, the rise of the family fortunes, the loss of the *Lagan* being the pit, the nadir, before the acquisition of the new boat, the *Judy*, the phoenix rising, to be followed by the *Meg*, and the *Sal*, the *Fran*, and the rest of the fleet.' Ring licked his lips. 'I could tell Dad wasn't happy with it, that he had to kind of endure the telling. The loss of the *Calabria* never got a mention, not a footnote. It was just one of the reasons they were out there that night.

'Any celebration – Christmas, a leaving party, a boat launch, whatever – the old man would get to his feet, the great patriarch. Dad would sit and listen, and I'd catch his eye and there was something there all right, something that said, *One day, one day, son, I'll tell you the truth.*'

'And did he?'

Ring pressed a hand against the curved metal roof of the cylinder, as if testing its strength. 'In 2003 – the fiftieth anniversary – they held a service on the beach and I took them, Mum and Dad; he'd retired by then, so maybe that loosened his tongue. That's one of the advantages of age: in one way, there's less to lose, fewer years to ruin. And there was no real danger. What was I going to do? Run to the police?

'When we got back to the house that day, I could see something was wrong. There were tears – there were always tears on the anniversary – but he just sat by the fire. Angry – that's what I felt, angry and ashamed. So I said, *Just tell me, for Christ's sake.* We waited until Mum went to bed, by which time the whisky was well down the bottle. Then he refused. Point blank. Said the past was the past. I said if he didn't tell me the truth, *I'd* start asking questions. I'd go to the police if I had to.

'I saw it then: the terror – no other word comes close – the *terror* he felt at the prospect of telling me the truth. But I told him there was no other way. If he didn't tell me then, I'd go and get Mum, and I'd make him tell us both.

'That did it. There were excuses first – or, if I'm being kind, explanations. The sea was bad, treacherous – it often is – but that night he said was a one-off, what they call a *thousand-year storm.* By the time they'd got the *Lagan* into open water, and they'd spotted the *Calabria*, the sea state was what we'd call flat white – so that's kind of boiling, but no waves. It's what you get at the centre of a depression, the eye of the storm. It's not good, because any way you go, you're sailing into bad water. And it's dusk, on a winter's night. But there was an opportunity too, because for a short while – a window in time – they could get alongside.

'Even though she was sinking, there was still a chance of saving her because Coram had a plan, a bit of local knowledge. There's a great horseshoe-shaped sand bank, called Roaring Island, and inside that – even at high water – there's an anchorage, a stretch of shel-tered water; we call it Holme Lake – you'll know it, Shaw. Not on any chart, mind. Sounds crazy, a lake at sea, but it's there, all right. It wasn't high tide – the water was backing out – so if they could get her into the lee of the sand banks, she'd have had a chance at least of sitting out the worst of the wind till dawn.

'They got the *Lagan* alongside and offered her a line. Crew turned that down flat – twice: once by loud hailer, once on the short-wave radio. No problem with language apparently, because the captain – Beck – spoke English. But, no. No help. Thanks, but no thanks. Why? Because saving the ship would have given the *Lagan* the right to a salvage claim. Did they think they could ride it out alone? Maybe. Brave, either way, because in that sea you'd be dead in seconds; with the cold, the sea state, you'd be dragged under.

'Dad said it was Coram who decided not to take no for an answer. If they could save the ship, they'd land a share of the value of the vessel, and the cargo – a fortune by anyone's standards along this coast in the fifties. Coram told them a number; that was the genius of it – thirty thousand each. Made it up, of course. She was carrying timber. But once it was said, it must have been like a spell, because back then that was the kind of money that could change your life.

'And they *could* save the crew as well. I think Dad clung to that, later, when he had the time to think. The *Calabria* was sinking, right there, in front of their eyes. If they could get her anchored in Holme Lake, they could take the crew off.

'Coram outlined the plan: they'd board her, put a line on, tow her to sheltered water. Later, they'd say Beck accepted the help, then reneged on the contract. That was the word Dad said Coram used, the one they'd have to remember if it got to court. *Reneged.*

'They left Dad on the *Lagan*, and he brought her right alongside. I think they knew, you see, that he was reluctant, that his nerve would fail if they asked him to board her, but Coram and the other crewman – Dell Craig – they were up for it. Armed too: the old man had a pistol he'd stashed on board since the war, and Craig could use his fists, but he took a fish gaff too. Coram's target was the bridge. Craig was to go below decks, after attaching the line. Dad said he saw nothing because he had to take the *Lagan* off, in the lee, and wait for a signal by light.' Ring poured himself coffee, his hand steady, colour flooding back into his pale skin. For the first time he looked into Shaw's eyes. 'There's an old word for it – piracy. It's the new word for it too – off East Africa, the Philippines. Back then, boarding a ship, armed, in international waters would have carried the death penalty.

'Dad said after six or seven minutes Coram flashed the signal to bring the *Lagan* back alongside. Craig jumped over first, alone, with his lip busted, and Coram followed, carrying the line, but without the pistol. Beck, the captain, had seen it coming, he said, and armed the crew. They'd been waiting with fish hooks and a couple of shotguns. Dad's theory – which we'll never know the truth of – was that they weren't carrying timber at all, but running something – contraband. Coram said the crew fired on them, then went below to the hold, although Dad never heard a shot. By that time the *Calabria* was actually awash at the stern, so there was no point getting a line to her anyway. So they gave it up.

'The swell came up – six, eight foot, then more – so they took the *Lagan* out a hundred yards, and then the *Calabria* caught a wave beam on. Dad said she broke her back, the *Calabria* – went down in two halves, in less than a minute. Coram sent up a flare, which lit up the sea, and they spotted the lifeboat, a mile off but gaining. But it was too late. Worst thing he'd ever seen, because a ship's a coffin, and he knew they were all aboard, probably down in the hold trying to fix the pumps.

'The lifeboat circled, and they swapped radio calls, but they never did find a body. The *Lagan* headed for Lynn. The lifeboat marked the spot and swung back in towards the coast and the South Beach, because by now the word had got out that the tide had broken the seawall and people were trapped.'

A buzzer sounded and Shaw, who'd leant his body against the metal cylinder of the chamber, felt the bolts unlock automatically on the hatch. As it opened, it seemed to expel its own breath.

'They were lucky, all of them, to survive the night,' said Ring. 'I doubt Coram's lost a night's sleep all these years, but it preyed on Dad – the contrast of it, I suppose: them drowning, while he and his mates survived. That night, the anniversary in 2003 – a year before he died – he said that things might have been different if they'd left her be, that they'd driven the crew below, that they'd lost the chance to abandon ship.

'Craig – even roughneck Dell Craig – I don't think he was ever the same again. Ended up with a tea hut on the front, just by the Spyglass. I reckon Coram bankrolled that. People like Coram, they keep their friends close, their enemies closer. It must get tricky in the end, telling them apart. He died a few years back, a care home up the coast.' Ring accepted a towel from one of the crew who'd come down with fresh coffee. 'Dad went a few months after that night, by the fire at home with the bottle of whisky. By and large he'd kept his secret, but I think it ruined his life. Men like Coram brush such things aside. Dad couldn't. Dishonour – it's corrosive. I think it undermined his own view of himself.'

'You think he told the whole truth?'

Ring, pulling on clothes, stopped, straightened his back. 'I guess. As much as he could. Depends how honest he was with himself. But he was still haunted, right to the end. Always was.'

Shaw thought of Dirk Hartog's body suspended in the sea by its tether, and Coram's tower-top room, with its eye-like balcony looking out over the beach – and, finally, a new image: Dell Craig's tea hut, with its rectangular view, seawards again, as if he too was condemned to keep a perpetual vigil.

FORTY-FOUR

arc Ross had been airborne for nearly two hours when *Free Spirit* slid over the Norfolk coast. The organizers of the fly-past had felt that the Ross family deserved at least some reward for their part in the discovery of Sunny Hunny's Zeppelin past. Donald had been offered the seat for the trip, but had nominated Marc instead; Donald, despite his passion for the depths of the earth, was scared of heights and wanted Marc to record the voyage using his considerable skills as a photographer. The airship's gondola, for pilot and passengers, was slung beneath the great balloon. Marc had his window open so that he could get the Canon outside, and pan down to the landscape passing beneath.

The Canon fired off a series of pictures capturing the scene below, as the remote seaside resort of Sea Palling slid under the airship. The pilot in the front seat waved a hand to the port side, indicating a fishing boat below, mobbed by gulls, but Marc ignored him, uploading a picture to Instagram using the onboard Wi-Fi.

Take-off had been at ten that morning from the vast hangars at Cardington, near Bedford, ninety miles west. That had provided Marc's first picture opportunity, as the cab from the hotel dropped him and his father by the vast double doors, already inching back on winches to reveal a dark, shadowy interior, in which the *Free Spirit* hung suspended in one corner, dwarfed by the shed that had once housed the R101 and the other Leviathans of the airship age.

A local newspaper reporter had cornered Marc, just as the ship began to edge towards the light, a crowd chatting excitedly behind a police cordon. He'd been spellbound by the gentle purring of the engines, the grace of the craft, and its fluid translation from one place to another, like some eerie, airborne whale.

'How do you feel?' the reporter asked.

Marc communicated with images, with photographs and sketches, but words always failed him. 'Excited,' he said, letting his dad take over.

Since take-off he'd kept his eyes open, his head to the open window, a large-scale road atlas on his lap, across which the pilot had drawn a rough approximation of their intended course. The images had passed beneath: the spaghetti string of the A1, the mushroom discs looking star-wards from the radio telescopes strung across the Cambridgeshire countryside, the roof of King's College Chapel, a trio of punts on the open river at Fen Ditton, then the patchwork fens like a chessboard, Ely Cathedral (he'd been told by Donald to note the octagonal central tower, like a single chamber of a beehive), and then the Norfolk hills, throwing shadows while the sun was still low, like a flock of sheeps' backs.

Editing the pictures as he went along, he posted selected shots, thrilled that his 431 followers would find the images popping up on their mobile phones.

Now they were over water, Marc's eyes locked on the patterns the waves made, and he took a series of pictures, which he then modified with the camera's various filters – noir, sepia, and tonal – until he had created a stunning image of mathematical beauty. Then came the serried ranks of breakers at right angles to the north-west wind, the swirls around the sand banks like soapy water going down the plughole, and the white horses, where the wind whipped the foam off the top, as if clipped by gunfire. Finally, ahead, he glimpsed the dim, blue outline of the Norfolk coastal hills, indicating that they'd swung round into the Wash and were approaching land. Below, two windsurfers rode the waves, one becoming airborne as he watched, spinning on the breeze, before splashing down.

The engine thrust dimmed, so that he could slide more comfortably back in his seat, and they seemed to hang in the air, motionless, above the shuffling waves, until – at an impossibly serene pace – the pier-head rig appeared directly below, the *MV Telamon*, the support tug, the great crane, and, standing off a hundred yards, the distinctive yellow teardrop-shaped hull of the lifeboat.

Over Cambridge and the fens, they'd been high, only just below a thin line of fluffy cirrus cloud, but now Marc could see that they'd dropped to a hundred feet, possibly less. Men on the deck of the *Telamon* waved, seagulls in a line on the wire that ran across to the jack-up barge rose as one, and in the blue marine water a skidoo traced a crazy path of circles and curves, a water canon playing on anything within range.

Gliding east, *Free Spirit* traced the line of the old pier. All the airship's windows were open now, and on the air they heard the unmistakable sound of a crowd cheering, and Marc thought of Eric and Jonah and his mum, watching the approach from the esplanade. The rest of the passengers were up and out of their seats, looking through the pilot's forward window, watching the approach of the red-and-white cliffs, the fragile tracery of the funfair to the south, and, beyond, the gentle whaleback of the hill behind the town, studded with its stately villas.

Keeping his chin on the sill, his eyes down into the sea, Marc took a picture to capture the light-filled, azure shallows, the pale sand of the seabed just visible now, in sinuous ribs.

Marc's talent for photography was in part a facility to recognize patterns. There were some below now, which he captured on film: the parallel ranks of the waves, the crisscross divergent lines created by the wind buffeting the surface, the network of the gulls, a lattice work of interlocking, swooping paths.

The twin lines of the old pier emerged, like some subterranean railway track, and he framed a shot, knowing his father would appreciate the geometry of the composition. Then a waterskier crossed his field of vision, and finally, just before the shallows really began, a shape that was almost an echo of a shape – little else but three lines, two of which promised to come together in a prow, the other a link, suggesting a brace against the curves. He took a snap, considered the ghost-like image, then posted it, forgetting it immediately as the miniature armada of protestors' boats passed beneath, a riot of placards and hooters, sirens and flags. And then, finally, matching now the onward crash of the breaking waves, they were over the beach and the teeming crowds on the esplanade, and Marc heard the band playing the theme tune from *633 Squadron*.

FORTY-FIVE

The helicopter dropped Shaw and Valentine back on the beach in front of *Surf!*, drawn to the giant fluorescent H in the sand like a hovering hawk on an invisible gyre. PPC Clay stood on the edge of the circle, holding on to her neat chequered cap, as the down blast ripped at her trousers and tunic.

Clearly, succinctly, she told Shaw of her visit to Alice Banks, and that the box of Milk Tray was on its way to the Ark for chemical analysis.

Valentine considered the sea, trying to look unimpressed.

'Where's Esther Keeble now?' asked Shaw.

'Bedford Prison.'

'So what are we saying?'

Clay removed an imaginary blond hair from her eye. 'That the sister-in-law was the intended victim, that Esther was just the *means* to an end, and that George was the killer.'

'Motive?' asked Shaw. 'It's still a mystery, just a different mystery. Get Esther transferred back to us, Jan. Then organize a car to bring her out to Empire Bank, to the house. We'll meet her there. I want you there too. This afternoon, if we can do it. And Jan . . .' She'd begun to walk away, eyes already on her phone. 'Great work. You've made George's day, but no doubt he'll tell you that later.'

From the south they heard the buzz of the esplanade PA system, and the jangle of the fairground music, as the crowds regained the beach, now cleared of any danger.

Clay walked away along the shoreline, trying to find a spot to pick up a decent telephone signal.

'Let's get a brew, George,' said Shaw, heading for *Surf!*.

Leo D'Asti, Lena's business partner, brought them a cafetière and saffron cakes, telling Shaw that Lena and Fran had got away on time for their flight.

Valentine sat patiently, watching a couple sip white wine in glasses blushed with condensation.

'Next move?' asked Shaw. 'I don't care what Ring says; someone just tried to kill him – specifically him. Why?'

'Coram's the key,' said Valentine, regretting the black acrid coffee, because it seemed to reawaken a visceral need for nicotine. 'He must have suspected this morning we were on his tail. He lied about the *Calabria*. Maybe he was prepared to kill to make sure we never found out the truth. Ring's right: it's piracy – at least it was in 1953. Now – who knows? But there's a law of the sea, right? Must be.'

'Well, inside territorial waters it would be any number of things, George – hijacking, assault, whatever. Outside, it's got to be international law, which is pretty much beyond my pay grade, and unless something's very wrong, yours too. It'll be a UN charter, something like that. I need to take advice – which is shorthand for I've got no real idea. But you're right that Coram's at the heart of this. There's something out there he doesn't want anyone to find: the truth about the *Calabria*. Somehow the pier, or the building of the pier, threatens to reveal that secret. This isn't really about *stopping* the pier. It's about *keeping* that secret.'

Clay appeared by the table, holding her mobile out as if it were an exhibit in court. 'St James' just sent a text – they couldn't reach you. Tad Atkins has just been found up at the pool. There was an issue with the water quality, so they closed it down for the day, drained the water out. He climbed to the high board and jumped. Environmental health officer, a woman, found him half an hour ago. She's on the way to hospital – shock. It's not pretty.'

'Guilt,' said Valentine, not unkindly, but as if it was a suggestion that might offer an excuse. 'He'll be Coram's man – got to be. And he'll have guessed we'd tracked down the watch to him.'

'Indeed, Coram's man,' said Shaw. 'One of many, I suspect. Let's check every inch of the pool and Atkins' flat for a suicide note. Then we go back to Coram himself. And this time, no warning we're coming. We know he lied. We need to confront him with that, but not *just* that. Let's dig a bit deeper on Coram's associates – especially Craig, the third man on the *Lagan*. While we're at it, let's get a warrant for the Old Lookout. The next time we interview Edward Coram, I want to nail him.'

'There's something down by the water,' said Clay, pointing along the coast, to the foot of the cliffs.

A group of people stood on the edge of the famous rock pools, where the tide was just beginning to splash white water over the seaweed-covered hogsback boulders. A woman emerged from the group, a hand to her mouth, dragging a small child away so violently that the little girl couldn't keep her feet and was hauled up the beach like a sack.

By the time Shaw reached the spot, it had formed a curved shape, like a sickle moon, with a rock pool at its centre. The tide was still exploring the spot, like a tongue searching for a filling.

At first, during the second it takes to match shapes to words, Shaw thought a dolphin or a seal had become trapped amongst the rocks. Pale, smooth, curved: the body lay curled in a strangely foetal ball, a limb encased in a wreath of green seaweed. Then he noted the tightly curled hair, the reaching, articulated bones of a human hand, the sand imprinted on the calf muscle of the right leg, the white trunks emblazoned with a Flume! motif.

Kersk lay face down, his back white in the flat noon sunshine.

Shaw knelt in the wet sand, turning the body over by the shoulder, feeling the coldness of the flesh and a hint of immobility, or stiffness, in the joints. The skin, marbled with blue veins, seemed solid and heavy, so that Shaw was astonished at how difficult it was to drag him on to dry sand, a hand under each armpit.

Valentine ushered the crowd back as Shaw administered a series of rapid chest pumps. It felt, and indeed was, utterly futile. Once, at university, where he'd volunteered for the lifeboat at Calshot, he'd helped haul a tourist out of the current in the Solent. Three of them had got him on to the beach, and as Shaw had applied a violent, downward, rhythmic pressure, he'd actually been able to feel the man's blood pulsing round the body, and had watched the colour return to his face, and then the flickering, miraculous flutter of the eyelids.

This felt different in a profoundly disturbing way. Theo's flesh felt solid, as if the blood had set in his arteries and veins. No hint of air troubled his lips as Shaw savagely compressed his lungs. The corpse – and Shaw had no doubt that it was now a corpse – appeared profoundly airless. The strangest aspect of the body was the placid face, and most of all the eyes, which were open in mild surprise, although one was full of seawater and Shaw could not bring himself to brush it dry.

It was the face of a man who had not expected to die.

The sickle-shaped crowd parted, and as Shaw stood, he saw that Valentine held the hand of a young woman, but she pulled free and ran towards the body of her lover.

FORTY-SIX

Ava told them Theo's story: a tale of love, but not just between them.

Kersk was, in fact, Ukrainian, from Sevastopol, not Romanian, and he had a childhood sweetheart called Oleysa. Ava had once found two pictures amongst Theo's things when she'd moved in and started taking the washing to the launderette: one showed them crushed into a passport photo booth, their faces pressed together; the other was a shot taken in the sea, both of them pointing towards a pod of dolphin fins, breaking an oily grey surface, a distant warship a shadow on the horizon.

Oleysa was Russian, her father in the navy based in the port, her mother a chambermaid at one of the hotels on the golden strand that had once catered for the Soviet elite, flocking to the Black Sea Riviera from freezing Minsk or desolate, ice-locked Archangel. They'd met aged fourteen, swimming off the beach in summer.

Theo had told Ava all of this when they'd first met, trying to make it sound as mundane as the rest of the family history, just the kind of biographical detail a boyfriend would tell a girlfriend on the first night they spent together: fathers, mothers, uncles, aunts, cousins and old girlfriends – he was comfortable sharing it all.

'Sometimes, in his sleep, he'd say her name,' said Ava, her eyes on the sea, as Shaw poured her more coffee. She hadn't shed a tear as yet, and her eyes were bright, even eager. 'Sometimes there was an email too, and I'd hear it ping, and he'd slip outside on to the balcony, or go down to the yard, and I stole a look once, and saw his face, lit by the screen, and the way he seemed to drink in the glow.' She took in a sudden gasp of air then, as if she'd forgotten to breathe.

Theo's story was the story of his generation, the Ukrainians displaced by the Russian invasion. They'd imprisoned his father, a merchant who'd traded European textiles into Russia, as *his* father had done, and *his* father, from a wooden warehouse on the waterfront embellished with a frieze of bears and eagles.

Theo, just seventeen, had received a letter telling him he had been conscripted into the army of the new autonomous republic of Crimea – a puppet state of the Kremlin. Oleysa and her family moved to a new secure compound by the docks. The lovers were forbidden to see each other.

Once, when he had drunk too much vodka at the Flume! Christmas party, he'd told Ava about their last meeting. They'd said goodbye in the water off the beach, at midnight, swimming away from each other in the moonlight. It seemed to Ava like an impossibly romantic parting, and she'd despised its childish perfection, and Theo too, for the crass insensitivity of reliving it now. Realizing too late he'd said too much, he never mentioned Oleysa again.

The Kersks' mercantile business was sold, and Theo's father was deported to Kiev. But there was to be no such an escape for Theo: his army papers arrived, a time and place was stipulated, and he would be taken by truck to a new training facility to the north. His father, with forty-eight hours of liberty before his exile, converted part of the sale price of the business into dollars. Theo was smuggled aboard a Greek coaster bound for Istanbul, where he hid himself within the great Syrian diaspora, migrating across Europe by train and on foot. In Macedonia he purchased false papers, emerging in Germany as Theo Kersk, born in Galati, Romania. As a registered EU citizen, he entered the UK by ferry at Hull, and began searching for work, moving down the East Coast from town to town, until he reached Hunstanton.

'Tad gave him a job, although I think he suspected his papers were false. He never said, but I think Theo confided in him. I don't know that, but I felt it. It's odd that water – just the love of it – can bring people so close, and perhaps he was a father figure.' She sipped the coffee. 'I think he told him too much.'

At last a tear fell, and Shaw wondered if it was that small betrayal – that Theo had shared his secret – which had released her grief.

'Tad made him do stuff. Theo said that if he refused, Tad would have no choice but to go to the police. If that happened, they'd send him back, and he'd lose me. So he did what he had to do. That's what told me: that it was blackmail. Setting the fire, out there. I think he deliberately botched it, so that no one would be hurt. Then Tad told him to follow the Dutchman, the one looking for his father's ship. He was sniffing around, asking awkward questions, and Tad wanted him scared off.' She shook her head, as if trying to dislodge a memory. 'He followed him out on a dive one evening. It was easy for Theo, of course, because he could free dive, so there was no kit, no gear, no clumsy oxygen tanks. The idea was to frighten him: intimidate him. It all went wrong. When he came home, he had bruises, a knife wound here.' She ran a slender fingertip across her hip. 'Theo didn't mean to kill him, but he said that the Dutchman panicked, thrashing wildly, and so Theo just held on until he was still.

'He lay in my bed and cried for him. After that, there was no going back. Tad told him that if he didn't sabotage the diving chamber, the truth would be out, that the immigration authorities would know all about his false papers. Today was supposed to be the end of it. One last task, Tad had promised. And a kiss – I got a kiss this morning, which was rare, and now, of course, I see it for what it was: a goodbye kiss, and a betrayal.'

Valentine, who'd been using the landline in the café, joined them, pulling out one of the beach chairs, folding his raincoat carefully on his lap. 'St James' have got witness support to send a car,' he said. 'They can take you home, Ava, and they've got a call through to your mum . . .'

But Ava hadn't finished her story. 'Theo lied, you see,' she said. 'I don't think it was blackmail at all. Tad's like a father to him; he wouldn't have told the police. Theo was paid, you see, in euros. I found these.' She had a beach bag, and she unpacked it now: a swimsuit, a towel, a book, sun lotion, a neat packed lunch – sandwiches, crisps, two apples. 'We were going to meet on the beach when he came ashore. A celebration. To mark the end of it. I'd have asked him then myself, but now I never will.'

She held out an airline travel wallet, with a ticket inside, issued by British Airways, in the name of Oleysa Oboyan, one way from Istanbul to London, Gatwick. There was an addressed envelope, torn open, but ready to post, with an address in Cyrillic. 'Inside there was money, in euros, and the note gives her the name of a ship and a time. The flight arrives Monday next week. I wonder when he would have told me. *If* he would have told me. So now I'll never know what I was. I know what I'd like to do, but you won't let me. I'd like to send the letter, and the money, and the ticket, and then I could go to Gatwick, and I could meet her at the barrier and tell her that we're both alone now.'

FORTY-SEVEN

Valentine trundled the Mazda past the entrance to the South Beach caravan park and for the first time they noticed Beach News, the shop George Keeble had run for nearly forty years. An out-of-sync neon sign flashed *24 Hours* and the window was full of videos and lurid magazines. A wire-mesh guard covered the door, and a security camera hung from a frayed cable over a new sign which read *Tattoos*.

A security prison van stood on Empire Bank, outside the Keebles' bungalow. The driver, in a scruffy uniform, leant on the bonnet, smoking, while Esther Keeble enjoyed the sun, sitting in her own front garden on a whitewashed bench, a small old-fashioned suitcase set neatly to one side.

'They wouldn't tell me where George died,' she said to Shaw, standing stiffly, her voice betraying again that subtle hint of determination. 'I don't understand. It's cruel. I just want to know.'

Valentine produced a set of keys and let them inside. The hallway smelt of pizza and the now ageing, ingrained reek of nicotine.

She stood in the doorway, surveying the room, no doubt noting the gas fire, set to one side to reveal the empty flue where her husband's suicide note had stipulated he'd hidden the rat poison: proof, if they needed it, of George Keeble's guilt.

She seemed reluctant to cross the threshold. 'I knew he wouldn't cook,' she said. 'They deliver, of course,' she said, picking up a pizza box. 'Otherwise, he'd have gone for fish and chips. George liked his food. We had this joke – I suppose. I'd bring in the plates, and he'd be sitting at the table and he'd hold his knife and fork vertically in his hands, ready to eat. We always laughed. So what's that – once, twice, three times a day for a lifetime. Maybe we didn't laugh, but there was always a smile. Do *you* know where he died, Sergeant?'

'They found him in his chair, Mrs Keeble. Just here. We're sorry for your loss.'

The office swivel chair, stuffed with cushions, still held his shape.

Through the front window they saw PPC Clay pull up in a blue-and-white patrol car. Valentine watched as she reached over the seats to take a plastic bag from the back seat.

Shaw asked the security guard to make tea in the kitchenette while they gathered around George's chair, all reluctant to take a seat – any seat – in case one of them was left with the office swivel. Valentine felt he'd been inveigled into some grim, sick version of musical chairs.

Shaw pointed at the forensic evidence bag Clay had brought in from the car.

She held it up, and they could all see the box of Milk Tray. Shaw took it carefully and placed it on the mantelpiece beside a framed picture of George Keeble receiving a medal outside the lifeboat house at Old Hunstanton. Shaw's eye lingered on the image, noting the familiar glint of the RNLI's bronze medal, and the date: 14th June 1953.

'PC Clay will explain,' prompted Shaw, and Valentine noted the pointed omission of the P for probationary.

Clay took a breath. 'I visited Alice Banks, your sister-in-law. She said you gave this box of chocolates to her three weeks ago, a present from your husband. The doctors had told her she was developing type-two diabetes, and she needed to be careful. So no more, please. She was allowed one a day, so the box would last long enough. And she asked you not to tell George. She feared he'd make the effort to visit. They weren't close, she said. A visit would tire her.'

Keeble reached out a hand for the swivel chair but thought better of it. Shaw took her arm and led her to the small two-seat sofa. Age seemed to overwhelm her once she was off her feet.

'They were *too* close,' she said. 'George once said that as children they'd been inseparable. Odd, isn't it? That's where hatred starts sometimes, when you can read someone else's mind, understand how selfish they are, how weak. George never forgave her for her cruelties, especially to me. I don't know when love turned to hatred, but it did.'

'A week later George gave you more chocolates for his sister,' said Shaw. 'So, rather than break your promise to her and tell him the truth, you took the gift, but handed them out in the bus queue, with fatal results,' said Shaw. 'And that set the precedent. It was only DS Valentine here who stopped you handing out another box. Once you were arrested, your husband must have hoped that Alice might yet finish the *first* box. So he waited. No doubt he always planned to confess. But he kept giving it just one more day. That reveals a quite extraordinary degree of hatred, Mrs Keeble. That he was prepared to see you in a cell, just to preserve the chance that his sister would die in agony.' He paused. 'I'm still not entirely clear of his motive? Are you?'

She avoided all their eyes, watching a seagull on the window ledge, its egg-white feathers ruffled by the stiff sea breeze.

'George never, ever asked her for a favour. She had money, but we were poor. I don't think either of us was worried by material things.' She looked at her hands. 'I asked him to break that rule. I couldn't have children, Inspector. We went to doctors, clinics, quacks. By the time we'd stopped trying, the NHS was offering IVF – but only to certain couples. I was too old – thirty-five. I wanted to try. The cost of going private was prohibitive for us. George asked her for the money. She said no. He asked again. He never said, but, knowing George, he begged. She still said no. He thought it was unforgivable.

'I think death – his death, the mere prospect of it – crystallized that hatred. He thought I'd be alone. If we'd had children, it would have been different. He wanted to die knowing I was all right – that I'd cope. She'd robbed us of that sense of peace.'

Shaw picked up the forensic bag and gave it back to Clay. 'At which point I suppose we should simply leave you here, Mrs Keeble. It's still home. We have George's confession. But. There is a but – isn't there? There's an uncomfortable truth here, Mrs Keeble. Because you kept silent too. Our forensics experts tell us that two of the chocolates on the lower layer in this first box are poisoned. Another week – ten days – it would all have been over. George was hoping she'd die, but you *knew* she was eking out the box, that she would, eventually, swallow a poisoned one.'

'I always took her chocolates. I'd done it for years. I thought George had started lacing them when he switched to the cartons – TopChoc. I had no idea. I knew what he'd tried to do, but I thought he'd failed.'

She'd kept silent so long that Shaw didn't think she'd succumb to cross-examination now. 'Indeed. And I suspect that is where that line of inquiry will have to end. We'll never know the truth of it, will we?'

For a few seconds they listened to the clock. 'There'll be a brief court appearance – here in Lynn,' said Shaw, moving on. 'The DPP will need to formally drop the charge of murder.'

He went back to the mantelpiece and took down the framed picture of the RNLI medal presentation. 'George's medal – it was for bravery on the night of the tempest? Back in 1953?'

From the back bedroom Keeble fetched a shallow blue box held tightly shut with a red ribbon. Unthinkingly, perhaps, she took her dead husband's chair and carefully unwrapped the box on her lap to reveal the bronze medal, which glowed dully.

'George would take it out sometimes and hold it, turning it over. Sometimes I think he felt cheated, that the world moved on so quickly. He would have given his life that night, for others. They saved so many people from the flooded houses, in the dark and the ice.'

She nodded once, twice, and then Shaw realized her head was shaking slightly, the strain showing for the first time. 'Earlier that night the lifeboat stood off a ship out at sea that had got into trouble. The *Calabria* – a Dutch coaster. Did he ever talk about that, Mrs Keeble?'

'Yes. He saw the ship sink. The inquest was held in the old town hall, up on the green. Just crew then, of course – it was years later they made him coxswain – so it wasn't his call . . .'

'His call?' prompted Shaw.

'The crew – the lifeboat crew – felt there was something wrong with the sinking of that ship. It just didn't seem the right time or the right place to make a fuss. So they kept their peace. Besides, the relatives were there, from Holland, but hardly any of them could speak English. George said that was the worst part – that they could see how distraught they were but they couldn't comfort them.'

'What was wrong with the sinking of the *Calabria*?'

'George said when they came in sight of the coaster, she was listing. Then she snapped in half, and the stern began to rise up. She sank in a few minutes. George said they never understood why they saw no one on the bridge, at the rails – nothing. The ship's lights were running on a generator, so they could see her clearly. They signalled and got nothing back. The radio channel was open but they never answered. George said – and he talked of it often, especially on the anniversary – he said that even if they were below trying to fix the pumps, they'd have come up when the back broke. It wasn't hopeless – it was worse than that. What's the point of trying to get the pumps working when the ship's in two halves? They'd have come up, and taken a chance in the sea. The lifeboat was on the spot within a few minutes of her going down, and they never saw a sign of anyone. George said the ship was big enough to leave a whirlpool behind, and when they got the lifeboat to the spot, they cut the engines and she just turned, round and round, like she was a top, until it slowed down, and then there was just the white water of the storm. And nothing. No bodies – ever.

'The inquest was over in an hour. Then they moved on to the others who'd died down on the South Beach. That took days. Not the time or the place for awkward questions. And maybe the crew *were* below decks. But George didn't think so. He said the crew either jumped ship before she went down or they were trapped below.'

FORTY-EIGHT

The pale body of Theo Kersk was taken directly to the morgue at the Ark. Within two hours it lay naked, eviscerated, blind beneath the Gothic unseeing angel that stood on its plinth in the east wall. The autopsy, performed immediately by Dr Kazimierz, had been of considerable professional interest, due to the fact that initial tests had revealed that not only was the teenager's blood severely depleted of oxygen, but it was also unnaturally free of carbon dioxide.

Dr Kazimierz's interest was further piqued by a note from Shaw by email: *I have a hook on cause of death here. Rare. Very rare. Ring me if you need info. Peter.*

While the first mystery lay in the blood, the second lay in the lungs, in that the pulmonary tubes on both the left and right sides were dry. She had sluiced the salt and sand from the skin herself, and she had the written report of the victim's discovery before her on a nearby workbench: *Washed up on Hunstanton beach, lower left leg entwined with green seaweed.* The victim's job description had also been helpfully added: *pool attendant, swimming coach.*

But *dry* lungs, and none of the characteristic carbon dioxide poisoning of a typical victim of drowning.

Dr Kazimierz had taken a tea break, standing by the corpse, the condensation from the mug clouding slightly her rimless spectacles. The body, now stitched closed, troubled her in a disturbingly nameless way. Death had clearly been caused by asphyxiation, but this had not resulted in the victim gulping down seawater in the final minutes of his life. Such a degree of self-control she knew to be impossible, and this therefore led her swiftly to an unavoidable conclusion.

She made several telephone calls to substantiate her deduction. The key conversation was with the chief medical officer of AIDA – the Paris-based International Association for the Development of Apnea – the regulator, according to its website, of the sport of free diving and its pool-based offshoot, static apnea.

Satisfied with her work, she fetched a metal stool from the forensic suite and sat beside the corpse. How many autopsies had she performed in her thirty-five-year career? A thousand? She closed her eyes and did the sums: five thousand, perhaps more. Of all those who had died conscious, perhaps only this sad young man had been unaware that death was a second away.

Kersk had died during an extended free dive – submersing his body without the support of either a snorkel or oxygen tanks. The key danger in such a dive was that the use of pure oxygen before submersion – or its substitution by hyperventilation – drove out the blood's natural carbon dioxide, during the process of packing the blood with oxygen. This removed the body's natural early warning that asphyxiation was about to take place. The irresistible urge to breathe is triggered by unease and pain, related to the amount of carbon dioxide in the blood; drive that out, and the victim is blissfully unaware that a danger point is approaching.

Such a danger was markedly increased if the swimmer over-exerted themselves physically. Any extreme effort undertaken during the dive could prove fatal.

Kersk had almost certainly fainted underwater, unaware that but for the absence of carbon dioxide in his blood, he would have been screaming with pain. His breathless body, devoid of buoyancy, would have hung beneath the surface, or danced above the seabed in the languid basal current, before it was washed ashore.

She composed a text to Shaw: *Kersk – asphyxiation during free dive. No evidence of violence. One detail. You were interested in watches. Pale skin, but indentation of strap on right wrist.*

She pulled the mortuary sheet up to the teenager's chin, looked once at his face, and then covered the head. 'Peaceful,' she said out loud. 'Thank God.'

FORTY-NINE

Hunstanton was enjoying its special moment in time: sunset. While along the rest of the East Coast shadows were beginning to creep across the sand, prompting families to pack for home, here the sun was boiling in a purple cloud, bathing the Victorian resort's seafront villas in a golden light. Shaw, standing on the high balcony of the Old Lookout, gazed out to sea. 'How bad are your eyes?' he asked, turning back to address Edward Coram, who was sitting behind his chart-strewn table.

The old man's hand rose to stretch the crow's-foot skin beside his left eye. 'Twenty per cent in the right; the left's blind. So, no better than a mole's, Inspector, and fading fast. The cataracts are breeding, it seems, and there's a problem with the blood supply to the retinas. I'll be blind in a year.'

It occurred to Shaw that his sight was so poor that he didn't know Shaw was blind too, even if it was only in one eye. 'So why is the view so important?'

Coram steepled his fingers to consider an answer, ignoring, or failing to detect, the belligerent tone of the question. Since Shaw and Valentine had arrived unheralded, with the younger Coram in tow, the father had been polite, almost serene. Shaw sensed in this over-confidence an opportunity.

'St Dunstan's, the hospital at Brighton for the blind – have you seen it? Rather a strange building, set high on a hillside above the cliffs, with a view to die for. That's the expression, isn't it? *A view to die for*. The residents love it. I entirely understand. It's a given, of course, that some senses, like hearing and taste, improve when we lose our sight. But what of new senses? Or long-lost senses revitalized? There's a certain bat-like skill in appreciating space, you see. Hearing space – can that be right? It's a great pleasure, and I'm profoundly relieved that I may be able to enjoy it in my extreme old age. My dotage.'

Shaw stood in the window, partly blocking the view. 'By the same token, you'd be able to feel you were in a prison cell?'

Valentine, standing to one side beside a bookcase, felt the hair rise on his neck.

'Odd question,' said Coram, affecting a smile.

'Let's take Captain Ring first, shall we? The father was always a weak link, I suspect. You gave him a job at Wells, in the back office; kept him close. Did you guess he'd told his son the truth? Or that he might one day tell the truth?' Coram sat quite still, the setting sun now shining directly into his blinded eyes. 'Someone tried to kill him today, in the caisson below the rig. A free diver, a pool attendant called Kersk, one of Tad Atkins' men. But then Tad Atkins is one of your men. We've just checked on his job application and you provided the reference, and you were a councillor back then – a man of influence. So he owed you everything.

'You'll know Tad is dead. Suicide. Death seems to haunt you, Mr Coram. You think this is all about honour and friendship, I suspect. But it's blackmail really. And it all started that night you took the *Lagan* out to sea and spotted a listing Dutch coaster. Do you regret the events of that night, Mr Coram?'

'This is fantasy,' said Coram, his lips set murderously straight. 'Thomas, can you get me the chief constable's office, please. Just mention my name.'

Tom Coram stood by the lift doors, his arms folded, but he didn't move, and for the first time Shaw wondered about their relationship, and the extent to which the son was merely another of the father's unwilling foot soldiers.

'Go ahead,' said Shaw. 'But you might as well wait and hear me out. Whoever it was who found Tad's body, in the pool, lying in his blood – nearly all of his blood – was understandably shocked. A young environmental health officer, I think. She called the emergency services. And the news spread quickly, of course. It's a small town . . . Who did you send round?' Tom Coram stared out into the dying light. 'It was only when CID visited the scene that they discovered the building had not been adequately secured. It looked as if the office had been ransacked. Did someone suspect a note had been left, an inconvenient confession? Clearly, they didn't find it as his bedsit was broken into, trashed.

'Actually, there *was* a note at the pool, in plain sight. My sergeant here found it. There was a PC in the office – actually on Kersk's desk, because Tad couldn't deal with the digital age, could he?

Loved telling people he still used pen and ink. That wasn't quite the truth. The screen was blank, of course. Easy mistake to make, thinking it was off. My sergeant simply touched the space bar. The computer wasn't off; it was asleep. Tad wouldn't have expected that – he thought the note would be there for all to see.'

Shaw took a printout from his inside pocket, unfolded it, and placed it on Coram's desk under a brass anglepoise lamp which had incised a golden circle on the wooden surface. 'That's a copy. It tells us all we need to know.'

'But doesn't prove he wrote it.'

'Right. Yes, if you're going to cling to something, try that. In the meantime, some of our forensic technicians are down at the pool, and others are at the bedsit. Modern science is a wonderful thing, and we live in hope. Three officers are downstairs now with a warrant to search these premises.'

Valentine, stepping forward, began to shuffle the various charts on the desk until he found a large-scale Admiralty map of the Wash. The father looked at the son, and the son looked out to sea, locked in some kind of guilty triangle.

'Which brings us to motive,' said Shaw. 'Underlying motive, fundamental motive. Good word, *fundamental* – same root as founder, which brings us back to the sea, and the *Calabria* – and the *Lagan*, of course.'

'I told you what happened that night,' said Coram, his blind eyes searching the desktop, until Valentine realized he wanted a drink: an empty wine glass stood next to a bottle of Merlot. The DS poured out a glass and set it by the old man, whose fingers encircled the stem carefully before he raised it to his lips.

'Yes, you did. But Captain Ring told us a different story, involving a failed attempt to salvage the *Calabria* by force. And then today we came across another version of the story which was much more disquieting. Do you know what I think happened? I think you went aboard and they fought back, and you either killed them or injured them to such an extent that they couldn't get off the ship. Or did you lock them below? Is that it?'

'Is this true?' asked the son, broken from his trance at last.

'Shut up,' said the old man, inadvertently spitting on the polished tabletop.

Shaw walked to the window. 'Which means that out there the

bodies of these men still lie in the wreck of the *Calabria* – proof of your act of murderous piracy, a dishonourable crime.'

'You might like to repeat that allegation in public.'

'I'll take the allegations in the order of my own choosing, Mr Coram. We'll start with blackmail, and then move on to conspiracy to murder. It will be several months yet before we get to the *Calabria*. We need to find it, or at least what's left. A wooden five-hundred-ton coaster in deep water – impossible to find in 1953, but today? That's what was so dangerous about Dirk Hartog's visit, of course. If wreckage from the ship was coming ashore, what might follow? Bones?

'Which brings me to the real puzzle . . .' Choosing a marine chart, he briefly scanned the depths marked, the hachured sand banks, the maze-like channels. 'Why are you obsessed with stopping the construction of the pier?' Coram didn't move, so Shaw slid the Cook's glass over the map, magnifying the features. 'The inquest accepted the accident report which placed the sinking of the *Calabria* here . . .' He placed his finger at a spot out in the deep water. 'But the lifeboat crew thought the ship sank here . . .' A mile and half north lay the edge of Roaring Island. 'Dirk Hartog planned a trip out to the island. He was on the trail of the *Calabria*. What led him there? My guess is he talked to some of the local fishermen. The island's a graveyard of flotsam and jetsam; I think he hoped to find more wreckage. It's a lonely spot, well away from the deep water channel. But it's not going to be quite so lonely if they build the pier – is it? A pier and a ferry service across the Wash, snaking through those long-forgotten channels. Is that what you're afraid of, Mr Coram? That one day they'll find the *Calabria*? Perhaps a winter's storm will reveal it once again? The fear is still alive, isn't it? The fear that someone will find her, and look in her hold?'

FIFTY

Over the next few days waves at last began to crash ashore on Shaw's beach, marking the end perhaps of the calm waters of summer. The Met Office predicted a seven-foot swell along the East Coast of England for the next six days, and so the surfing crowd had arrived in force, the sea dotted with black wetsuits, bobbing as the sets rolled in, the breakers reaching to within fifty yards of *Surf!*.

Lena and Fran had been in Jamaica a week, and Shaw had arranged their postcards behind the bar, depicting Caribbean sunsets and crystal blue seas, although no white breakers. The café was as busy as ever, the usual clientele boosted by the moneyed surfing set, their expensive waxed boards in a rack by the shop.

Shaw and Valentine, off duty for the first time in weeks, sat before a bottle of white wine in a cooler, watching Jan enter the sea with one of Valentine's stepdaughters.

A waiter spun past with a full tray, offloading an iced bottle of Spanish beer in front of Valentine, who deftly picked the slice of lime from the neck and tossed it into the sand.

'Cheers,' he said, his eyes on Jan's swimming cap, now out beyond the breakers.

Shaw raised his wine glass. 'To the scales of Justice.'

That morning, they'd witnessed Edward Coram's first appearance before magistrates in Lynn, to face a specimen charge of conspiracy to pervert the course of justice. The serious crime unit was building a wider case, which would include charges of conspiracy to commit arson, incitement to murder, and murder. Tad Atkins' suicide note underpinned their case, alongside Ava's account of Kersk's role in carrying out Coram's orders. The team was carefully building a raft of circumstantial evidence to support their case at Crown Court.

The sinews of Coram's criminal operation were now clear. Atkins' note described how Coram had controlled him by threatening to deprive him of his job. *He said it would only take a word*, Atkins had written. Atkins' job was his life, the one thing that had kept him from the chasm of despair that had opened up after he'd killed Josh Ridding in his car, drunk at the wheel. A job that had facilitated his rehabilitation in the community he loved. In his turn, Atkins used his hold over Kersk to subcontract Coram's orders, suggesting that the Ukrainian could, with the right amount of cash, get his lover out of Crimea and to the UK. In a limp attempt to salve his own conscience, Atkins had treated his protégé well, making sure he got all the overtime on offer, and even making a gift of the Leander Club watch he'd been given by the WaveCrest salesman for securing the club's bulk order.

Kersk had been responsible for the series of criminal attacks on the pier, including the violent assault on Dirk Hartog, whose quest threatened to divulge the secret of the *Calabria*. Was Hartog's determination to locate the wreck of the *Calabria* really motivated by a desire to reunite his parents after death? Esther Keeble's description of the inquest suggested another scenario: perhaps the relatives of the lost crewmen of the *Calabria* had somehow picked up the suspicions of the lifeboat crew. Did Hartog, perhaps, suspect that the truth lay in the hold of the lost ship?

The device uncovered by the Ross family had now been fully analyzed at the Ark. A minute particle of paint on a metal fragment had been traced to a high-street provider of white goods and heating supplies, suggesting perhaps the use of a kitchen boiler to encase the explosives – a mixture of garden-centre fertilizer and TNT. Extensive inquiries through Coram's shipyard had revealed a possible source for the explosives. One of the construction teams working on the new offshore windfarms near Skegness, regularly serviced by Coram's tugs, had reported the theft of TNT on three separate occasions the previous year.

The device had been designed by Coram, built by Atkins, and buried by Kersk, and included a commercially produced tip detonator, designed to trigger an explosion when Blue Square began the second phase of their project, the construction of the pier outward from the shore to the new pier head, on its caisson foundations. Roos and Lester, it was now clear, had operated independently, and were being held on remand, facing charges relating to vandalism, criminal damage, and breach of the peace.

So far Edward Coram had pleaded not guilty, although – given the growing weight of evidence – this might well be altered at Crown Court, if he decided to take refuge behind a principled motive: that he had sought only to delay and abort the construction of the new pier. The events of the night of 31st January 1953 were unlikely to be aired in court at all unless they could find either the wreck of the *Calabria* or a credible reason why halting the construction of the pier was related to an act of violent piracy more than six decades ago.

'This doesn't help,' said Shaw, using his hand as a sunshade so that he could reread the email he'd received that morning from the chief constable:

> Shaw. Re your request for the diving unit to locate the wreck of the *Calabria*. I've attached costing from DI Forbes: you will note that the figure of £150,000 comes with no guarantee of success. You concede, I think, that the vessel may simply reappear on the sands. Even if located there, it is extremely unlikely – Forbes' words – that any human remains could be located. It was a relatively small wooden vessel. We are not even sure the crew was aboard. It is possible they abandoned ship and were lost in the storm. I can't sign off on this operation. Coram is behind bars. The charges are of a serious nature. He'll serve the rest of his life in prison, or at least at Her Majesty's pleasure. Your job is done. Give my congratulations to the team. CC.

Jan appeared, dripping, grabbing a towel, her eyes on the surf where her daughter was bodyboarding. She had the kind of flushed skin tone that seems to be an emblem of good health. Seated, she poured herself a drink.

'Do we have to have this on the table?' said Valentine, taking the dull-russet plastic canister of ashes that they'd discovered in Hartog's hotel room and placing it below on the sand.

'Hartog wanted to sprinkle them on the spot where his father died,' said Shaw. 'It was, admittedly inadvertently, his final wish. I just thought we should take a boat out to Roaring Island and do the deed. Unless you've got a better idea.'

'Hardly a last resting place,' said Jan. 'With burial at sea, they weight the coffin, so they get to lie on the seabed. But this is just ash, atoms – they'll instantly be diluted, flowing with the tide, who knows where? Doesn't seem quite right.'

Valentine drained his Estrella, not bothering to lift his elbow from the table. 'We've decided to move from Greenland Street,' he said, adopting the tone of an official announcement. 'Out here, God help us. A terraced house in Wells, on a backstreet. No sea view.'

'But the quayside's five minutes' walk,' added Jan, smiling.

'So we're not on your doorstep, Peter. No panic.'

Jan slipped her arm through Valentine's and pulled him close. 'You can just feel the enthusiasm, can't you? The excitement of it all.'

Valentine caught the waiter's eye, tipping his wrist with the empty Estrella bottle clasped in his fingers.

'I thought – *we thought* – that Julie could do with some peace,' he said. 'Truth is, I've been haunting *her*, not the other way round.'

Reaching down, Jan put the urn of ashes back on the table. 'Why don't you weight the urn? Then the whole thing will sink to the bottom.'

'What about you?' said Shaw, topping up Jan's glass. 'Wells must be full of memories. It was your old man's manor. Local copper for twenty-five years. He's the father of your children. Won't you see him about the place – shop windows, a passing squad car?'

Jan shook her head. 'Kids have grown up. Beth's getting married in the spring,' she said, nodding towards the waves. 'That makes a difference, because it's like her story's being written over mine, over ours.'

Shaw looked along the beach, thinking of the childhood hours he'd spent here with his father. Sometimes, walking on the sands, he imagined finding their footprints.

His phone buzzed intermittently, struggling to make contact despite the poor signal. 'It's Lena,' he said, checking the screen, concerned it was bad news. Disentangling his legs from the picnic table, he jogged up the beach to the dunes where the signal was best.

Lena's voice was suddenly clear. 'Peter?'

'Yes. I'm here. Signal's good.'

'We're fine. Look, reception here isn't good – it's down to luck. I just wanted to touch base; if we lose you, don't worry. I'll call later in the week. The service is Friday, at Black River, then we'll bury the ashes in the churchyard.'

'OK.'

'We're in Half Way Tree. At Milly's. Jessie's enjoying herself. Fran's amazed that she's part of this. I think they know why Mum wanted to be buried at Black River, but they're not telling. Not yet. I can tell there's this secret. They're just bursting to say, but they can't . . .' Shaw heard a mumbled conversation. 'We better go. Fran wants a word.'

'Dad? Listen. Two things. Go on to Instagram and look at my pictures; I've kept a kind of visual diary of the trip – yeah? Check it out. Also, you know that kid who went up in the airship – Ross. He's on Instagram. The pictures are, like, amazing. You can see *Surf!* and everything. You do know how to do that, right?'

An hour later Shaw was alone, his laptop open, *Surf!*'s Wi-Fi connecting him to Marc Ross's Instagram feed.

The teenager had created a gallery of about a hundred separate images chronicling his journey in *Free Spirit*, from the first shot of the airship's nose poking out of the giant hangar at Cardington, to the last images of the dunes, right here, above Shaw's beach.

Flying north, Marc had caught rowers on the Cam like water boatmen, the geometric perfection of Ely Cathedral, a great Tudor house with sheep dotted beyond a ha-ha, the giant wind turbines at Swaffham, and then the harbour at Wells, dotted with boats, leading out to the mathematical patterns of the buoyage, marking the channel out to deeper water, the wind leaving grey wave patterns on the open water.

Here young Ross had posted a comment: *Now we've left the land behind it's like we're not moving at all, just hanging. And the engines are so quiet, you can't hear them for the wind, and the sea.*

The next picture showed a coaster, the deck layout sharp as a pin, with gulls in its wake, and then a shot of a skidoo, and a little flotilla of windsurfers, indicating that land was close. The long windless summer had left the sea preternaturally clear, so that the images soon began to reveal the sand banks below, until the *Telamon* appeared: an intricate, jewel-like puzzle of mechanical structures.

And then the subtlest of images, the one that Marc Ross had almost not bothered to post: a ghostly shape, made up of three broken lines, two curving to create the echo of a ship's prow, the third a blunt stern. And now Shaw could see what young Ross had missed with his own eye: just off centre, as if dislodged from its precise mathematical position by time, the clean, crisp icon of a circle, marking what looked to Shaw like the once-sooty chimney of a stout tug.

FIFTY-ONE

As Shaw tumbled backwards off the dive unit's boat, he lodged the image above in his mind as if in farewell: a wrack of cirrus cloud, the white morning light. Once the fizzing mass of oxygen bubbles cleared, he found the sea itself still unusually clear, thanks to the long windless summer, untroubled even by the return of the surfers' swell. For a moment he hung in the salty, dense seawater, waiting for the familiar to return: a sense of up and down, of light and darkness, and – heard but not seen – the sudden implosion of the next diver entering the water over his head. Within a minute the three of them hung, suspended, at the corners of a watery triangle. Then the underwater lights thudded on, the camera pointing to the seabed, and they spiralled down.

Using Marc Ross's aerial picture, they had made a rough estimate of the location of the wreck glimpsed in the clear summer waters from the airship above. Using the *Telamon* as a fixed point of the fly-past route, they had accurately set GPS coordinates for the wreck. It had taken four dives to make contact with the sunken boat. An underwater image, captured on camera, showed the prow and the distinctive ogive curves of a ship.

The exact wreck position was now marked by a moored diving platform above: an awkward, rectangular block which Shaw could just see, framed in silhouette against the sunlit surface of the sea. Descending, the seabed appeared, the low-gravity jolt of his touch-down raising plumes of silt, which cleared to reveal the three of them within a tight circle of blazing light, across which ran one line of the stunted wooden footings of the old pier. Three divers: Shaw with the red helmet, the dive leader with the yellow stripe, the cameraman in blue.

The dive leader checked a hand-held compass to obtain a bearing to the wreck, and as they waited, a miniature shoal of minnows twisted in the circular space between them like a living knot. Shaw felt the sudden presence of something larger, which threw a shadow over them in passing, making his heart quicken with a rapid double beat. Turning, corkscrewing down, it swept past them, slipping through the circle of light, and they saw it for what it was: an aged, battered dog fish, the shark-like shape scarred and mottled, the teeth parted to reveal a flash of the dark gullet beyond. Close enough to touch, the grey, padded, dry flesh was also pitted, Shaw noted, with the wounds of dog fights, the hallmarks of decades of feeding frenzies, here on the unseen plane beneath the sea.

The dive leader prodded the fish with a baton and a dull spark buzzed, the fish skittering away in terror. They watched its retreat from black, to grey, to the echo of a shadow, before following the leader north, towards the other – unseen – line of pier footings, moving across the striated sandy floor, with its curious, curving, parallel rib-lines, as if they were traversing the surface of a giant fingerprint.

They were over the wreck within fifty yards. Shaw, who'd drifted away from the others, was on the port side and therefore the only one who saw the stencilled name on the metal hull: *Lagan*.

The underwater camera was running, but Shaw had a smaller stills model, and as he hung in motionless dead water, he recorded the nameplate, confirming in the single image the implications of the discovery: the *Lagan* lay a thousand yards off the low-tide mark, not three miles south-west of Holme – the position recorded in the inquest papers. The *Lagan*, its deckhouse ripped away by more than half a century of underwater currents, but its hull, protected by the sand, still settled in its seabed grave.

The hull plates of the metal tug – riveted in the dry dock at Hull in the 1940s – still held fast. But the deck plates had popped, dislodged perhaps by the bomb blasts on the beach. The hold now gaped, a black rectangle twenty-five feet by eighteen, into which the camera lights were tilted, to reveal a cargo of railway sleepers, stacked neatly, the surface eaten away to a pitted, curved, organic skin.

And three skeletons.

All lay within the still, trapped water of the hold. Shaw's eye, allied with his imagination, fixed on one that lay by the brass port-hole, the skull perhaps a foot from the glass, which reflected the camera lights, as did the small, oval lenses of a pair of spectacles that had fallen to embrace the neck of the victim, lying on the chest bone. Did he edge towards the glass on that stormy night in 1953, seeing, perhaps, the fleeting lights of the town before the *Lagan* struck disaster, to sink within sight of land? Had the tug been staved in by a railway sleeper, or, in the chaos of the storm, had it struck the pier itself? The other two dead lay fixed in a tableau in the middle of the hold, their lower arms held together by what looked like leather bonds.

Shaw had little doubt this was the last resting place of the crew of the *Calabria*, that they had been incarcerated in the hold, bound, and that they'd died here, in the terrifying darkness of that night, while the crew of the *Lagan* had fled to the sanctuary of the South Beach.

Across the scene the shadow of the dogfish flashed again, and as Shaw looked up to catch its passing, it twisted along its spine and, with a single violent flexing of its tail, was gone.

FIFTY-TWO

Events moved swiftly in the hours after the discovery of the wreck of the *Lagan*. Edward Coram instructed his solicitor to inform the Crown Prosecution Service immediately that he would be entering a plea of guilty to all charges on appearance at Luton Crown Court, on the date set in early October. His next public appearance was to be a bail hearing in Lynn just twenty-four hours after the discovery of the wreck. Through his solicitor he made an application to the magistrates seeking permission to make a statement in court, indicating that he wished to give a full account of the events of 31st January 1953. Given the narrow time frame, relatives of the *Calabria*'s crew were unable to make the journey, although the Dutch consul indicated that he would attend on their behalf. Permission was granted for the statement, although the move was perhaps cynically interpreted by the prosecution as a ruse to help secure the defendant bail, on the grounds of failing health.

The court was packed, Shaw and Valentine observing from the upper gallery.

Coram's solicitor confirmed that his client would be pleading guilty at Crown Court to two specimen charges of manslaughter and murder: the victims named as Dirk Hartog Senior and his son. Under English law, he was as culpable for the murder of the second – for which he had procured the help of Atkins and Kersk – as he was for the manslaughter of the first, in which he had taken an active, leading role by recklessly imprisoning the crew of the *Calabria* in the hold of his boat.

The solicitor then read Coram's account, explaining that the prisoner had been advised by his doctor to remain silent, as he was suffering from stress. Coram sat in a wheelchair behind the dock, blind eyes looking down into his lap.

The narrative sounded, to Shaw at least, curiously objective, as if Coram was merely the storyteller, not the prime mover. Perhaps it was by this gift of distancing himself from his own guilt that he had survived the intervening years, unlike his crew. Shaw considered the contrast with Ring, who had been unable to tell the entire truth, even in a private confession to his own son.

Coram's statement took them rapidly to the point where the two ships had come alongside that night. Ring had indeed been left aboard the tug while Coram and Craig, both armed, had boarded the *Calabria*. And the original plan had, as Ring stated, been to secure a line and force the crew to accept the offer of salvage, towing the ship into the nearest port. But events aboard the ship moved too quickly for the plan to hold. Beck, the captain, had a gun up on the bridge, but he had not, in fact, armed the crew – they were below decks struggling to fix the pumps. Coram and Craig were fired on and took refuge below, where they overcame the other two crew members and, using their prisoners as hostages, forced Beck to hand over his gun.

The problem was that while Coram and Craig were below decks they were witness to the desperate situation of the ship. Water cascaded into the hold, visibly rising. Coram devised a change of plan: they would secure a line, tow the *Calabria* into the sheltered waters off Roaring Island, while stowing the crew below deck on the *Lagan*. Salvage was still possible – but only if they could get the coaster beached. They bundled Beck, Hartog and Spaans over the side and into the tug's hold, securely bound, and, in at least one case, chained by cables. They then managed to secure the tow line. The *Calabria*, however, was losing its battle with the storm, listing alarmingly, and beginning to wallow in the swell. To save their own lives, they were forced to drop the line and let the storm blow them south.

Coram, ever resourceful, reformulated the plan. They would now 'save' the crew. The tug set out for Lynn, but was staved in by a railway sleeper. But she didn't sink out at sea. *Their* pumps did work, and they fully expected to make it to shore, but within a thousand yards of the South Beach the rudder broke away, and they were dashed against the pier superstructure, where the *Lagan* sank. The crew had seconds to save themselves: Craig managed to get the dinghy overboard, but then all three of them were swept into the sea and had to swim for dry land. It was only later, after the discovery of the dinghy on the beach, that they were able to agree a version of events that cleared them of all blame and obscured the position of the wrecked tug.

'In the chaos of the moment there had been no time to release the Dutchmen from the hold,' read the solicitor; a profound silence greeting this blunt statement.

The chairman of the bench intervened. 'Is the prisoner really unable to articulate any part of this statement himself?'

Solicitor and prisoner traded whispers. 'I'm afraid so,' was the answer.

An audible hiss came from the body of the court.

The solicitor continued. In the years following the loss of the ships, Coram discreetly surveyed the spot. There was no sign of the wreck from the pier itself. The usually murky waters of the North Sea had drawn a veil over the superstructure, until the ship was, presumably, buried by the encroaching sands. In the late seventies, fire destroyed the pier, making it even less likely the wreck would ever be found. The stormy winter, had, however, remade the sandscape, and, at this very point in time, Blue Square had secured funding to rebuild the pier directly over the grave of the *Lagan*.

A single shout of 'Shame!' came from the relatives as Coram was pushed in his wheelchair down the wooden incline from the dock and out of the court to the cells.

Local TV reported that evening that the prisoner had been taken directly to North Sea Camp, an open prison a mile from the sea near Boston, in the north fens, where he would await his scheduled appearance in October. Shaw imagined him trying to sleep that night, his ears searching the silence for the gentle whisper of the distant surf.

FIFTY-THREE

After dark the Ark's former identity, as a Methodist chapel, seemed to creep out of the stonework and haunt the echoing interior. There was something spiritual about the peaceful gloom of the interior. A single desk lamp played down on a desktop in Hadden's forensic laboratory, reflected in the glass wall that separated it from the autopsy suite beyond.

'Peter,' said Hadden's voice from the shadows, as Shaw entered through the original west doors. 'Thanks for coming. I thought you'd like to know . . .' The forensic scientist was at his desk, but leaning back, balancing his chair on the two back legs. 'I always think it is our job to secure the truth, not take someone's word for it. Especially someone as manipulative as Edward Coram.'

Shaw was instantly grateful for Hadden's unhurried scientific methods. The whole of the team had felt the speed of events had slightly overwhelmed the inquiry, and there were always lingering doubts in such situations that they'd missed some vital clue or made a disastrous assumption.

On the desk, brilliantly lit, lay a plastic forensic evidence bag containing a single bone – the proximal phalange, explained Hadden, indicating that section of the index finger below the second joint.

'With the families in Harlingen so keen to help, it seemed like too good a chance to miss,' said Hadden, rubbing the sallow freckled skin of his cheeks. 'So we got the bureau in Amsterdam to take DNA swabs. This little chap's from the *Lagan* – the skeleton by the porthole. We asked the Home Office lab to extract a sample and attempt a match.'

Touching the space bar on a wide-screen computer, he lit up an image of what appeared to be two supermarket bar codes. 'The unknown remains from the tug are on the left; Captain Beck's grand-daughter's DNA profile is on the right. If I slide them together, you can see the degree to which they are a nice, tight fit. I won't bore you with the maths, but let's say if this degree of concurrence occurred by a process of random coincidence, it would represent a chance of one in thirty million. Add to that Coram's confession, which places Beck in the hold of the *Lagan*, and I'd be happy to stand up in court and say there was no doubt.'

Hadden stood, straightening out his back in a series of plastic clicks. 'The families approached the coroner about exhuming the remains and taking them back to Harlingen for burial. Unfortunately, the last few weeks of high surf have shifted the sands. The local sub-aqua club says there's about ten foot of the stuff over the spot right now. It could be years before it remerges. The relatives will be disappointed – they wanted to take them home – but the coroner feels it's appropriate to leave them in peace. And it's her call.

'It's what? Sixty-three years ago that these men died. The spot will be designated a grave, so that should keep any organized dives away. One unintended consequence may fall to Blue Square. They'll have to build over the spot, and that raises issues. Talking to Beck's grand-daughter, she said the company had been in touch with the relatives, and they wanted a meeting, so maybe there's a way forward. Or maybe not.'

Three of Hadden's team returned from the canteen, and the lab's various hot desks began to light up, screens full of data.

Shaw reactivated his phone and noted a missed international call from Lena. Seeking some privacy, he pushed through the heavy plastic strip curtain into the autopsy suite. Of the three aluminium tables, only one held a corpse, shrouded in a zippered white bag. The old chapel's single angel was lost in the shadows thrown by the roof beams.

For a few seconds Shaw listened to the phone signal bouncing from one exchange to another, making its way, no doubt, out of Kingston and along the coast towards Black River. He took his phone to one of the old lancet windows through which the street light shone in dull amber.

'Peter?' Lena's voice was light, even joyful, and remarkably clear.

'It's a good line.'

'It won't last. I'll get the boring stuff out of the way. We're back Sunday, arriving early morning, so we'll see you by noon. Can you be home?'

'Yes.'

'The case is over?'

'Yes. A result. I'm pleased. You?'

'A result . . .' In the background he heard laughter and recognized Fran. 'She wants to say something. But first, my news.'

He heard Fran's light laugh again and then a darker, softer voice, at a much lower tone.

'Who's that?' asked Shaw.

'It's my father, Peter.'

Shaw let a few seconds pass. 'Your father died when you were ten.'

'Apparently not. His name's Isaac. Isaac Greenidge. I'll send you a picture. It's imagination, of course, to some extent, and maybe wishful thinking, but you can see Fran – in the arc of the eyes, and the cheekbones.'

'You'd better explain . . .'

Lena laughed. 'I'll send you a picture of the place too. It's called Long Cove, about a mile from Black River. There's dunes, and a beach facing west. No café – well, a hut, just like the old one in the pictures of our beach. Isaac lived here, in a shanty town behind the dunes, out of sight. Poor people could hire chalets for a holiday. Isaac and his father did odd jobs, fixed the roofs – stuff like that.'

Shaw heard the joyful scream of a child in the sea.

'Mum came here in 1982, with the family, for a holiday. I say the family – her dad stayed in Kingston because he was after work. They had one of the huts. She was nineteen, Peter – but a bit of a looker. Milly and the cousins have pictures. Anyway, she fell for Isaac.

'End of the holiday, they all went back to Kingston and Mum's dad announced he'd got a job, in London, as a hospital porter. So everything changes, and there's chaos, and in the middle of it she finds out she's pregnant with me. I was conceived here, Peter. On Isaac's beach.'

The lights had begun to go out in the forensic lab, so Shaw went back through the plastic doors, joining the rest as they made their way out into the car park. 'How did he find you?'

'The funeral. I'll tell you everything when I see you – but it's made me think, about how much Mum knew. I shook him by the hand at the church door after the service, and I said, "Did you know Mum?" and he just wouldn't let go. It explains things, doesn't it? Why I'm different from Jessie and Marcus.'

He heard Fran's voice, clearer and insistent. 'Mum, you promised. It's my turn.'

'OK. OK. She wants to tell you about the surf, and the food – my God, the food! Anyway, we went to the spot where she wanted her ashes buried, beyond the wall of the graveyard. Isaac came too. The church is on a hill, Peter, so the view's for ever. And he pointed and said, "That was our beach."'

FIFTY-FOUR

One year later

The winning design for the new Hunstanton Pier, to replace the conveyor belt of boxes planned by Blue Square, was based on a joyful, seaside game: ducks and drakes. A flat stone spun horizontally into the water will hop once a long way, twice a little less, a third time perhaps, and then sink. Experts can achieve much more. The Cambridge-based architects who won public support for their vision of the pier made sure the local papers had all the necessary information to fuel the town's enthusiasm for the ducks-and-drakes concept. The US record for ducks and drakes was eighty-eight skips. The British record, always awarded to the longest throw comprising more than three hops, was set in a disused slate quarry in Scotland and stretched an incredible 169 metres. The architects pointed out that the design had international appeal, in that almost every major world culture had at some time attempted to spin a stone to skip across the surface of water. Shaw's favourite was the expressive Italian version – *rimbalzello* – although the Greek, which translated as 'little frogs', was Fran's choice.

The second stroke of architectural genius was to reverse the pattern, relative to the beach, so that the shortest spans came first, then gathered speed, as it were, as the graceful longer arcs opened out seaward, until the very last span – an eye-watering 280 yards – seemed to leap into the arms of the end-of-pier pavilion, a theatre and cinema venue, with a café and viewing deck. From the far end, ferry boats left each day in season for the distant smudge on the western horizon that was the town's twin resort of Skegness, the boats propelled, it seemed, by the sheer energetic exuberance of the lengthening spans of the pier itself. Once completed, the delicate tracery of the structure supported a single-line miniature monorail – with a central double-track section allowing two trains to run at the same time – one seawards, one landwards.

Blue Square's leaden design had been rescinded by the local
council on the grounds that it broke several of the strict stipula-
tions contained in the original planning application, this news
coinciding with a decision in Brussels to call in the £77 million
grant set aside for the project on the grounds that there was evidence
Blue Square had improperly lobbied MEPs to smooth the path of
public funding. Given that the caisson was in place – at a cost
of £15 million – a decision was taken to launch a public competition for a new design to join the pier head with the beach. The
lightweight construction of the ducks and drakes blueprint, alongside its aesthetic grace, made it a clear winner.

Shaw had watched the construction with a mariner's eye from
the beach in front of *Surf!*. The series of landward arches, narrowly
spaced, were out of sight, hidden by the gentle curve of the cliffs,
so that by the time the vaulting structure came into view the spans
were already lengthening, like a runner's legs stretching out for the
final lap. Mimicking its Victorian forerunner, the pier was narrow
but high, held nearly fifty feet above the sands of low tide by the
narrow tracery of curved steel. This allowed Shaw to see *through*
the pier, to the sea beyond, as if the structure itself was no more
than a flying arrow, its target the horizon.

A week after the grand opening, Shaw met Valentine at the pier
entrance, a semi-circular platform which supported a café, ice-cream
parlour, and various smaller concessions.

'It's a mile, probably more,' complained Valentine after Shaw
declined the chance to catch the next train to the pier head. 'You've
seen that,' he added, gesturing towards a newspaper billboard by a
gift shop: *TOWN KILLER DIES IN JAIL*.

'Twine rang me earlier,' said Shaw.

Edward Coram, who had been unable to stand trial due to ill-
health, had died at North Sea Camp, quietly in his sleep. Twine
reported that the newspapers had contacted Tom Coram, now retired,
for a comment. The son had said simply that he now wished to
fulfil his father's last wish: that his body should be cremated, and
the ashes scattered inland, beyond sight of the sea.

Shaw, shouldering a small rucksack, lengthened his stride. 'Come
on, George. The walk will do you good.'

After a hundred yards he paused to let his DS catch up, while
he considered the receding coastline. This summer had been wild,

with hot spells sparking thunderstorms. Over the Norfolk hills he could see a great cloud brewing, its heart a murderous black.

'It's going to rain,' said Valentine.

'How's the new house?'

'She wants a dog now.'

'That'll want walking,' said Shaw, setting off again.

Wooden benches marked the long trek out to sea, each one bearing a silver disc inscribed *STP*. Tom Coram, cautioned for his bungled attempt to find Tad Atkins' suicide note, had otherwise been cleared of any involvement in his father's crimes. So he had been in a position to personally wind up the anti-pier campaign once the new pier's design and specifications had been agreed. The balance in the fighting fund £196,000, was donated to various schemes related to the new pier – the benches, solar panels on the seaward side of the pavilion roof, and a series of free telescopes, mounted at the halfway station and the end of the pier.

Shaw used one of the telescopes now at the halfway station to look back at *Surf!*. On the beach, sitting with a straight back on one of the café's wooden chairs, he could see Lena's father, Isaac. He had been with them a month and would fly back tomorrow. The old man seemed to bring a rare stillness to their lives. Lena, certainly, seemed to thrive in the presence of a man who explained so many of the contradictions in her life. At dusk the night before, around an open fire, they'd even discussed the dream of building a café at Long Cove.

Shaw and Valentine walked on until he found the plaque set in the wooden boards of the pier.

> Below this spot lie the bodies of Arjen Beck,
> Rafael Spaans and Dirk Hartog,
> trapped within the wreck of the *Lagan*,
> lost 31st January 1953.
> This plaque was erected by their relatives from
> the Port of Harlingen, on the Frisian coast.
> *The only villain is the sea, the cruel sea,*
> *that man has made more cruel . . .*

Shaw swung the rucksack down to his feet and slipped out the urn Dirk Hartog had brought to Hunstanton. Its heft, he noted, now included the pebbles he'd added from the beach. A second urn contained Hartog's ashes and was similarly weighted. He wrapped both in two identical Dutch flags and handed one to Valentine. Leaning over the rail, he repeated the last line of the plaque's inscription, by way of a blessing – a request made by Hartog's niece, who had been too ill to travel to the UK for the ceremony – and then they dropped their offerings together. There were two small splashes, and the flags spread out, then floated west on the tide, leaving nothing behind on the surface. Beneath, Shaw glimpsed the grey shadow of a dogfish, gliding over the unseen grave, as if in welcome.